all the
broken
girls

all the broken girls

LINDA HURTADO BOND

Entangled Publishing, LLC
644 Shrewsbury Commons Ave., STE 181
Shrewsbury, PA 17361
Visit our website at www.entangledpublishing.com.

Amara is an imprint of Entangled Publishing, LLC.

Edited by Robin Haseltine
Cover design by Elizabeth Turner Stokes
Stock Credits: Shutterstock/TheOldhiro,
Shutterstock/Alvano Vino, and
Shutterstock/AY Amazefoto
Interior design by Toni Kerr

Print ISBN 978-1-64937-214-7
ebook ISBN 978-1-64937-229-1

Manufactured in the United States of America

First Edition September 2022

AMARA

ALSO BY LINDA HURTADO BOND

Alive at 5
Cuba Undercover
Flatline

broken girls blossom into warriors

CHAPTER ONE

On a normal day, I'd be first in the conference room, laptop open, eager to impress El Jefe and my TV news colleagues with a list of exclusive stories to pitch—mined from my confidential, well-placed police sources.

But this is not a normal day.

Today, my center spins in one anxiety-fueled funnel cloud as I, the disgraced crime reporter back from suspension, walk into the lively afternoon content meeting.

I present my best journalistic poker-face as I parade through the room in my only pair of red-bottomed stilettos. I pray that, despite my nerves, I'm pulling off a *got-no-worries* look. No one needs to know my goal is simply to survive my first day back without getting in trouble. Or worse, fired.

I intend to grab an easy assignment and not screw up. *Sencillo. No pido mucho. Easy. Not asking much.*

My various coworkers stop the daily debate over story priority and stare. Today, I'm fish food for their curiosity. I smile at the afternoon anchor with the perfectly blown-out hair. She raises her eyebrows and glances to the other side of the room. As do I.

There are only two open seats in the room packed with managers, producers, writers, reporters, and photographers. One chair is next to the afternoon anchor. The other is at the end of the elongated conference table, directly across from El Jefe.

The Boss.

I deliberately head toward the seat across from Mr. Payton.

I'm running fifteen minutes late after driving my Abuela Bonita to her doctor's appointment. But that's not bad, actually, for Cuban time. Of course my statement high heels click on the uncarpeted floor like my abuela's disapproving tongue and all I can think of is that silly commercial with the tagline "Wanna get away?" Except I can't escape. It's my first day back at the TV station after two weeks at home with no work and no pay. I'm still on probation, and I need this job like I need water and air.

Speaking of which, the thought makes me notice how parched my throat is and I'm afraid my voice will crack when I talk. My lungs are so empty I'm not sure I can deliver any story pitches, even if my job depends on it.

Which, it does.

Reporting is in my blood.

But my paycheck—also a necessity.

I rub my right wrist. The red rope bracelet is there. The pea-sized, black gemstone dangles from it. I roll the azabache charm between my fingers, silently going through my routine: twist the stone three times to the right, three to the left. Six times in all. My lucky number. I swear I'll never go to a crime scene again without the charm. I've learned my lesson. *Asi es. Truth. That's how it is.*

I pull out the chair across from Mr. Payton and

accidentally scrape the floor. It's loud. *¡Qué escánda-lo!*

More stares cut my way. The air conditioning kicks up a notch, but that means nothing to the sweat rolling down my back, sliding into the most inconvenient places. I ignore the wet tickle and stand even taller before taking a seat.

My boss drills me with that intense stare that says everything he's not allowed to vocalize for fear Human Resources will reprimand him. "Thanks for joining us, Ms. Álvarez."

"Had to drop off my grandmother at her doctor's office. She doesn't drive." I sit and twist the water bottle on the table until the label faces me. I look at El Jefe and force the corners of my mouth up. Abuela Bonita always told me, no matter what's going on inside, you can win over the world with a warm smile.

"Let's continue." Mr. Payton looks at Paul Johnson, our political reporter.

Paul clears his throat. "As I was saying, the governor is going to hold a press conference on the opioid crisis at a local…"

I cross my ankles to keep my leg from bouncing. It's clear my boss doesn't trust me anymore. Not since my serial killer story got the station sued.

I catch the ambitious, crime reporter wannabe eyeing me from the right corner of the room. Bet she's dying to know what happened to warrant my suspension. *She probably already knows.* Secrets don't stay secrets for long in a newsroom.

What the hell had gone wrong?

Abuela Bonita calls it mala suerte. She insisted I

wear the azabache bracelet today to ward off the bad luck following me. I find the charm again and twist.

I will fix this. Don't know how. But I *will* repair my damaged reputation.

"Álvarez?"

I flinch in my seat.

"You have anything to add to the meeting?" El Jefe taps his engraved pen on the table in a slow, rhythmic pattern.

"Well, Mr. Payton." He likes it when we use his last name. "I thought I'd do a feature on a young girl in New Tampa Hospital who needs a kidney transplant."

"That from the crime beat reporter?" I hear the words he isn't speaking.

"I know." I answer in my head. *"Eleven Emmys, and I still messed up that last crime story, didn't I*?" Out loud I say, "She's an artist—truly amazing gift—and she's willing to auction off her paintings to raise money so people can get tested to see if they're a match. We could save her life by sharing her story."

My boss nods but says, "Busch Gardens is showing off a new baby sloth this evening."

My cheeks burn. I sit back. The heat floods down into my chest. "A baby sloth?" I'm pretty sure this is what a public castration feels like.

"We have enough crime, corruption, death, and destruction today. We need something positive after Weather. Sloth baby it is. Can't go wrong with baby animals," he says.

Can't get the station sued again, you mean.

"You're on that, Álvarez."

"Gracias." I close my eyes and visualize a sloth

picking at El Jefe's bushy, needs-to-be-cut eyebrows with those two big claw-like toes. In slow motion, of course. "If our viewers see what I'm envisioning, they're going to love it." I smile. Warmly.

Whatever. It will keep me employed for at least one more day. My sister Izzy and Abuela are counting on me.

My phone goes off. I look down, fumbling it as I try to flip off the ringer. "Sorry. Sorry." It's not someone calling. It's my home RING security camera alerting me. My pulse takes off like an F-16. *Someone is at our front door.* My heart stalls. And falls.

"An important source?" El Jefe asks.

A scoff from the right corner of the room. "Baby sloth police calling?" Crime reporter wannabe gets the room laughing.

Wannabe must have missed her café con leche this morning. I join the laughter and wink at her, despite the slow scalding heat I'm feeling. Abuela Bonita also taught me you get more with honey than vinegar. "No. No. Sorry." Just my sister's boyfriend of the week, who is not supposed to be at our house. I shake my head.

"Álvarez?"

My spine straightens. "Yes?"

"You can take the new photographer, Chris Jensen."

That pulls me back to the moment. "But I always work with Orlando." A big eyeball fills the RING camera at the front door, but it isn't Izzy's new boyfriend. His eyes are as blue as the Florida sky. Isabella's are dark brown, so dark you can't tell where the pupil ends, and the iris begins. Izzy pulls back and yells at the RING camera, "Stop spying on me! ¡Consiguete una vida!"

My younger sister is telling me to get a life of my own.

Snickers flicker across the room.

Every hair on the back of my neck rises. The audio on my iPhone is still on. *Wanna get away?*

I glance at my friend Kiara. She smiles and shakes her head. I appreciate her support. Time to turn the sound off my iPhone.

"Everything okay?" El Jefe's features remain constant. He doesn't chastise me for my sister's outburst, even though she interrupted his busy news meeting.

"Yes sir, I'm fine." *Wait till I get home, Isabella Álvarez!* "I'm fine."

He nods, but his eyes narrow.

I sit through one of his nerve-wracking, wish-I-knew-what-he's thinking pauses.

He says, "You can take Orlando."

I exhale.

El Jefe is throwing me a peace offering, I think. Or maybe he believes I can't even handle an animal story with the newbie photog, so giving me Orlando is like tossing out a safety vest.

Wow.

Two weeks ago, I would have rolled my eyes at the insult of such an easy, nonrelevant assignment. I would have been deeply offended by the shade of making sure I had a veteran babysitter with me.

Tonight, I'm grateful for it.

Even though I know I can't possibly screw up a baby sloth story, right?

CHAPTER TWO

"Orlando, how do you feel about doing a story on a baby sloth's birth?" *When you usually shoot Emmy award winning stuff. Relevant, important news stories.*

"What's not to like?" Orlando's eyes are glued to Dale Mabry Highway as we cruise north toward Busch Gardens and our date with Tippy Toe, the newest addition to the theme park's sloth exhibition. "Easy, breezy. I'm feeling a little lazy tonight."

I smile at O's attempt to make a joke. He's never been lazy.

I find my charm bracelet and roll the black azabache charm between my fingers. Count to six. Muscle memory.

"Easy, breezy," I repeat, putting the words out into the universe, a conscious manifestation of my hope and desire. Get to the theme park, do this story, get off the clock without any unexpected problems.

Should be easy. Should be breezy.

But my stomach wobbles like guava with the bad feeling that's been stuck in me lately.

"Signal 7."

A dispatcher's voice blasting out of the scanner in O's assigned TV vehicle makes me start. My heart stutter steps because I know what a Signal 7 means. So does Orlando.

The voice on the scanner says, "521 Hesperides."

Heat drains out of my cheeks. "That's near here." My neighborhood since childhood, in fact. Not my street, but close enough. I start running through who lives on Hesperides. Izzy's old boyfriend. Abuela Bonita's pharmacist.

The voice continues to crackle. "Paramedics on scene."

"Dead body and others hurt?" This could be a lead story. *¡Carajo!*

"Shit," Orlando echoes me. He's pursing his lips and shaking his head.

Normally, we'd divert and head to the crime scene. We'd do breaking news for the night newscasts.

"I'm thinking we gotta check this out."

The way his shoulders slump, and the hesitation before he presses on the gas, tells me he's as reluctant as I am.

"I don't think El Jefe will like this." *I don't like this.*

"I'll call the station," Orlando says.

I nod. Usually, I make the calls while O drives. I fiddle with the water bottle, making sure the label is facing me.

Signal 7.

That could be an old man dead after a heart attack. Awful, but not a news story.

Could be a suicide. And a loved one hyperventilating. Sad. No, devastating, but still not a news story.

Could be a murder scene.

And that would be it. The one thing I dreaded would happen today. Breaking news that might put me back in the path of more bad luck.

And more death.

I close my eyes and try to remember which Santería saint Abuela Bonita says protects me. I can't remember the orisha's name, but it's the one that helps you with justice.

"Help me face whatever awaits us." I open my eyes, still rolling the azabache bead between my fingers. It's warm from my worry. I follow the prayer with the Catholic sign of The Trinity. "In the name of the Father, the Son, and the Holy Spirit. Amen."

I do both silently, without using my hands or my words, praying in my mind's eye only. Not sure Orlando will understand this odd mixture of mine.

"Got it. I'll spray the scene." Orlando gets off the phone and makes a quick turn off Dale Mabry. We're on Hillsborough Avenue, close to Hesperides. "They want me to get video before the police block off the road, put up the tape, and force us to a command post."

"You don't have to explain." I know how this works.

My phone dings. The text is from El Jefe: *Remember. You're on probation.*

Like I could forget. I text back. *Yes, sir.*

El Jefe: *If you must do interviews before the second crew gets there, don't talk to officials unless they will go on the record.*

Second crew? I'm a veteran reporter. I fight back the burn of fresh tears. My fingers hesitate over my phone. Oh, the reply I'd like to send him.

But my boss beats me to it. *In fact, stay in the car until your replacement arrives.*

My replacement.

El Jefe: *You're off the crime beat for now.*

What?! "Who are they sending?"

Orlando cuts a glance my way. "Chris Jensen and Jessica Spencer."

I groan; I can't hold it in. The new guy and crime reporter wannabe. "Are you kidding?" I turn toward the window so O can't see my face. It's burning like a brush fire.

"Not kidding. Sorry."

My gut is blazing, too. I know I screwed up, but to send the newbie and the woman who wants my job? What an injustice. To me. And to O.

My trusted coworker is unusually quiet and focused. Is his ego combusting like mine?

"You okay?" he asks.

"Fine," I answer on autopilot. "No, really. I'm fine." But my cheeks are as hot as red coals.

I can barely breathe.

Orlando turns onto Hesperides Street. He passes The Waffle House and the elementary school I attended and drives by the single-story homes once the glory of Tampa, now part of its rich, cultural past. Most of these familiar places could use a new roof and additional landscaping but the owners have outgrown their ability to do heavy repairs.

Something white catches my attention. A dress billowing in the warm August wind.

A couple is standing in the middle of the street, their backs to us. They're not moving.

My stomach lurches. O is looking at me, not the road.

I point toward the street. "Watch out! We're going to hit them."

CHAPTER THREE

Orlando slams on the brakes.

My heart's beating like Abuela's fingers on her secret drum.

"Why the frig aren't they moving?" He smashes the horn and swerves to miss the couple.

Tires screech.

The couple turns.

A man puts out a hand as if that will stop our big ole Ford SUV. But it does.

We stop inches from that hand.

I exhale my gratitude.

Smoke rises between us, and the smell of burned rubber rushes up my nose. "We almost hit them."

"Even the damn roosters got out of the way." Orlando's chest is also rising and falling.

The couple comes into focus, and I understand why they thought they could face death by SUV and survive. It's not unusual to see a Santera or Babala-wo in our West Tampa community. They are dressed as a priestess and priest of my abuela's Afro-Cuban religion, Santería. But I thought I knew all her fellow Santería followers here in West Tampa. The man's face is new.

He towers above the woman, his lanky limbs covered in cool dress pants and a white cotton Guayabera shirt. His outfit is topped off with a fedora. The woman is rounder in that middle-aged kind of way. She's wearing a house dress, street slippers, and a head wrap trimmed with one giant red rose. Their clothes, and their beautiful skin tone, tell me they're Cuban. The fact they're dressed in mostly white means they must practice Santería.

I roll down the window, stick my head out into the misty, thick humidity of a late summer afternoon in Tampa. "Lo siento." I can't help that my apology is breathy, because their sudden appearance may be a sign.

Neither speaks. While still looking at me, the woman points down the street.

"Holy shit on a stick!" Orlando's voice rises. He points down the street at the same time.

My gaze follows their fingers. Color lights up the normally quiet neighborhood. First responders pack the narrow streets. The strobes on their sedans and vans slap red and blue onto everything in their path. It looks like a deathly disco dance floor.

Normally, I'd be itching to jump out of the news vehicle, hit the streets, and start asking questions, especially since I've learned people answer truthfully when you're first on the scene. But tonight, I've been handcuffed. I need to stay in the car, like El Jefe said, to keep bringing home the family paycheck. I'm the only one working.

"The focus is on the house at the end," Orlando says.

We're too far away to make out details. "Get closer. Before the police rope it off," I answer automatically because this feeling, this anticipation, this desire for the deep dive has fueled me for so long. Reporter's curiosity is the blood rushing through me.

And now I have to rein it in.

O drives again, slowly, so he doesn't hit the abuelos and abuelitas, or the families gathered in the street, gawking at the unusual spectacle.

I glance out the back windshield. The couple in white has vanished into the crowd. *They're fine*, I reassure myself, making note of the nearest house number with the porch lights on. It's the only one where residents aren't standing in the yard, gossiping about the action down their street. That's an interesting detail. I file it away for future reference.

Orlando rolls down his window. "Media coming through." He repeats this as he drives slowly through the crowd and maneuvers into a tight spot near the house with all the activity. I'm surprised we're able to get this close, but the scene is still hot.

He slams the car into park. "I'm jumping out."

"I'll call Busch Gardens and tell them we'll be late."

Orlando's at the back of the van grabbing his camera. He stops and looks at me.

I bluster as I say, "Hope the sloth baby can wait up for us." Sarcasm eases my pain.

He shakes his head. "This sucks."

"Todo bien." I wave him away, and he takes off toward the house. "Todo bien." But it's not fine. I lick my lips and twist my azabache bead. I'm not sure I actually believe in Abuela Bonita's old school Cuban religion. *But just in case.*

Police officers buzz around the house, a one-story, faded, yellow concrete block home like ours, but a little smaller and more rundown. I squint because the lights are bright and sting my eyes with their rhythmic slashing.

My gaze stops at the entranceway.

My breath stops with it.

Blood.

Even in the dimming light of dusk I see lots of it dripping down the pathway, oozing from one step to the other, flowing like a slow-moving, thick waterfall.

Tropical storm-like waves roll in my gut.

I need oxygen. I open the door. Step out. Gulp the sticky warmth of August air.

All the sounds — the sirens, the voices of the paramedics barking orders, the flurry of Spanish from concerned neighbors, fade into white noise.

The buzzing hurts my head.

Turn away. Walk away. Go away. But I can't help myself. My gaze follows the trail of blood up the steps. My heart skips, not from joy, but from dreaded anticipation. Then I see it. See *her*. A woman collapsed in the doorway as if murdered as soon as she answered.

I step forward and almost fall over the curb. I catch myself.

The woman's right leg twists into an awkward angle. Her bata de casa is hiked up in an inappropriate way, showing legs fat with age and inactivity. Her middle is wet, red. Impossible to tell anything except someone knifed or shot this mother, wife, sister, friend. Whichever it was, it wasn't just once.

The attack had been savage.

The fast-food rice and beans I ate about an hour ago rush back into my throat. I swallow, pushing the food back down.

Why don't they cover her?

A flash goes off. Techs taking pictures.

I should look away. Get back in the car. But I can't.

Did the doorbell ring first? It's around six thirty. The family was probably fixing dinner. Maybe Ropa Vieja or yellow rice and chicken? Tostones? Was anyone else home?

I look around for family, but all I see are professionals. Forensics snapping pictures of the dead body. A uniformed cop interviewing the next-door neighbor, who is flapping both hands in wild gestures. An investigator drops a yellow cone on the ground, signaling something of significance.

A red Kia Soul pulls in front of me, partially blocking my view. The doors open and two girls rush out, one with dark braids, wearing a St. Catherine's uniform. An older girl follows. A sister or cousin? Her hair is held back in a tight bun, and she's in a leotard mostly covered by gray sweatpants and a Mary Jo's glossy jacket.

The younger one takes off toward the house, braids flying behind her like two loose ropes.

The image ignites a memory. And a raging, painful fire deep in my chest. In my very soul.

A cop in a blue uniform darts after the younger girl, but he's not fast enough. She's running up the steps, taking two at a time, blind to the blood.

Her white sneakers are turning dark.

I can feel the girl's heart pounding, because mine is pounding, too.

She gets to the top step and drops to her knees. I

know she's about to fling herself over the woman's dead body.

Exactly what I'd wanted to do.

The girls scoop something off the patio where the woman's body is splayed. A bloody what? I squint. Step closer. A doll? The size of a Barbie, with broken, plastic arms swinging with the unexpected motion.

A man in jeans grabs the young girl under the armpits and pulls her up and away while she kicks and claws at him. She drops the doll.

Her sobs are horrific, the sound unspeakable.

I know that wail.

The grief starts in your belly and rises into your chest with a pain so intense you think you'll pass out from the intense pressure of it. The sound rips out of you, tearing everything you know into shreds.

Tears heat the back of my eyes. I blink, but I can't stop them from coming, hot reminders sliding down my cheeks.

I stumble back and clutch the door. When I close my eyes, the world starts spinning, but I don't open them.

Because I can smell it again.

The chicken fricassee Mamá cooked that night. The smell of the base sofrito, strong with onion and garlic swirling around the room like a permanent accessory. And I can see it now—the steam hanging low in her kitchen, thanks to the hot oil boiling to make my favorite fried plátanos.

My heart hurts with longing to see the most important person in my life one more time.

CHAPTER FOUR

A car door slams.

In that instant, I jerk back to the present.

Breathe in. Breathe out. Think positive thoughts. Maybe I should go back to therapy.

Orlando is standing a few feet away, behind some yellow crime tape. He's shooting video of the murder scene.

The older teenager, in the ballet jacket, stands behind the younger girl. They're to the side of the doorway, out of the way of the working officers and investigators. Two uniformed officers stand between them and the woman's body like guards, so they don't touch any more evidence. Those girls need hugs, not sequestration.

The younger girl is no longer kicking or screaming, but her face is red, and her shoulders are shaking. The older teen with the tight bun doesn't try to comfort her and doesn't appear to be crying. In fact, she's like stone, a statue standing out in this garden of misery.

She's holding in all the pain, like cement hardening inside you. Someone has to be the rock holding it together.

I should get back in the news vehicle, call Busch Gardens, check on a baby sloth who is probably sleeping. But all that's irrelevant right now. So who the fuck cares?

After trauma like this, if you don't talk to someone, the memory will eat you from the inside out.

Three questions will consume you forever: *Who? And why? And how could I have stopped it?*

You'll try to control the visions and the guilt by controlling everything else in your life. Your hair, your weight, your sister, your house.

Which way your water bottle faces.

How many times you twist the azabache charm.

I know this to be a cruel fate. I have to help these girls.

But I have to think of Izzy and Abuela first. I head to the news car to do what my boss ordered, but my mind is ahead of my feet. I trip over the curb, twisting my ankle, and yelp. The world is so focused on murder and its aftermath no one is paying attention to me. Not even Orlando.

I move my ankle. It's not broken.

I look up at the scene.

Broken.

Those two girls have been broken—their pain is more relevant than anything I'm feeling or a silly assignment I'm avoiding.

I can't let those teenagers suffer without a few words of comfort and advice on what to do next. And I can't walk away from the first crime scene to trigger some type of connection to the worst day of my life. The scenes are eerily similar.

I'm going to stay here, at least for a while, even if it gets me in trouble at work again.

I shut the SUV door, but leave it unlocked for Orlando. I finger my azabache charm again, careful not to break it. I need it tonight, even if it's a placebo. I have to get to the girls. It's wrong, but I can't ignore them like everyone ignored me—someone needs to assure them life will be normal again.

Someday it will. Right?

I must do this. The old man and woman—the Santería practitioners—literally pointed me in this direction. Maybe the orishas, the Santería saints, are leading me to information through the religious couple. That's how my grandmother told me it works.

I take off across the street, bounce off an approaching cop car, and jump the curb. Heart sprinting, my breath barely keeping up, I lift the yellow crime scene tape, knowing full well what could happen if I walk under it. But for these broken girls, I'm willing to cross the line.

So I do.

CHAPTER FIVE

Orlando is spraying the scene. His heavy camera, up on his shoulder, points at the front door and two forensic experts. One tech takes pictures, the other notes evidence with small yellow cones. I want to get closer to see what's being singled out as potential evidence, but my gaze shoots back to the older teen. She doesn't even blink as two medics push a gurney in front of her, a bag on top for the dead body.

The girls come first. They are broken but still alive.

Her younger sister, the one wearing the stained shoes, wobbles as her knees give.

My heart stretches. I step toward her, too far away to help.

A petite female in plain clothes flings her arms around the girl, stopping her fall.

I stop, too.

I don't take my gaze off the girls, though. The female investigator positions her arm around the youngest, bloodying her detective's shirt, but the woman doesn't pull away. Her head is low like she's offering encouragement to the victims as they all walk toward an unmarked car about three cars down from me.

On the *legal* side of the yellow crime scene tape.

Thank you, orisha of mine. You must be watching

and helping me.

I lift the tape, about to slip back under it. A quick glance around to make sure no one—

¡Carajo! An athletic-looking guy in jeans notices me, stilling me with his concentrated, connecting gaze. He's too far away to ask me where I'm going or what I'm doing, but the questions are evident in his stiff body stance. I'm betting he's a cop. I step to the legal side, drop the crime scene tape, and turn my back to the man. If he's heading this way, if he catches up with me, he'll likely tell me I can't have access to an active crime scene or the victims within it. And he's right.

Or, if he is a detective, he could charge me with entering an active crime scene illegally.

My breath literally arrests, but I don't have time to ponder my fate. The victims are no longer within the crime scene borders, and their law enforcement protector is walking over to talk to—well, look at that—none other than beefy guy. That should keep him away from me for a minute. Or two, if I'm lucky.

I take a deep breath. Now's my chance to talk to these victims without interference, and I head toward the girls.

"Where ya going?" Orlando steps in front of me, blocking my progress. "I came to tell you the boss man is trying to get a hold of you."

I glance at my phone. El Jefe's number is on the recent call list. He's called three times. *¡Carajo!* I didn't even feel my phone buzz.

"He asked if we'd left for Busch Gardens yet. He also asked why you aren't answering your phone."

"My phone's on silent. I'll call him." But I'm not

going to. I'm looking at the older girl, the one who needs to cry, and I'm already planning to throw my arms around her and hug her until she realizes I mean her no harm. I'm going to—

"Mari, you hearing me?"

"Yes, Orlando." I throw up both hands. "Boss called. Go interview the sloth. Got it."

He shakes his head, his dark eyes alarmed at my answer. "Our backup arrived. Boss says if we don't bring back that damn sloth story and meet our deadline, we're both in deep shit. Let's beat it."

I look at my wingman, my photographer for the last five years. He's the man who knows my deepest, darkest secrets, and I can't for the life of me tell if he's going to cover for me after I tell him the decision I've made. His job is on the line, too. He was my photographer on the serial killer story, and he'd voted not to run my off-the-record information linking the city council member to the deaths of several young girls. Orlando had said it's important to prove a man's guilt before sentencing him to a public hanging. Figuratively, of course.

I did it anyway, editing in the lines myself. I had a damn good source.

"I'm staying. I'm going to help these girls. You go and shoot the B-roll and interview at Busch Gardens. I'll Uber to you when I'm done. We'll write and edit the story in the Busch Gardens parking lot. It'll be fine."

"Marisol… Don't do this." O never uses my whole name.

"It won't take long." I can't even look at him as I move my feet. "I promise. We'll get the sloth story done." I can feel him following me, and his energy is blistering. "I need to talk to the oldest girl."

He grabs me, and I jerk to a stop.

"I'm not going to broadcast anything." I break from his hold and spin around. "This is personal." I can hardly spit the words out. "This is the first time since the murder that I've felt a connection to a crime scene. I have to follow my gut."

His face is hard, eyes so wide I wonder if his eyeballs are about to explode.

"Reporter's instinct." I lower my voice. "Please."

He doesn't respond or break eye contact. We're in a stand-off. Not our first.

"Hey, who let the media over here?" We both hear the voice at the same time. Probably another cop who'll try and make us move.

Orlando breaks first. He drops the camera to his side. "No trouble here, okay? And you meet me at Busch Gardens in an hour."

CHAPTER SIX

I stride toward the older teen standing outside of the cop car. Her younger sister is already seated in the back seat.

I'm doing everything I can not to run. Or look back at Orlando or the two detectives.

The girl with the bun is biting her fingernails, which I find odd, considering the rest of her looks so perfectly put together.

I surprise her when I touch her shoulder and say, "Hi, I'm so sorry for your loss."

The girl jumps away from me. "You knew my mother?" Her face lightens a shade.

"No…I—" Okay, the dead woman *is* her mother. "What's your name?" I reach out my hand in a gesture of comfort and respect. "I'm Mari Álvarez."

She doesn't take it. "The girl on TV?"

"Yes." That she's heard of me could be a good thing or a bad thing.

"I'm Anastasia Rodríguez."

And I'm surprised she's telling me—a reporter— her name. Her flat tone convinces me it's because she's in shock and on autopilot. "And your mom's name is?"

New emotion, either hate or anger, flashes in her eyes like a blast of heat lightning. "You don't remember?"

"Should I?" I dig for a reason I'd know her mom. I couldn't see the dead woman's face, and I haven't been to this house before.

"Natasha."

"Excuse me?" I'm still trying to place the news story where I might have met her mom.

"My mom's name was Natasha Rodríguez."

The name sounds familiar.

"She's dead."

Those two words linger in the damp heat of the evening. "I'm sorry. Someone murdered my mother, too."

At my words, the older teen's stiff, controlled features melt. First, her bottom lip quivers, then her eyes well up. She puts her hands up to cover her face.

She's ashamed of her lack of control. I remember that feeling so well my own cheeks are flushing.

Her shoulders rock, but unlike the other girl, probably her sister, no sound comes out of her.

I reach out and fold her into my arms, hugging her as if I'm her mother, and her body molds with mine. There's no resistance. It's what I wanted someone to do to me that night. Show me some compassion and give me comfort. But no one had.

I stiffen when I realize someone is watching us. A man in a dark, sweatshirt type hoodie. Close, personal contact is totally inappropriate for a reporter and the person she's interviewing. I don't give a damn. Grief is a motherfucking roller coaster ride—without a seat belt. "I know exactly how you're feeling." And once grief has whipped you around too many corners, you form compassion for those taking the same jarring journey.

The girl's tears wet my neck. What else can I tell her? What do I wish someone had told me the night a murderer massacred my mother? "You need to get into therapy. It will help you survive this."

"What?" Her voice cracks.

"Therapy will help. You need to talk about this." Before it turns your heart to stone.

The girl shoves me away. "What do you want?"

I don't blame her. I've offended her. "I want to help you. What do you need?"

She grabs herself, wrapping her arms around her own body, pressing her fingertips into her jacket until the tips of her fingers go white.

"You have any idea who might have killed your mother?" I'm rushing now because I see the athletic-looking cop in jeans in my peripheral vision. He's pointing to me.

"No." The girl with the bun says, "I...no—"

The female detective starts long-stepping our way.

"An angry boyfriend?" I ask.

The female cop is talking on her radio, mouth moving fast. The other detective strides behind.

"Did your mom owe anyone money?"

Ballet girl shakes her head.

No time for a slow warm up. "Was that doll yours? Or your sister's?"

She shakes her head at a quicker pace. "Someone stabbed the doll in the eye." The teen trembles. "Ripped it out and jabbed the doll in the chest. Just like—" Her voice morphed into a sob.

I bring a hand to my heart. *Creepy.* "You know why?"

"Why someone stabbed a Barbie doll? And killed my mom?" Her eyes are wide pools of rippling terror. "No, but I...but she..."

"But she what?" I take a deep breath. No time to go easy. "This could be important information I can use to help you."

"My mom had a huge, gold coin covering one of her eyes. The other was wide open. Staring at me. But...but not seeing me."

"A gold coin?" *Creepier.* And what's with the one eye open, one shut?

"I think it was a coin. I... I...couldn't bear to look at her like that. Dead." The girl's voice cracked.

"You recognize the coin? Maybe it was your dad's?"

"My dad is dead."

I freeze.

The young woman's face is ashen, her world burned to the ground. "I'm sorry." And I am. I really freaking am. "You have other family?" I'm no longer asking for clues about the murder. I'm consumed with helping this kindred spirit. This beautiful, broken girl.

"A brother." More tears hover on her lower lashes. She swipes them away. "He's in prison."

Ah, damn. "Who is going to take care of you all now?" And it hits me like a big stone to the head, this young woman and her siblings need protection. I jerk off my azabache bracelet and roll it onto her wrist. I know it's both forward and odd. It's also necessary.

She grabs at my hand. "What are you doing?"

But I'm not letting her take it off. "It's an

azabache charm." I yank her hand up, probably a little too forcefully, until the important black charm dangles in front of her face. "It's evil eye protection."

Her eyes round, big, and white. "I don't—" She pulls her hand away like I'm burning her.

Heat prickles the back of my neck. "As long as you wear the charm, it will protect you against the evil eye." I ignore her backing away. "As long as you wear it, nothing can harm you. No one can—"

A hand on my shoulder.

I jump. Turn to see the guy in jeans towering over me, his eyes glowering.

The female detective tries pulling the older teen away from us, but she resists, twisting away from the cop.

Beefy-in-jeans glares at me. "You should be ashamed of yourself."

I lift my chin. "Who are you? And what's your problem with me trying to help her?" I sneak a look at the teenager.

She's pushing the bracelet up her arm, hiding it beneath her clothing.

So they can't take it from her? *Good.* She understands sometimes you must hide your beliefs from the nonbelievers.

"I have a problem with reporters selling lies," Beefy-in-jeans says.

He knows I'm a reporter? Of course he does. I should bite my tongue, but I'm so pissed I might bite it off. "What lie?"

"The evil eye. What the fuck is that?"

I pull back, stunned by his use of profanity—and his question. So he saw me give her the azabache charm? Does he even know what it is? "Let me guess. You're a good Catholic boy who doesn't believe—"

"Altar boy," he interrupts. "Sacred Heart. Attended Jesuit High."

"Well, good for you." *Aren't you privileged?* Private school boy versus me, the West Tampa street girl. "Well, I'm a good Catholic girl, too. Baptized and confirmed at St. Lawrence. Attended Academy of the Holy Names." *On scholarship.* But that still counts. "I'm as *educated* as you are."

"And yet you—"

"And yet I believe everyone has a right to believe what they believe."

He cocks his head, and those dark eyes narrow further. A slight smile and a barely there shake of his head follows.

"You need proof, right? Because you're a detective." I make it a statement and not a question.

He doesn't correct me. I was right. He is a cop. "The proof is in the history. Hinduism preaches that the evil eye is the most powerful point at which the body can give off energy. Jews have sought to ward off the evil eye with amulets, particularly Hamsa. The evil eye is even found in the Islamic doctrine—"

"I don't remember reading anything about it in the Bible."

The female detective is pushing the girl into the car with her sister. I want her to hear, so I speak louder. "Jesus referenced the evil eye in his Sermon on the Mount. If your eye is evil, your entire body will be full of darkness."

The female detective slams the door, but I'm sure

the girl heard me.

Beefy detective steps closer, whispers, "You're selling false hope and unproven protection."

"I'm not selling anything. Sometimes faith is all the protection you need." My response surprises me because, despite my background, I'm not a religious person, in the traditional sense. After Mamá's murder, I stopped going to church on Sundays. I've never gone to confession, even though I've got plenty to confess. And I grew up questioning the old school Cuban beliefs I am now defending.

"I believe what I see, Ms. Álvarez. I don't believe in silly superstitions."

It's the word silly that makes my blood pressure rocket skyward. Because what does this man know? What do any of us know, for sure?

Then I realize this cop has addressed me by my name. ¡Carajo! What else does he know about me?

CHAPTER SEVEN

"You know who I am, right?" I regret those words as soon as they exit my mouth. Because, I mean, who wouldn't want to put someone in their place with a pair of handcuffs and a career-ending trespassing charge when they sound as arrogant as I just did? *¡Ay, Dios mío!* I'm my own worst enemy.

"I do know who you are, Ms. Álvarez."

His smirk and his narrowing, dark eyes tell me that's not a good thing. Of course he knows. After that damn article in the *Tampa Bay Times*, every freaking person in Tampa knows about the lawsuit and my suspension after my serial killer story. The fact I've become a victim of my own profession shouldn't stun me. But it does.

"I saw you enter the crime scene under the tape. I'd think a reporter knows better than to break the law to get a story."

¡Carajo! Damnit! "Was just doing my job." Not an admission of guilt.

The man points to the crime scene tape like I don't see it. "Your right to do your job stops where the crime scene tape begins."

I wonder if that line is in some Tampa Police Department rule book.

"I was still on a public sidewalk." I give him a sweeping gesture pointing out the obvious. "So I had every right to be there." Which, of course, is in every Journalism 101 textbook.

"A crime scene trumps public access." He lifts both eyebrows and looks like he's trying not to smile.

He's got me. Ignoring that truth, I go right into reporter mode. "Got any suspects? Any idea who would want to kill their mother?"

"The Public Information Officer will be here shortly."

Touché.

"We'll be setting up a command post down the street at…"

I don't even hear him, much less retain the location because I know he's blowing me off, which pisses me off. As does the fact this man, standing in the Florida humidity, which makes my hair morph into an ugly Brillo-pad, looks perfect. His slicked back hair acts like a protective shield. The scruff on his face is manscaped into a perfect goatee. His bronze skin is flawless. Not even a drop of sweat. He's too good looking. I know the type. Probably another macho, playboy Latino, who doesn't respect a woman for her brains and ability.

"I only wanted to help the girls. Especially the older one, who hasn't cried since she arrived." Had he even noticed that? "She's in shock."

His left eyebrow crooks up. "You want to help her like you helped that Tampa City Council member?"

My spine straightens, even though his tone is factual, not condescending. "Police suspected the city council member of murder." The heat rises into my cheeks again. This time it stings.

"I arrested him."

Hmmm. Beefy in jeans is homicide. Must be new. "Well then, why did you let a guilty man go free?"

The detective's chin rises.

I've offended him with my blunt, journalistic honesty. He's not the first.

"I didn't." He takes a step back but doesn't look away. "The State Attorney decided not to press charges."

Humidity rises like a barrier between us. "Does it matter to you that a murderer may be walking free?"

He's drilling me with an interesting look. "Does it matter to you that a justice system only works when you follow the rules. Like—don't cross crime scene tape."

I cringe but hold a poker face.

"The State Attorney followed the rules of law—as currently written."

Well, isn't that official sounding. "Releasing him was a mistake."

The cop reaches behind his back.

I stiffen. Is he going for his handcuffs? He's actually going to arrest me? For three seconds on the wrong side of the crime tape?

El Jefe is going to kill me. Right after he fires me. *Shit*.

"I agree." A stick-thin man, also in blue jeans and a black baseball hat, saunters over with even more cop-like swagger than muscled cop.

But he may have just rescued me. So, instantly I like him.

"Releasing that prick was bullshit. Hey," the new cop says, his tone one pitch too high to be his normal, talking voice, "It's City Council Killer."

"Excuse me?" I look around to see who he's talking about. It's me, of course. So much for liking him. "My name is Mari. Not Mary. Not Marie. Not City Council Killer. It's Mari. Rhymes with sorry." Which he will be if he calls me that again.

"Mari, rhymes with sorry. That's the headline you wrote, right?" new cop says.

My serial-killer story strikes again. And again. "I didn't write the headline."

"Works as a title for you now, doesn't it?" New cop is sneering.

Or maybe that's the way his mouth always looks. *Weird*. Like he can't close his lips and his teeth always show. "I don't get what you mean."

"Your story literally killed the city council member's career." The new cop shoves his unusually large hands in his front pockets. "Whether he's innocent or guilty, he's done professionally. You are"—he points at me—"a city council killer."

Is he trying to be funny? Or throwing shade? Finally, I say, "The city council suspended him pending the investigation." Now *I* sound like the cop. "But I'm sure he'll be fine." Especially if he wins his lawsuit against the station and files one against me.

The cocky new guy, who's about twice my height—okay a slight exaggeration—has an unremarkable face, except for that weird, constant half smile.

He shrugs. "Off the record, I agreed with your

story." New cop lifts the cap and winks at me.

Fit cop tilts his head and shifts, looking as uncomfortable as I feel. "You're not in homicide anymore, Hanks."

New cop is named Hanks.

"But I used to be. One for all, all for one, right, García?"

Fit cop's last name is García. *Cuban?* He's the kind of guy Abuela Bonita keeps praying I'll marry.

"Hey, I might be able to help." Hanks plays with his cap. A nervous habit? "Mind if I check out the crime scene?"

Suddenly, it's like I'm not even in the conversation. I could be insulted, but a good reporter knows when to shut up, watch, and listen. I'll let the two Alphas wrestle with words. Maybe I'll learn something valuable. Like do they both work for Tampa Police or is the new guy FBI? Or maybe I'll not get myself arrested.

Either is a win.

"What's your interest now?" García asks, his arms crossed against his chest, which shows off his flexed muscles.

Hanks pauses. Crosses his arms, too.

Men. I roll my eyes.

Hanks looks at me and smirks. "Well, I'd tell you, García, but I'd rather not have details of an open investigation repeated incorrectly on tonight's fake news."

"Wow." The fake news part did exactly what I'm sure Hanks wanted it to—it annoyed me. *What a dick.* I bite back a nasty reply. Fighting with either won't get me what I want.

"Make sure you sign in like everyone else," García says to Hanks.

"Got it." Hanks tips his baseball cap in an exaggerated gesture. It's a Tampa Bay Lightning hockey hat. Has to be, with that giant lightning bolt.

"You a hockey fan?" I throw out.

"What? No." Hanks turns to García. "Document my presence. Will do."

Hanks, who's probably a detective, too, walks past the crime scene tape.

"Hey." García's touch on my shoulder makes me jump. Hanks is almost at the house.

"Is that guy a cop with Tampa, too?"

García nods. "Former homicide. Works cold cases now."

"Cold cases?" I ask out loud, without even thinking. "And he's here? Interesting."

García's eyebrows cave, and he says, "Why did you bother those girls? They don't know what happened. They weren't here. And they're both grieving right now."

My shoulders hike up. "Why do you think I bothered them?" Why do people automatically assume reporters have a deceitful intention? "Maybe they were thankful for my help."

He nods, but I don't see agreement in his eyes. "And maybe you wanted the lead story, and you're willing to exploit a traumatized family for a soundbite, so your pretty face can be on TV."

So condescending! "You know nothing about me." He knows nothing about how to talk to women, either, although he probably thinks he does.

He doesn't look put off. In fact, the way he shifts

back and further examines me makes me think he does consider me pretty. He adds, "You've been reckless with the facts and a city councilman's reputation."

Now my thermostat is rising. "You arrested him."

"As I recall, your boss suspended you for reporting your opinions. You didn't stick to my police report."

"I based my reports on your police statement." And one well-placed anonymous source deep inside the police department.

He licks his lips and looks away. Maybe I hit a nerve?

"I'm sorry, I didn't get your name."

"Detective Antonio García."

He smiles with his eyes and for one minute I think he's enjoying this tit-for-tat.

"But friends call me Tony. Or García. Want my badge number, too?"

He is enjoying this. Of course he is. I know his type well. I don't answer his question—make him a little nervous about my intentions. Now I'm enjoying this, too.

"Mari, Mari, Mari,,,"

My shoulder's hike up. I can tell by that voice the crime reporter wannabe is here. I turn to face Jessica Spencer. But I say nothing.

"What are you still doing here?" she asks.

"I'm leaving."

Jessica eyes García with an appreciation that makes me want to roll my eyes again, but I hold my poker face. I'll hold it until he leaves, even if it kills me. At least Jessica didn't bring up the damn sloth.

"I'm here to relieve you, so you can go solve the mystery of the baby sloth birth at Busch Gardens." She flicks a flirty grin at García, but he's looking at me, both eyebrows raised.

We're not done with our conversation, but I choose to address my coworker. "I turn the crime scene over to you, Jessica, with pleasure." *Smile. Warmly.* I ball my fists until my sharp nails pierce my palm. Now, I face García. "Detective García, meet Jessica Spencer." Jessica, who's still smiling at García, steps in front of me and holds out her hand. Her long nails look recently manicured. García takes it. He never shook mine. "The detective is about to tell you to head to the command post and talk to the PIO." Now García checks her out. And they're still shaking hands. How expected and disappointing. "But hey, maybe I'm wrong." They're not even listening to me.

"Nice to meet you, Detective." Jessica, with the long blond hair of TV news legends, looks down at where their bodies are connecting.

A horn honks.

I jump and turn toward the sound. O hasn't left yet? He leans over from the driver's seat and puts down the passenger side window. "Hey, Álvarez, sorry I'm late with the car."

I exhale. He's saving me. I can't even look at García. Or Jessica.

He reaches over and opens the passenger side door. "Jump in. We've got a sloth story to rock."

Orlando, even after I pissed him off, comes to my rescue. My black knight in invisible shining armor. I love him. I truly love him.

As soon as I jump in the car he moves, but he can only creep through the crowd still gathered in the street.

"Why do you engage with her?" he asks.

"Because she wants my job." We both know Jessica is gunning for it. "And I'm not going to make it easy for her."

He swerves to miss a man in a black hoodie who's standing next to a group of teenagers playing soccer in the street, as if a dead body in a doorway was nothing unusual. The kids play on, but the man in the hoodie looks up. I think I recognize him. Was he the guy lurking around the scene earlier? When I was comforting the girl? Has to be. Or maybe I've seen him at some other story before?

"But you *are* making it easy for her," O says.

He's right. I let Jessica get to me. I wish I could control my envy and insecurity. What did Abuela say? When you're at the top of your game, the devil comes for you. The devil being envy and ego?

He shakes his head. "How 'bout we go to Busch Gardens and hang out with less dangerous creatures?"

I take a laugh. He's trying to make me smile. Take the edge off. "Okay."

"Okay?"

"Okay." I cave, because suddenly I'm exhausted. I want to lean back and close my eyes until we get there.

Then I see her, the beautiful, dark-skinned woman dressed all in white. A headdress hides her hair. Her flowing skirt is undulating in the soft breeze, dancing around her. The woman we almost hit earlier, the one who's been watching me, who pointed me down the street. Maybe she has a message from my orisha saint. I can't even remember his name. My Abuela Bonita would want me to stop and listen.

Sometimes faith is all you need. Isn't that what I told Detective García? Sometimes faith is following what you can't see. "Stop."

O smacks the steering wheel with the palm of his hand. "I'm not stopping."

He does slow down, though, because he knows me. I'm a singled-minded, stubborn woman, and O knows I will do what I want, with or without his cooperation. "I'll meet you at Busch Gardens."

"If you don't, I can't protect you." The car rolls to a stop. "I want to protect you."

I should stay and let him.

Instead I open the car door, jump into the street, and walk quickly toward the unknown.

CHAPTER EIGHT

The lady in white tells me she's a new neighborhood friend of my Abuela Bonita's. She ushers me through her house, bypassing the cluttered kitchen which smells of delicious sofrito bubbling on the stove. That's highly unusual for a Cuban host, considering the kitchen and conversation over food is the heartbeat of our culture. I stop, inhale the familiar scent, my heart aching as I relive the joy of my friends feasting on Mamá's magia en la cocina. She did make magic in the kitchen. My mouth waters. As do my eyes.

My abuela's friend tugs on my wrist, pulling me out of the memory and down a hallway. Her urgency ignites fireflies of worry, lighting up my already overtaxed brain.

So I follow her into the back area of her house and into a screened-in lanai, stopping at the entranceway. My mouth drops open.

Tall, lush tropical plants cover the porch from floor to ceiling, isolating us from anyone's prying eyes and also acting as an audio cushion for the cries and sirens continuing down the street. Music is playing, loud enough to add another layer of protection. I recognize the same Afro-Cuban rhythms my Abuela Bonita loves. Music—no words—and a beat that makes your body move unconsciously, like the pounding of the drums possess your muscles. The room smells of tobacco smoke, fingers of which dance in the warm breeze kicked up by a floor fan.

The man Orlando and I almost ran over is sitting in a simple rocking chair in the corner. His back is straight, his posture regal.

I know this man is a Babalawo. My heart races, sending waves of anticipation rippling outward. Abuela Bonita shielded me from her backroom religion, mostly because my mother didn't approve. But after Mamá died, Abuela Bonita began to open up when I asked questions. Still, I have no idea how to properly address him. So I transfer my weight and shift automatically into my blunt, reporter mode. "Why am I here?"

The man strokes a small lap dog. Long, patient strokes.

Despite the hum of the fan on the floor, little droplets of sweat form on my forehead and under my arms.

He finally glances up, warmth in his dark brown eyes. "People come for various reasons. For their health—"

"But I'm not sick." I want to inhale those words as soon as they're out, but I can't. I know I've disrespected him. I also know he's right. I don't have the flu, but my heart is broken, my faith in justice… severed. I'm sick with grief that's never healed. I swallow, sweat bubbling now in the lower crook of my spine. The ground fan is only recirculating warm air.

The Babalawo's eyes darken. The Christmas-type

lights, strung around the lanai, reflect in his pupils, reminding me of the cops' flashing lights outside.

"Your abuela sent you to me," he says.

It's a statement, but— "No." I glance behind me. Where did my abuela's friend go? "No, I think my orisha guided me to you. And it has something to do with the murder down the street."

"I see." He lights a candle, one clearly used a lot. It's almost burned down to the white plastic plate. "What is it you seek?" It fizzles and pops but finally lights.

"I seek justice." The truth spills out of me, as if ignited by that flame. "I'm driven by it." *Recklessly*. "I need justice for my family." I can't take my eyes off the dancing finger of fire. "Justice for the family down the street, too."

He begins to rock back and forth. "You seek an eye for an eye?" The rocker creaks as the man moves back and forth to the music.

Every hair on my body stands. But the music is hypnotic, and my words follow the beat. "I don't know."

He stops the rocking and reaches for an object on a side table, rolling it between his fingers like it's a cigar. It's a bronze thing that looks like a cross between the pestle I use to grind garlic and a musical instrument you might find in a kindergarten class. "If justice is deserved, does it matter how it's served?" he asks.

The room is starting to fade around the edges. Why does that question make me dizzy?

He shakes the bronze thing, but it makes no sound. His haunted eyes appear to go unfocused.

He doesn't speak.

The music pauses, and I hear the whirl of the fan.

I can't stand the silence anymore. "I've got to—"

The sound of a shekere starts. The hollowed gourd, dressed in a skirt of multicolored beads, swishes as if sand is inside. The shaking sound blends perfectly with the beat of both bongos and drums.

I blurt out, "I want to know who killed my mother." I'm not sure where that came from.

His eyes focus, and his body stiffens. He grows taller in his chair.

"I *need* to know who killed my mother." I'm not even sure I said it out loud this time. Doesn't matter. Recognition sparks in his gaze.

"I don't know who killed your mother." He places the bronze thing down. "But you do."

I step back. *Really?*

"I don't." Would I be here, risking my damn job, feeling awkward at best, at worst…scared…if I already knew who killed my mamá? "I don't. Who told you that?" I look around the lanai, not even sure what the hell I'm looking for. Spirits? Orishas? My abuela's friend?

"Child, you must lean on your orisha and stand on your own two feet or these questions you ask will crush someone you love dearly. This is what I see."

"Okay." I inhale. But I have no idea what that means. "Those girls at the scene down the street, they reminded me of my sister and me. It's the first time I've felt a connection to my mother's murder. I've been waiting ten years to feel…feel something. Learn something. Have the police finally proven something."

"There is a connection." He's still now. "I feel it." The dog wiggles off his lap and bounces out of the lanai. "Follow the path of your thoughts."

"The older girl I met at the crime scene acted like I should know her mother, and her name did sound familiar. I meet so many people in this job."

"Everyone in our neighborhood knows her mother."

The new voice startles me. I look behind me and see a floating red circle on the other side of the lanai. It gets brighter, hotter. It has to be my abuela's friend, the Babalawo's sister. She's been sitting quietly in the far corner all this time?

I shiver.

"I felt the calling from Cuba to visit my sister," the Babalawo says. "I felt compelled to leave my beautiful Playa Hermosa. Now I know why."

A cold streak hits my spine. He came from Cuba? To see me? *Okay, this is getting weird.*

"What do you do when you need information?" The Babalawo picks up a glass and sips what looks like dark rum.

I wish he'd offer me some. I know he expects me to say, *I go to a Babalawo.* I probably should, but I can't lie. "I usually visit Google."

He smiles, his eyes gleaming under raised eyebrows.

"Right." I grab my iPhone and type in the name *Natasha Rodríguez — Tampa.* Headlines pop up. *Day-Drinking Deputy Neglects Teen Shooting Suspect. Deputy's gun used to kill 6-year-old neighbor girl.*

It all comes flooding back.

Natasha Rodríguez, the deputy, drank on her day off and slept through an accidental shooting at her house. I close my eyes, blood pressure rocketing as I recreate the image. The corpse in the doorway tonight, who reminded me of my mom, was the former deputy. The mother of the teen who shot and killed a six-year-old neighborhood girl three years ago. Sofía Figueroa. The young victim had delicate features with large, beautiful lips. It was a huge news story. But at the time, the mom went by Nat Rodríguez or just Deputy Rodríguez. Her son shot his best friend's six-year-old sister with her department-issued weapon. The son spent some time in juvie, but the mom never served any time as I recall. "But that shooting didn't happen at the house on this street."

"They moved." The sister tilted her head back and let out a halo of cigar smoke. "Wouldn't you?"

I had to move in with Abuela Bonita after Mamá was murdered. I could never walk through that front door again. "But it happened in this neighborhood, a couple streets over, right?"

I click on YouTube, because it's all coming back now. What I need to see is video. I want to see faces. Because my reporter's instinct is burning like the Babalawo's candle. Ironically, my fingers go cold. If I'm right, I fucked up. I saw the six-year-old victim's father on the street only moments ago. I interviewed him years ago. His haunted eyes are unforgettable. But how could I have known in the moment? O and I were trying to miss hitting him. He was in a black sweatshirt. With a hood, I think. He's probably gone now. And yet, maybe still only a few streets away. My heart skips like a flat stone over still water.

Maybe the police can still get him. *Oh God.* I slip my fingers under my sleeve, searching for the azabache charm. Three to the right. Three to—

It's not there. I gave it to the broken girl. To keep *her* safe. My head flops back against the wall.

"Marisol, tell me what you're thinking, ángel mío," the Babalawo asks.

I'm thinking that I'm no angel. "I let him go."

"Who, Marisol?" The lady in white lifts from her chair in a cloud of white cigar smoke and waddles over, arms outstretched.

"The victim's dad was in the crowd tonight." I fall into her arms because I want to hide. She's softer than my Abuela Bonita, but her energy feels the same. Welcoming, accepting, loving, nonjudgmental. The only difference—she smells of strong Cohiba cigar smoke. I exhale and whisper, "Justice was never served for that six-year-old girl, Sofía Figueroa." I sense more energy. Reluctantly, I pull away from the lady in white's embrace. "Maybe it was finally served up tonight. Maybe her dad killed Natasha Rodríguez."

The Babalawo is standing next to me now. He says nothing.

"I have to go." I've got to find the by-the-books detective. What was his name? García. I need to tell him I have a potential suspect for him. The man in the hoodie. The man Orlando and I almost hit as we were leaving. That man in the street could be Sofía Figueroa's father. Why would he be wandering around the scene of Natasha Rodríguez's murder tonight? Maybe the murder was committed by this grieving father, finally serving justice himself?

Killing the mom who slept through his beautiful daughter's murder. The deputy who had unloaded her weapon but failed to check for a bullet in the chamber. An accident—but a deadly one. My heart is beating so hard I can hear it above the bongos.

"Thank you," I say to the Babalawo. Not because he gave me this information, but because he cleared my mind enough to think and find it myself. He cleared the mental weeds for me to see the path.

He nods and points toward the door.

My phone buzzes. I grab it out of my pocket. *¡Carajo! Orlando!*

He texts: *On your way?*

My breath stalls. How could I have forgotten about O, Busch Gardens, and baby sloths?

He texts: *I know you're not. I'm tracking you on Snapchat.*

Damnit. I didn't sign out.

He texts: *It shows me you're still on Hesperides. Leave now and text Julie in PR when you arrive.*

I don't want to read the rest. But I do.

She'll meet you at Gate Three. Hustle. We can't miss deadline.

¡Carajo!

What I learned after my mom's death is that sometimes justice is not served, even if it is deserved. And I won't move onto the next stage of my life until I see justice done. So I have to do it myself. I can't let a killer walk free, even if it's not my mom's killer.

I text Orlando: *Got a tip on possible suspect in tonight's murder. If I'm right, this is going to be a big story. So, here's the plan. I have the press*

*release from Busch Gardens with me. I can write
the story here, record audio on the iPhone, and
email it to you. You can edit in the parking lot of BG
and feed in a complete news story with my voice
on it. No one will know I'm not there with you.*

What I mean is El Jefe won't know.

I type: *If the police decide to take in my suspect
for questioning, I may be the only one who knows.
I know where the suspect lives. I'll get the video
with my iPhone.*

I hit send.

No way I'm letting those two sisters suffer like
Izzy and I suffered. Ten years we've been waiting for
police to nail Mamá's killer.

Between the time that's past and the memories
that surfaced at the crime scene, I'm beginning to
believe we'll have to do it ourselves.

But tonight, I can be the one to make sure justice
is served for someone else.

That's when I notice the Babalawo's rocking
chair. It's still rocking, but he's not in it.

I sprint over to the chair and with one hand stop
the rocking. But my heart is still zip-lining toward it,
because I remember another one of the secrets
Abuela Bonita whispered to me in her extra-large
closet at the back of her bedroom.

Never let a rocking chair swing by itself.
It means death is approaching.

CHAPTER NINE

Back on the street, I push through the growing crowd of residents gawking at the crime scene. Those returning from their day jobs stand with their friends, speaking over each other, trying to reason away what had happened in their tight-knit enclave tonight.

I recognize and nod at a few of them. Abuela Bonita's pharmacist, Roberto González, holds a weekly dominoes tournament on his front porch. The lady who runs a small, assisted living home next to Roberto is standing on the front lawn.

Izzy's high school boyfriend, Raúl, used to live on this street. He always drove a brand new Ford Mustang that he bragged about. His parents still reside in the corner house, but when Izzy broke it off with Raúl, she forbade me to talk to his family anymore.

A new Mustang is sitting in their driveway. This one is shiny red and black. *Fancy.* I recognize Raúl's dad standing in their front yard, but I'm glad I don't see Raúl. He's rumored to be dead. Never did trust him. Still, I wonder about whatever happened to the possessive, destructive gangbanger.

A slight movement in my peripheral vision makes me still. I turn toward their house. The drapes covering a bedroom window move back into place, fluttering like my thoughts. It's as if someone was watching the crime scene, but when I showed up, they didn't want to be seen. My heart hardens. Has to be Raúl's mother. After my mamá made Izzy break it off with her son, Raúl's mother shunned us, too. Apparently, she still does. Fine. Like I care.

The spread of worried words rolling through our neighborhood rises and falls, like football fans creating a stadium wave. Until it fades.

The street falls silent.

I stop, curious.

And watch.

The medical examiner's van drives by, and people part to let it pass.

The break in the crowd gives me a chance to search for Detective García. I've got to tell him my theory about Sofía's dad as a suspect and see what he does next. He has to at least question Mr. Figueroa, right?

Forensics is still on scene. One tech is over six-four, tall enough that when you see him, you remember him. He's crouched down near the front steps using what looks like large eyebrow tweezers to pick up something out of a pool of blood. It's as if Forensics Freddy senses my sudden queasiness. Or my presence. He looks up, catches my eye, and nods.

I nod back. I've got more than a few questions for him, but not now. We have our own Woodward and Bernstein methods of delivering off-the-record information. So as not to draw attention to our connection I'm about to turn away, when a line of light from an investigator's flashlight hits the baggie Freddie's holding up. It looks like a necklace made of red and white beads. Or maybe white beads stained with blood.

I turn away, the vision unsettling.

And there is Jessica, crime reporter wannabe, across the street interviewing a neighbor. The woman, in a floor-length house dress, waves her hands as she speaks. She points to the house where the woman died, almost to where I'm standing.

My breath catches. I slide behind a truck so Jessica can't see me. If she does, she might call El Jefe. ¡Carajo! I feel like a kid who's playing hooky and my damn teacher shows up.

Then I notice a truck parked where the female detective's unmarked car was. An empty, cold feeling flutters over me. I wonder where the girls will end up tonight. *Please not emergency foster care.* The stories I've done about that mess—sometimes foster care is worse than the nightmare at home.

I still don't see Detective García. Inside the house, maybe? I'm probably not getting past the patrol cop standing at the end of the driveway, but I can at least leave a message with him. I have information García needs to know. Tonight.

Someone grabs me at the elbow.

I jerk around. All I see is a black hoodie like the one Sofía's dad was wearing when we almost hit him.

I hold my breath. Step back.

"I thought you'd left," the man says in a voice I don't recognize.

I lean forward to get a better look at the man's face. Air rushes out in relief, and my shoulders drop.

It's not Sofía's dad. I'd interviewed him years ago, after his daughter died. "I'm sorry?" Hoodies are common but in my estimation, one only wears a black hoodie on a hot, Florida night if they're trying to hide their identity. "Have we met?" There's a second guy wearing a hoodie at a crime scene? Coincidence? My instinct says no.

"I've seen you at a couple crime scenes."

The man, probably around forty, can't be a TV news reporter. Maybe he works for *The Times?* "You're a reporter?"

"A crime writer. Like you."

The streetlights cast light and shadows across angular features, but the hoodie hides much of his face. I can tell he's got a nose like a boxer's, broken at some point, and he sports a goatee of dark hair.

"I'm a big fan of yours," he says. "You're the queen of local crime news."

Well, not really, but— "Thank you."

"You cover my favorite kind of stories."

Now he smiles, and that's weird. Warning bells ring in my head. I wish I could see if that smile makes it all the way up to his eyes. I hear that often—the fan thing. But not the "queen" thing. So why are my reporter senses tingling? "You watch my station?"

"I watch you."

The hair all over my body rises. There are fans. And there are *fans*. I don't need any creepy creepers creeping on me tonight. *¡Ay, Dios mío!* Maybe he means he watches my crime segments on the news. "Thank—"

"This scene reminds me of your mother's crime scene."

I stiffen.

"Don't you think?" He steps closer to me.

Every part of my warm body breaks out into a cold sweat. I should be asking: *What the Jesus, Mary, and Joseph are you talking about? What do you know about my mother's murder? Who the hell are you?* But after the cold flash hits me, a sense of calm takes over. I need to know what this man knows and freaking out isn't going to get me what I need. "What part of the crime scene?" *Engage him.* "I'm curious if you see what I see?" *Challenge him.* "I respect your opinion." *While also flattering him.*

"I see another mom shot down in her front doorway."

"Aren't you hot under that hoodie?" I need to see his face.

"But this time her kids weren't watching."

He must have seen the girls arrive.

My heart whacks against my ribs. How does he know I watched my mother die?

"You were watching, weren't you? I mean, did you actually see your mother take the bullet, did you—"

I almost expect him to call me Clarice. Like he's freaking *Silence of the Lambs* serial killer Hannibal Lector taunting me to tell him my secrets, in exchange for his. "I'm not sure what you're trying to do, but I'm not playing. I've got to go."

"I have a theory," he says.

He grabs my elbow again. This time it feels more like I'm being taken hostage. I glance around looking for help. At the same time, I need to stay out of Jessica's line of sight and off her radar. No big scenes. This wouldn't be happening if I'd gone with Orlando like I was supposed to.

"Don't you want to hear it?"

"A theory on what happened with my mom?" I'm buying time till I figure out how to carefully extract myself from this odd situation.

"Also what happened tonight." He pulls me closer, and I smell his excitement. A little body odor mixed with that potent whiff of sexual energy, like this was turning on this real-life Hannibal.

"I follow things," he says. "You know, like you do." He leans in like he's going to—

Oh, hell no! I pull away. But he's not letting me go, and that stalls my words. His fingers dig into my elbow, and since there's not a lot of flesh there, it hurts. I wonder if that's what he's trying to do—hurt me.

"Hey, we got a problem here?"

I exhale. *Detective García.*

"No."

"Yes." Hoodie Hannibal and I speak at the same time.

Detective García looks a little less fresh now. His hair is no longer perfectly plastered back. He's rolled up his sleeves as if the heat has finally penetrated that cool, cotton, button-down look of his. But he still looks glorious to me, especially compared to the man still holding onto my elbow. "Can you please let me go?"

Hoodie Hannibal drops my elbow. I'm sure it's not because I asked him to, but because the man with the badge and the gun is eyeing him.

"Ms. Álvarez, you know this man?" García asks.

"No, no." Why does it irk me that he calls me Ms. Álvarez? "I was about to ask for him to—"

"Can I see some ID please?"

That request rocks Hoodie Hannibal onto his heels. "I haven't done anything wrong, Officer."

"Detective." García reaches out his hand. "You're at a crime scene, holding a reporter who looks to me like she's trying to get away."

"I'm not holding her." He looks at me.

"You were holding me." I'm not backing down, Hoodie Hannibal.

The man turns toward García, who still has his hand out. "We were discussing the crime scene."

García isn't backing down either. "ID, please."

The man pulls out his wallet and his ID. Good. Now we'll know his name.

"Detective, this man was about to share his theory on what happened here tonight." I turn to look at the man who thought he could grab and hold me. "Why don't you do it now? In front of the detective working on—"

"Can you please take off your hoodie?" García asks before I can even finish.

Wow. He must be catching the serial killer vibes, too.

Hoodie Hannibal stiffens. "Am I under arrest?" He puts his hand out for his ID.

The detective doesn't hand it back. He stares. Doesn't say a thing.

"I'd like to leave. My ID?" Hoodie Hannibal has balls. Cojones grandes, actually.

The detective hands over the ID.

Hannibal turns to me, his eyes glassy. "Wanna go

somewhere and compare notes?"

"Stay away from Ms. Álvarez," García responds with a voice edgy and intimidating.

Hoodie doesn't move. He's still staring at me.

My cheeks fill with heat, my head with worry. My heart beats like a bat in a box.

"Until we meet again, Marisol." He takes off.

None of my friends call me Marisol. It's just Mari. But Marisol is the name I use on TV, so maybe this guy actually is a news junkie obsessed with TV news people. Or maybe he wants to be one himself. Maybe he's not dangerous. Just weird. Or jealous.

"I got his driver's license number." García's words bring me back to the present. "I'll do a background on him."

"You think he had something to do with this murder?"

"No, but I think you need to be careful. I don't like how he was holding you or looking at you."

I check out the detective, surprised at how he'd been checking out the man who was checking me out. "Aw, García, you care."

His eyes narrow. But he also smiles.

Not everyone smiles when I challenge them, I kinda like it—going toe to toe with an equal. I can't stop myself from smiling back.

"I want to see if he has a record. He could be stalking you."

"Or he could be a super fan. Don't bother. I get this sometimes. I never get used to the feeling people know me because I'm on TV, even though I don't know them."

He flips shut the notebook he'd been writing in.

"Not all people have good intentions, Ms. Álvarez."

Well, that's for sure. "Hey, on the subject of good intentions."

He looks toward the crime scene—I'm keeping him from his real work tonight.

He arches an eyebrow. "Yes?"

"I have a theory, too."

Both eyebrows go up.

"Oh God, I sound like that fan." I shrug.

"Are you being serious, Ms. Álvarez?"

"Please, call me Mari." I explain who else I saw in the crowd tonight, in a similar hoodie. "I thought I recognized him. When I googled Natasha Rodríguez's name, a bunch of articles came up. I think the man we almost ran over was Sofía Figueroa's father." I explain the connection and speculate why he might be here on the night of this particular murder.

García keeps a poker face the whole time. "And you're thinking the six-year-old's dad came back to seek justice, three years later?"

"You have a better suspect at this point?"

The air stills around us.

I'm not sure how much more García can take of my no-nonsense, tell-it-like-it-is personality. I know it's blunt and even borderline rude.

But he eventually throws up both hands and says, "No. I don't."

I appreciate his honesty. "The only thing that bothers me about the dad as a suspect is why not shoot the teen who actually shot his daughter? Why target the mom?"

García looked at the crime scene like he was

seeing something new there. "The son is in prison. Can't get to him. And the mom, as a deputy, is responsible for her weapon and what happens with it."

He's tracking the case he wasn't on three years ago. *Interesting.* "And the deputy's husband?" I know the answer. The girl at the murder scene told me. But sometimes you ask a question to fill in the details you haven't been able to uncover.

García shifts his weight and looks away. "They divorced, and he died from a bullet to the head last year."

"He was shot?"

"Shot himself." García meets my gaze.

We don't cover suicides. "Oh my God." It hits me that García may know tonight's victim. "You were friends with Deputy Rodríguez and the family?"

He looks down, shakes his head. "Didn't know her personally. Just in passing. And when she resigned…" He looks back at me. "But the department will make sure the kids are taken care of. All the kids."

Even in the low light, I see his cheeks color.

"I'm making sure of it." His tone is not to be argued with, but also tired.

It hits me. García is a good-looking, cocky, gym-going dude. But he's also an empath. *So am I.* And sometimes, it hurts to feel the pain of others while carrying the burden of your own.

He clears his throat. "Aren't you supposed to be at Busch Gardens?"

I know he's changing the subject on purpose, but it does make me glance over to where Jessica is interviewing the neighbor. She's no longer there, which means she could be anywhere. "Heading there now." Might as well go, if García isn't biting on my theory and bringing Sofía's dad in tonight. A second thought pops into my head. "Or, maybe I'll go interview the father myself. Maybe I can rule him out for you."

"Please don't do that."

I smile at him. "You *are* interested in my theory."

García rolls his eyes, which makes me sure he is. He starts to walk away. "Go to the command post for any further updates, Ms. Álvarez. Have a good night. Stay safe."

"Thank you for coming to my rescue, Detective," I yell after him.

He stops dead in his tracks. Turns to look at me. "Is that what I did?"

I straighten up, stand as tall as I can. "Isn't it?"

"Maybe."

He smiles and for one moment that's all I can see.

"Or maybe," he says, "it's *you* I think I need to keep an eye on."

As García says that, I notice two things. The first thing I notice is my forensic friend—also my inside source—flips me a sign. He's on the other side of the street, at the edge of the crime scene, holding two fingers up. He puts one to his ear, the other to his mouth, like a telephone.

The second thing I notice is Hoodie Hannibal standing across the street watching us. He flips up two fingers as well. A peace sign.

I don't think so.

He points to his eyes and then at me, as if to say, *I'm watching you.*

CHAPTER TEN

It's a new day. It's also Friday, the last day of the work week. Only one more day to get through, and I plan to be one of the first in the news meeting.

I'd set my alarm early and taken back roads to avoid traffic jams. I didn't stop for café con leche, and still, as I walk in, I realize the room is already packed. Did it start early or something?

I've got three options. One: sit across from El Jefe again. Two: sit next to Jessica, which feels a little awkward after last night, although I don't want it to. Three: sit next to Orlando, who hasn't answered my texts today.

Okay, I never did make it to Busch Gardens last night. But what's the big deal? My plan had worked. The sloth story aired last night with my voice on it. No one said a word to me. To us. So why is O not looking at me?

I sit next to him.

He adjusts so I get more of his back.

I swallow and shift in my chair, aware of eyes on us.

I almost asked Abuela Bonita to say a prayer over me last night, to protect me from ill will and malicious wishes today, but I stopped myself. She would have asked why, and I would have had to explain about the bracelet I gave away last night.

The azabache charm had great meaning to her because her mom gave it to her as a baby in Cuba. I still can't believe I gave it away, but in the moment, my intentions were good. I want to ask her if the blessing passes on to others. It should, right? If not, what a waste of a most precious gift. Abuela will be hurt, but even worse, if I tell her, she'll worry about my health and my physical safety, and I don't want her to worry. She's been weak with dizzy spells lately. The doctor says she has a weak heart, although I disagree. She has the strongest heart I know.

But out of respect for her, I made a promise to myself. Show up early today. Have an acceptable story to pitch when asked. Already got it figured out.

I won't even ask to work with Orlando today.

That way, I can go visit my forensics friend sometime during the day. Freddy had motioned for me to call him last night but didn't answer his cell today. I know where he lives, and since he worked late last night, chances of him being home today are good.

I took care with my hair and heels today. Put on the red lipstick. Mamá always told me when you're feeling down or a little unsure, dress to impress.

I glance over at Jessica. She looks up from her iPhone. Our gazes meet.

My hand goes to my wrist. Nothing to twist. Not even a water bottle on the table.

I break out my sugar and spice and everything nice smile, me pongo la cara de niña buena, and quickly look away. But not before I see her raise her hand.

Mr. Payton calls on her.

She rehashes last night and updates the room with a few details in case they didn't watch the eleven o'clock news. Mainly that the neighbor she'd interviewed witnessed Natasha Rodríguez arguing with a man right before he pulled out a gun and shot her. Gotta say, I'm impressed with all the details Jessica got.

If I have time today to drive by that witness's house and talk to her, I will. I have a few questions still to ask.

"A black hoodie covered his head so the witness couldn't see the face, but she's sure it was a man and—"

A man in a black hoodie shot Natasha Rodríguez.

Jessica didn't report that in her live shot last night. Not sure why. My temples throb. Lack of caffeine, maybe. More likely it's that I can now identify *two* people who were at the scene of a murder wearing dark hoodies. Sofía's father. And Hoodie Hannibal. What are the chances there was a third guy, the shooter, wearing one, too?

Sofía's father had motive. But could Hoodie Hannibal be the shooter? I didn't see any blood on him.

Do I speak up now? Tip my hand? Impress the boss, or maybe piss him off more, because I wasn't supposed to be at that scene last night for more than ten minutes. I wasn't supposed to get out of the car. I was supposed to be at Busch Gardens.

Orlando is burning me with a *don't you dare say shit* look.

My phone buzzes against the table. I slap my

hand on top of it, but not before El Jefe's gaze drifts my way. As does the room's attention.

"May I take this?"

He nods, watching me as I push my chair back and shuffle out of the meeting.

Lately, walking in and out of these meetings feels like walking across fire. Barefoot. Under a full moon with howling wolves watching.

I look at the phone — a number I don't recognize. No, wait, I do. But I don't know who it belongs to, so I've never answered it. And the caller has never left a message. *Which is weird.*

I walk-run to the makeup room and close the door. Could I have manifested this into existence? Hoodie Hannibal said he'd been watching me. Has he been calling me, too?

I answer. "Hello." I'm breathless.

No answer. But I hear breathing. Someone else is breathless, too.

I get the heebie-jeebies listening. *¡Solavaya!* I pull out the makeup room chair and fall into it.

"Hello." I say a bit louder this time.

"Hey, sorry. It's me." *Freddy.*

I exhale. Forensics Freddy. That's what I jokingly call him. "I didn't recognize this number."

"Burner phone."

I pause. "Why do you have a burner phone?"

"So you can stop calling me on my real number. Don't you watch *Law & Order*? Cell phone calls are always the first thing cops check when a crime is committed."

I cock my head. "Are we committing a crime?"

A pause before, "Girl, I love being your secret

source. It makes me feel naughty." He chuckles. "But I would not love getting fired. Ya hear?"

"I hear." I can't help the smile spreading ear to ear. "I have questions."

"And I have answers, but not a lot of time, so honey, you're going to have to shut that big, love-to-hear-my-own-voice mouth and let me speak. 'Kay?"

"Go."

"Did you know the victim was shot six times?"

Whoa! Only the medical examiner could determine that. "You're sure?"

Freddy scoffs. "Got it from the ME this morning."

"You think there's any significance with six shots?"

"Don't know yet," Freddy says.

"What do you know about the victim having one eye open, one eye shut?" I ask.

A low whistle. "Chica, que buena. I know there was a gold coin keeping one eye closed on the victim."

"Know that, too. The oldest daughter told me."

"You interviewed her? Good job. Can't believe the junkyard dog let you."

"Junkyard dog?"

"García. Lead homicide detective."

"Met him." García definitely didn't have jowls or a pushed in face like a junkyard bulldog. "Hmmm, he looks more like a German Shepherd to me."

Freddy makes a noise that comes close to a squeal. "Girl, that dog will bite you. Be careful."

I shove an image of García and his perfectly groomed hair out of my head. "What can you tell me about the coin? Know who owns it?"

"The coin didn't come from the U.S. mint. Like, you're not using it at the grocery store."

"A rare coin?" I always love talking with Freddy. He makes even my smallest discovery feel like the unearthing of a new Egyptian tomb.

"I don't know that it's rare. I know it's made of real gold."

"Do you know what was on the coin?" I ask. "A president's head?"

"A crown."

"Like a queen wears?"

"I guess like a queen would wear. Or a king."

Instantly, two thoughts converge into a tornado inside my head.

First, I see the spray-painted sign of a crown on our door a couple of days after my mother's murder. Izzy told me it was a warning by the local West Tampa Kings to keep our mouths shut about Mamá's murder. That Raúl, her ex, may have turned narc against the gang and that's why Mamá was killed. If we talked, we'd be next.

The second thought overpowers the first. Hoodie Hannibal said to me tonight, "*I'm a big fan of yours. You're the queen of local crime news.*"

"What?"

"Did I say that out loud?"

"Honey, I'm about to have lunch with Roger, but I can drop what I'm doing and come see you. You're talking to yourself today."

I don't mention Mamá's murder, and the gang symbol left on our door a decade ago. I do say, "It's something a man said to me last night at the crime scene. He said he was a fan. Called me a queen. He was wearing a black hoodie and wanted to talk to me about crime scenes. Specifically, my mother's and Natasha Rodríguez's."

"Have you told the German Shepherd about this?"

That makes me smile — I've never had a guard dog. "García actually saved me from him. The guy was making me feel uncomfortable."

Another low whistle.

"Anything else stand out?" I asked.

"Glad you asked. Cause I'm about to drop the big bomb, light the final firecracker, sing the show-stopping finale."

I laugh out loud. "Go for it. I'm ready."

"We found a half-naked Barbie doll on top of the victim."

"I already know. One eye missing."

"Damn. You trying to take my job?"

"Tell me about the necklace I saw in the evidence bag. Was the necklace red and white, or white with blood? Who does it belong to? What's its significance?"

Freddy exhales in dramatic fashion. "I collect the clues. You and García will have to figure out what they mean." I hear a voice in the background. "Gotta run."

"Thanks, Freddy." I wish he could talk longer.

I look at myself in the makeup room mirror and say out loud, "Well, change of plans." I'm going to have to go find García and tell him what I know now, without telling him *how* I know, so he'll check into my fan, like he'd originally suggested. Sofía's dad, too. I can place them both at the scene. In black hoodies. Both of them could be the murderers.

My life could be in danger now. Or am I being dramatic? Only one way to find out.

I open the door and stall in the doorway.

Jessica is getting water from the cooler, which happens to be right next to the makeup room. How long has she been there? "I thought you were in the meeting."

She takes a sip. Makes me wait, then says, "And I thought you were off the crime beat."

I swallow. The word is stuck in the back of my throat. I push it out, pissed. "Eavesdropping?"

"Who is Freddy?" She puts one hand on her hip and drills me with a look that answers my previous question. "And what exactly is your change of plans?"

I'm not about to tell her.

CHAPTER ELEVEN

A couple of things are clear to me as I walk down the sterile, third story hallway in the downtown police department—García in front of me, Orlando to my right. First, it's eerily quiet. My heels click on the floor like stiletto rain drops. It's not what I expected after hundreds of visits to this busy police department.

Second, neither Orlando nor García are happy to be here with me.

García answered my earlier call almost immediately. But since I arrived, he's maintained a solemn face and kept conversation to a few words.

Orlando, assigned to work with me by El Jefe, continues to drag his feet like they're concrete blocks.

Whatever. I need to tell García what I've learned about Hoodie Hannibal, ask him if he's checked the guy out or brought Sofía's dad in for questioning. 'Cause I don't want either of them coming to find me if they're killers.

The uncomfortable silence, and the way neither García nor Orlando look at me, raises the red flag even higher. *This is going to be as easy as covering a hurricane from a rowboat.*

A woman in ironed, straight-leg slacks and a white blouse rushes out of a room with a phone in her hand that she gives to García. He takes it immediately, stops dead in his tracks, listens for a moment, motioning for us to wait. He and the woman walk a few steps ahead and turn their backs to us. As they do, I notice she's left the door open.

And, you know, I can't help myself. I'm a reporter.

I glance at Orlando, who's on his phone, too, giving me his back. We still haven't talked about me not showing up at Busch Gardens last night.

I bump the door open with my behind, keeping my gaze on the three parties who might not approve. I don't dare enter. In case there's surveillance video. These days you must always assume you're being videotaped.

No one is inside, so I can feast on the details of what must be homicide's war room safely from the doorway. I only have a few seconds. As I scan the room, my breath catches. I've stumbled on a reporter's treasure chest. First, I take out my smartphone and snap a few pictures to review later for clues.

Now, I look around. A large, white eraser board has red writing on it. *West Tampa Kings* is prominent in the middle, with a circle around it, and a question mark. *Kings. Crown.* The West Tampa Kings are the local West Tampa street gang that spray painted our front door a decade ago and are still active in our community today. Maybe that's what the crown on the coin means? My heart speeds up. I'm seconds away from being busted for snooping, but I can't stop now.

Behind that board, which is on wheels, a cork board is secured onto the back wall. It's full of various crime scene pictures. There are pictures of murdered Natasha Rodríguez and clues García must have deemed important, like the red and white beaded necklace I saw at the crime scene. My pulse beats like fast hands on a bongo because the beads look like the ones the Babalawo wore when I visited the other night. Different color, but otherwise, strikingly similar.

"Hey, whatcha doing?"

I spin around, and the door clicks shut behind me. *¡Carajo! Who the hell just—*

"Well, lookee. It's City Council Killer."

I recognize the man in front of me immediately. Not only by the stupid nickname he gave me, but he's got the same Lightning baseball cap on, with a clean white button-down shirt, jeans, and that same crooked smile. The cold case detective at the crime scene. "Mari, remember?"

"Of course. Whatcha looking for, Mari, rhymes with sorry?"

I could say I'm looking for the restroom, but the reporter in me thinks only the guilty lie. "Looking around, Detective Hanks." *Not a lie.* "Entertaining myself while everyone else is on their phones." *Also not a lie.*

"Looking around can get a reporter bounced."

"No one told me I couldn't."

García, from a distance, catches my eye.

Heat slaps my cheeks.

He frowns.

The heat intensifies, and I look away.

Detective Hanks wags a long, lean finger in front of me. "Doing what you know isn't right is bad ashe."

Bad ashe? "Excuse me?" My spine straightens, my attention on Hanks now.

The cold case detective leans against the door he caught me peeking through. "Negative energy. Bad ju ju—"

"I know what ashe means. I'm surprised you do." Ashe is a spiritual energy thing from Cuba, by way of Africa. Detective Hanks is about as white as you can get. "How did you learn abou—"

"This way, Ms. Álvarez." García's voice cuts off my question. His tone is calm, even as his gaze tells me he knows what I've been doing, and he doesn't approve.

Hanks steps away from the door. "Hey, came here looking for you, García, but found something else instead." He directs a sly smile at me.

"I've got this." García places his hand on my back. "I'll text when I'm done," he says to Hanks.

"You know your girl was—"

"Not my girl." García doesn't stop, but I feel the tension in his touch. "And yes, I know what she was doing."

He doesn't look at either Hanks or me as he leads me away from the war room.

I must admit, García is a pro at holding in his temper and acting professional. I don't know why, but I wonder if I could break that super self-control of his. It's the rebel in me rising. I shake that side of me off and concentrate as we walk in silence. García and I are so close, connected by his fingers lightly guiding me. I almost forget Orlando is following, until he clears his throat.

I pull away.

García steps closer. He guides us into a much larger office space. This one is filled with tight cubicles and worker bees, most not in uniforms.

Homicide.

Finally! The hair on my arms tingles. I've always wanted an invitation into the mostly man cave. I must admit, I dig there's at least one female homicide detective in the man's club.

García gestures for us to take a seat in the two chairs in front of a cluttered, working man's desk. I'm assuming it's his. Surprising to me—I thought he'd be more, I don't know, orderly? Like the way he dresses. Like the way he acts. Almost too perfect. This work space is anything but, but I kind of like that. García can't control everything in his life.

He wouldn't be able to control me.

Orlando clears his throat again.

Did I think out loud again?

We sit. The space is so tight our legs are touching; even though O tries to move his leg away, there's no room.

"Now, what can I help you with, Ms. Álvarcz?"

So formal again. "Please, call me Mari." I smile. I hit him with my best compliment. Un piropo. "I decided you were right. I'd like you to look into the past of the man who grabbed me last night. I never even got his name."

The detective leans back in his office chair. "What made you change your mind?"

"Jessica, you remember her?" I ask.

The corners of his mouth go up and a sparkle hits his eyes, but he says nothing.

Neither do I, because a little envy hits the back of

my throat.

"She's the reporter who was covering the crime scene on Hesperides last night," Orlando offers.

O obviously missed the lightning bolt connection that surged between Jessica and García last night. "Have you heard from her today?" The break in my voice probably gives away my concern.

He shakes his head.

"Jessica says that a witness she interviewed saw a man in a black hoodie shoot and kill Ms. Rodríguez. I told you the father of the six-year-old had what looked like a black hoodie on last night, right?"

The detective nods. "And the man who grabbed you had on a black hoodie as well." He cocks his head and taps a pen on his desktop. "Which is why I wanted to look into him. You should have trusted me, Ms. Álvarez."

"Well, if you had told me that little, missing detail about the hoodie, instead of letting me find out later from a fellow reporter, I might have."

Orlando kicks my foot.

I ignore it and continue. "The man-fan told me he'd seen me at different crime scenes. But I don't remember seeing him. Is he a crime scene junkie, or maybe a stalker who shows up to crime scenes hoping I'll show up, too? Does he sit and listen to a police scanner all day? What's his deal? And why reach out to me now?"

Orlando jumps in, "You have no proof this man—"

"Edward Jones." García leaned forward. "That's his name, by the way."

"You have no proof that Mr. Jones has done

anything illegal." Orlando wasn't looking at me. He's definitely pissed off El Jefe assigned him to work with me today.

"My 'fan' called me the queen of local crime news, and since there was a coin with a crown on it covering one of the victim's eyes, I thought—"

García stands behind his desk. "How did you know that?"

¡Carajo! I glance at my hands. I can't tell him about Freddy. *Think. Think. Think.* Were there pictures of the coin on the wall in war room? I didn't see them. But they have to be there, right? "Deputy Rodríguez's daughter told me about the coin." *True.* "As for the crown on it, I saw a few crime scene pictures on the wall of that room back there."

García says nothing. He sits back down and places his elbows on his desk. He intertwines his fingers, creating a prayer-like triangle.

Is this some cop training thing to make me nervous?

He rests his chin on his hands. "I'm counting on the fact you know that evidence is crucial to our case and should not be reported at this point. It's not in the public record." He shakes his head. "And you had no right going in there."

"Well," *Don't say it. Don't say it. Don't say it.* "I didn't actually go in. The door was open."

García cuts a glance at me that would light an entire city on fire.

A young woman walks into the office and puts bottles of water in front of the three of us. I turn mine so the label faces me. It makes me feel better, despite Orlando's side eye. I take a deep breath and say, "Not sure how the West Tampa Kings fit in." I hold my breath, waiting for García to erupt.

His features barely move, but his stare hardens.

"But I do know they're in my West Tampa neighborhood. Mostly kids, but some adults, too. Maybe my fan is a member?" I shrug. "Now that I have more information that connects Edward Jones to suspicious activities, it warrants bringing him in for questioning."

"Good idea, *Detective*," García says.

I ignore the sarcasm and the fake title. "Does Mr. Jones have a criminal record?"

"He does." García breaks his earlier pose and sits up straight. "Would it surprise you to know your fan has been arrested for assault? Has documented mental health issues? Has been Baker Acted, twice in fact?"

Baker Acted? *¡Carajo!* Held for observation against his will. Not good. I'm glad García already checked Jones out even though I told him last night it wasn't necessary. That was nice.

"And the last place we had contact with him was outside your TV station."

I grip the side of my chair.

"Last month."

"Holy shit." Orlando turns to look at me. "Are you serious? Why didn't you tell me?"

In that moment I know, even if O is mad, he'll get over it. He still loves me because he looks scared for me right now. We've been working together for five years, and we have a bond that is strong and unbreakable, despite our standoffs, which have been happening more often lately. "I didn't know about this *fan* until last night."

"You have to tell Mr. Payton." Orlando is now playing with the keys hooked to his belt. "Station security should be notified." He looks at García, then back at me. "Damn." To García he says, "You got a picture of this guy? I want to be prepared if he shows up at another crime scene. Get video of him. Something."

García opens a file, pulls out a picture, and slides it across his desk.

Orlando studies it while I keep pushing García. "What if you brought in both the stalker—"

"Mr. Jones," García says.

"And the six-year-old's father? What's his name…Thomas Figueroa. Can you bring in both for a lineup and see if the witness Jessica interviewed can pick either out? Maybe she'd recognize the way they walk, a tattoo, a mannerism or—"

"Happening at five-thirty this afternoon," García says. "Had to wait for Mr. Figueroa to get off work, and we have to find Mr. Jones. The address on his driver's license is his parents' address. They say he comes and goes at all hours."

That makes me shiver, and not with delight.

Orlando flicks me a concerned look.

"I'd like you to be here to look at the lineup as well, Ms. Álvarez," García says.

I sit back, caught completely off guard. But now I know why García responded to my call immediately and set up this meeting within the hour. "Even if I can identify them, I didn't see either of them murder anyone."

"No, but we're bringing in other witnesses who

did see the shooting, but not a face. We're trying to put the pieces together. You can help us with one part of this puzzle."

"In exchange for an exclusive?" I have to ask.

García cocks his head, but smiles. "That's not how it works, Ms. Álvarez."

"Mari?" Now Orlando is almost coming out of his seat. "You crazy?" He points to García. "This man is trying to help you. You have a crazy stalker following you."

"I'm asking for your voluntary cooperation because it is the right thing to do," García jumps in. "Because there's a killer we need to catch. Before he kills again."

"Before he kills you." A vein in O's temple is throbbing. "Or both of us!"

"Stop it, you two." You don't say things like that. *Killing both of us*. You don't put the words out into the universe because they could manifest and become true.

And I'm not ready to die.

Even though a charm can't deflect bullets or unwind hands around my neck, I wish I had my abuela's azabache back. I'm starting to feel warm and a little achy, like you do when you get a low-grade fever. I'm also thirsty and tired. What a wild twenty-four hours. "I'll stay and do this lineup." Mr. Payton will have to say yes.

But I need to do something to protect myself first, and I need to do it now. Now that it looks like I'm protecting myself from more than someone like Hoodie's jealous evil eye. I may be protecting Orlando and me from a killer.

CHAPTER TWELVE

I've watched more episodes of *Law & Order: SVU* than I can count. I think Mariska Hargitay is one of the best actresses on TV. So I have to admit there's a part of me bubbling with anticipation as García escorts me to a room deep inside the Tampa Police Department. It has that reverse-mirror thing—I'll be able to see the suspects—they won't be able to see me—like on the TV show. I'm buzzing with eagerness.

I force myself to focus on why I'm here. I want to pick Hoodie Hannibal out of the lineup, so García has incentive to investigate him further. And if he's not a killer, Hoodie has nothing to fear.

I want to do this quickly so I can go home. I think I might have a fever. Now my lower back is aching. Abuela Bonita would say these are all symptoms someone is giving me the evil eye. And without my azabache charm, I have no protection. "Can I have a bottled water?"

"I'll see if I can get one for you." García stops at the door and hesitates. "Detective Smith will take it from here." He points toward a woman wearing a black suit and a simple, classic white blouse. She has a badge on her belt next to a big, black gun.

This is a different lady than before. She looks just as bad ass.

"Orlando can wait for you in the lobby."

My heart trips up. "Orlando can't come? He was there, too."

"Detective Smith will answer any questions you might have," García says.

"But you know the case." Don't want to admit it, but I'd like García to stay.

"And that's what makes it against protocol." He smiles and reaches out to reassure me with a touch. But he stops short.

"Detective Smith is running the lineup." García's tone says, "I'm sorry."

"This way, Ms. Álvarez." She gestures for me to move through the door.

I turn, but García is already walking away. He looks back.

I lock into his gaze. My feet don't want to move.

He doesn't move, either.

Detective Smith nudges me forward, guiding me into a different room. She sits me in a seat facing the window.

I feel empty but I know I have an important job to do.

"Detective Browski will be administering the identification procedure," she says.

Detective Browski, sitting across from me, nods.

I nod back.

The room is dark, the only light coming from the lineup room.

It gets so quiet I bet both detectives hear my heart thumping against my ribs.

I adjust the folding chair, trying to get it perfectly straight, since I have no charm or water bottle. It screeches as the legs drag against the floor.

The female detective puts a hand on my shoulder, and I jump, even though her touch is gentle.

"Relax, Ms. Álvarez. You don't need to be nervous." Her voice fills the air, although the room isn't empty. There are a couple other men in here with us that I'm assuming are cops, too.

"Ms. Álvarez," Detective Browski says, "six men will walk into the room."

Six. Coincidence? I shiver. No damn way.

"The suspect may or may not be among those presented. You are not obligated to make an identification. Neither Detective Smith, nor I, know who the suspect is."

I nod, but I'm still buzzing like I've had too much caffeine and the room is a little off-kilter.

"The investigation will continue regardless of whether you recognize anyone from the Hesperides scene last night," Browski continues. "Do you understand how the proceedings will work?"

"Yes." He's so formal, and that's making my legs restless—I'm fighting to stay still.

"Can you please sign here that you understand the instructions?" Detective Smith hands me a paper and pen.

The door opens and six men enter. There are no height marks on the wall like in some *Law & Order: SVU* episodes. My pulse hums because I recognize one of the men instantly, but only one of them. Where is the other man? I turn to Detective Smith.

She smiles, but also puts a finger to her lips.

Another male detective speaks into a microphone placed in the center of the table. His voice blasts into the next room. "Please stand with your back against the wall. Step forward when your number is called. Number one step forward."

I don't even bother to look at number one—he isn't the man we almost ran into or the man who grabbed me by the elbow.

I zero in on Thomas Figueroa, the father who lost his six-year-old daughter.

His cheeks are red like he'd been partying hard last night. But the rest of his visible skin is pale, like he's ill. He slumps against the wall, crossing his arms against his chest, anger radiating from bloodshot eyes. He's glaring right at the mirror.

Right, I think, *at me.*

I don't know what I expected to feel other than anticipation, but I wasn't prepared for the wave of indecision washing over me. I'm flushed, and yet my skin is clammy.

If Hoodie Hannibal had walked into the room with his busted nose and dark goatee, I would have said, "Yep, that's him."

But with Thomas Figueroa? I understand why this man would want to kill.

In my darkest hours, I dreamed of finding my mother's killer and shooting him or her. Right in the chest, like they'd murdered my mamá. An eye for an eye. And in those dreams, I never felt remorse.

The lack of any guilt, that's what woke me up those nights, gasping for air, gripping the sheets, sweating. It wasn't that I'd killed, it was my fear someone would sense this darkness in me. And tell the world. Or incarcerate me forever because of it.

I don't want to be a killer.

But I understand the desire for revenge, especially when you know justice was not served.

The District Attorney charged Deputy Natasha Rodríguez with negligence, but later, the judge sentenced her to probation.

Only.

Turns out the judge grew up in West Tampa with the Rodríguez family, among families that had members born in Cuba. Neighborhood snitches there would report your activities to the government. Here, in West Tampa, you protected your own. You did not snitch. And when one of your own got in trouble, you did what you could to help them. I understand that, too.

The fourteen-year-old's case moved to adult court, but the same judge ruled he could be a youthful offender, meaning his procedures were private. Not even the media had been allowed in, and court records were sealed. I heard from police sources the kid was doing "time" in a comfortable juvie lockdown his sister referred to as prison. He'd get out soon, probably serve probation. Sofía wouldn't get a second chance.

Pretty much everyone in the community knew justice had not been served. But no one spoke about it over dominoes or at quinceañeras. Everyone felt sorry for Thomas Figueroa, but no one wanted to see the Rodríguez family ruined, either. The deputy had helped many on the streets of West Tampa get out of trouble. Natasha also volunteered at Metropolitan Ministries and often directed those in need to services in town. Her fourteen-year-old son was a typical teen, who made one stupid, deadly mistake.

Surely, he was not a monster.

It was such a gray area.

Watching Thomas Figueroa squirm against the wall, I can understand why he'd break and want to take matters into his own hands.

It was hard to take sides in a situation like this. Simply no winners.

"Number four step forward."

Thomas Figueroa is number four. "That's the man we almost ran into. He was there, near the murder scene last night." I'm a little sick as I say it; I have no ill will toward him. But two girls and one troubled son are now without parents. Nauseous, I drop my gaze. "I don't recognize anyone else. Can I go now?"

Detective Smith walks me out of the room and to the main lobby. She thanks me and she's gone.

I'm standing here, shaking. Where is Hoodie Hannibal? Why didn't García bring him in? He's the reason I came.

As if my thoughts are manifesting him right before my eyes, I see Detective García standing next to a water cooler.

He walks over and offers me a cup. "Sorry I couldn't get this to you sooner."

He's been waiting here for me? With the water I asked for? I'm glad.

I take the cup and drink slowly, watching him, thinking it was nice of him to stay. Thinking also about what I've just done. "What happens now?"

"You're excused. You can leave. Orlando is waiting for you outside."

"That's not what I meant."

"I know." He sticks out his hand. "Thank you for coming."

I don't shake it. "You know, I feel for the man. He lost his baby girl. She was shot and killed at six years old. Her life was broken, and it wasn't her fault. Or his."

"And his wife." García drinks from his own cup of water. "Also broken." The stain under his arms as he drinks tells me he's been sweating this, too. He looks up at me when I don't respond. "You didn't know?"

I shake my head.

He leans back against the wall, sipping slowly, eyeing me.

My body still aches, and that throbbing in my temples is now the start of a real headache. Could García be giving me the evil eye? Unintentionally?

"I find it interesting that you members of the media will follow a story every day. Say suspect names on TV. Blast the accusations repeatedly. But once the sentence is handed down, you drop the story like it's a nuclear bomb. These people you report on, they have lives. That bomb destroys everything. Their lives are irrevocably damaged."

I can't even swallow. I've felt media hate before, especially lately, but this smack down hurts. I'm speechless.

"After his six-year-old daughter was shot, Mr. Figueroa started doing drugs."

I know too much about the physical feelings that come with grief.

"I know this because he has a previous arrest record. He lost his job. Lost his wife. Finally, his home."

"I didn't realize." My voice breaks.

"Figueroa has been staying with his son who still lives in the neighborhood. His son happens to be a leader of the local West Tampa Kings."

The crown. On the coin. "You think the crown means—"

"I can tell you that local police busted Figueroa for petty theft, drug-related things. All public record. His son's been in trouble, too. Not that I blame him. He witnessed his sister's murder."

"And now maybe Figueroa will be charged with murder?"

García doesn't confirm that. He says, "There are no winners here today."

I see the storm in his pupils. "We can at least agree on that." He takes his job seriously.

"Would you like me to walk you out?"

I let him guide me down the hallway toward the exit. Again, he barely touches the curve in my back. Still, I'm very aware of his energy. His ashe. I have one more important question for him. "What happened to bringing in Hoodie, I mean Edward Jones?"

"We couldn't find him."

"Oh." Now I'm even more tired and want to go home. And lock the damn door.

"If you're worried, we could explore a restraining order."

That does nothing to ease my fears. "In my experience, people who are Baker Acted don't care about a piece of paper that says you can't come near someone."

He rolls his lips in but says nothing.

García's phone goes off. His ring tone is a

Spanish song I love by a local band, Orchestra Fuego. He answers, then flicks an irritated look my way.

Just when I was appreciating his cool taste in music. I cross my arms.

He shakes his head. "I have to take this." He points to the exit and turns, walking away. He stops, his back to me, and runs a hand through his hair. Whatever he's hearing, it's not good. And if it involves this case, I want to know what it is.

He finally gets off the phone and turns to look my way.

I'm standing where he left me, both hands on my hips.

His eyes narrow, but he doesn't look surprised to see me still here.

Finally, he walks to me.

"What is it? You looked pissed," I say, surprised I'm being so informal with him.

"Figueroa's attorney is demanding we either charge him or release him. Now. The attorney plans to hold a news conference on the steps of the police station in an hour. He's called the media and says he has evidence his client is innocent and that we, the police, are guilty of harassment."

CHAPTER THIRTEEN

I'm standing next to Orlando on the steps of the Tampa Police Department. His camera is on a tripod; our station microphone is on a mic stand on the steps while Thomas Figueroa's attorneys prepare to speak. A half-dozen other local and state media members are standing shoulder to shoulder, waiting for the news conference to begin. García is with a group of detectives watching from the side. Including Hanks.

I can't remember how many of these events Orlando and I have covered during the past five years, but this one is very different.

First of all, it's not just the two of us. Jessica is standing next to Orlando, in my usual place, and I swear to God, it's making my skin itch. I'm not mad at her. The itch is due to my overwhelming annoyance that El Jefe sent her here.

I understand why he did it—I've become a part of the story.

Mr. Payton called to explain I can't be an unbiased reporter if I picked Thomas Figueroa out of a police line-up because I saw him at a murder scene.

Still, I don't like the way Jessica falls so easily into my place, standing so close to O. I hate myself for spending precious moments being jealous when there are clearly more important matters at hand. But there it is, the truth. La verdad.

I am here, despite feeling crappy, despite being pushed onto the TV news sideline, and despite telling El Jefe I was heading home. I want to find out what proof Figueroa's attorney has that his client is innocent. If they've got video evidence, that changes the game. It would mean my stalker—Hoodie Hannibal—moves up to suspect number one.

That's not a good thing.

I shake it off and focus on what's unfolding in front of me. Figure out what I need to do next. Concentrate on what I *can* control.

Thomas Figueroa stands behind his attorneys. He's a small man but has a brain big enough to realize the importance of hiring an attorney like J.P. Feinstein, the biggest, kick-your-ass and take-your-money attorney in Florida. The one who has enough cash to run about one hundred commercials each day. Rumor is Feinstein wants to run for governor. This case might be what puts his name in the media spotlight for an extended time, earning him free publicity.

Like he needs it.

"My client, Mr. Figueroa, is devastated by the allegations the Tampa Police Department is sharing with the media, and therefore, the world," Feinstein says. "My client is a resident of the West Tampa neighborhood where Ms. Natasha Rodríguez lived. And yes, he was in the neighborhood last night when someone shot Ms. Rodríguez in her own doorway." Feinstein throws his arm out dramatically. He points to Figueroa, whose head is down and whose hands are clasped in front of him.

Bet Feinstein coached him to do that.

"And yes, my client has a history with Ms. Rodríguez. He lost a six-year-old daughter to an accidental shooting at her home. He also lost his wife to divorce because of the residual stress. His son, who witnessed his sister's murder, is struggling. These events wrecked my client. And now, TPD investigators are treating him like a murder suspect, despite the fact they have no proof."

I look at Orlando.

He's all business behind the camera.

"Why now?" Feinstein, famous for his Emmy-award winning rhetoric, shrugs like the whole world is wanting to know the answer. "My client's baby girl died years ago. The false accusations at this time do nothing but inflict pain and suffering on my client and his remaining family." He straightens at the podium. "My client is innocent. And to prove that I've released surveillance video from a home Mr. Figueroa visited last night as an invited guest. It will be evident"—Feinstein emphasizes the word evident—"Mr. Figueroa is playing soccer in the front yard from about five thirty p.m. until sometime after six thirty p.m. The video shows him eating dinner with the family. In all, my client is occupied for three hours, during the exact time the medical examiner says the murder took place. The only time Mr. Figueroa is not seen on surveillance footage, he's using the bathroom. We don't understand why police ordered him to take part in this lineup."

I swallow. *I'm the reason.*

"We have video, which will air exclusively on

WTVB tonight at eleven p.m."

What? I glance over at Jessica, who looks like the cat that swallowed the canary.

Orlando doesn't look surprised. He stands taller and looks superefficient and super-cool doing his job.

Did he know about the video and not tell me? Did the attorney give it to O or to Jessica? I shrink, fold my shoulders in, and hide behind another photographer from a different local TV station. I told El Jefe I was leaving, so I don't want to end up on another station's eleven p.m. newscast or on the live stream on another station's website.

"I gave the video to Ms. Jessica Spencer because I trust she will get the story right. Police are harassing my client because of recent trouble with the law that has nothing to do with what happened on Hesperides last night. My client has nothing to hide. I will take questions."

Feinstein delivers a verbal punch to my gut with words as hard as an iron fist.

My colleagues throw out questions like loaded grenades, but all I can hear is, "My client has nothing to hide."

But maybe I do.

My head hurts, and my body aches like I've worked out.

The man I ID'd as a murder suspect has an alibi that makes what I told García sound like a lie. But I did see him in the street and O can back me up. Why isn't he saying something? *Something's not right.*

And why is he allowed to work this story if I can't?

Someone tugs at my elbow, and I'm so in my own world, I jump.

It's a teenager, in too-big basketball shorts and a dirty, white T-shirt that must have been washed so many times the lettering is unreadable. He looks out of place for a TPD news conference. "Yes?"

"Hey, you the crime reporter, right?" The recognition in his eyes is unmistakable.

"Yes."

"I'm supposed to give this to you." The teen hands me a newspaper clipping. It looks pristine, like it's been in between the sheets of a photo album. Pressed. Preserved.

"Who asked you to give this to me?" I glance at the clipping but don't really see or read it.

"That dude." The teen points away from the news conference.

I look across the street.

The air in my lungs stalls.

"Hey, you okay?" The kid reaches out to stop me from falling. "I'm not in trouble, right?"

I'm no longer listening. All I see is a man in a black hoodie, staring at me from across the street. It's like he's been waiting for my gaze to catch his. The man's face is half hidden because he's wearing a black baseball hat under the hoodie, but I can tell he knows when I see him. He lowers his head and, with what looks like a quick wave, jumps on a city bus.

Hoodie Hannibal.

I want to yell, "Hey García, it's him!" Point and cause a distraction. I could also bolt across the street and try to jump on that bus so I can confront him.

But what? Hold him for García? After what

happened today?

My track record sucks. Would García even believe me?

What else can I do?

I look at the newspaper clipping. Instantly, I recognize it. Because *I'm in it*. Front page of *The Times*, almost a year ago to this day, when I'm interviewing another detective about a different crime. Shantay Grimes, a cashier getting off work at the Stop-N-Go, is going to her car. Eric Richardson, her boyfriend, is waiting for her. They argue and get into a physical fight. Grimes pulls out a knife and tries to stab Richardson. He pushes her off him. She trips, falls, hits her head on the curb and dies. He gets off, because of the Stand Your Ground law in Florida. There were witnesses who say she had the knife and was going after him. But later I interviewed family, who told me Shantay was a victim of domestic violence for years at the hands of Richardson. She refused to report him to police because they had kids together and didn't want their daddy to go to jail. Because there was no record of violence with police, and Richardson claimed self-defense, the state attorney never charged him.

I'd always thought justice wasn't served, and a broken woman died trying to stay alive.

I wish I had my azabache charm on, because *Edward Jones is fucking with me*. Hoodie Hannibal gave me this news article for a reason. My next mission is to figure out why.

What to do now?

"Hey, you okay?" Orlando asks.

The Q & A has wrapped up. "I've got to go."

O narrows his eyes and grabs me by the arm. "Where?"

I shake my head. "Not important."

"Oh no." He knows I'm lying.

I know I'm lying. Why do I lie? I hate liars.

"You're telling me," he says.

"I'm not." But I do. I show him the article and fill in all the details.

"Wait until I can pack up my stuff."

"You have to stay and work with Jessica."

My phone *dings*. Forensics Freddy's burner phone.

Text: *Got a hot scene. Could be related. Stop N' Go.* The address follows. What are the chances?

"Holy shit!"

O grabs my phone. "What the…?"

Hot scene can only mean one thing in Forensics Freddy's world. "We've got another murder."

CHAPTER FOURTEEN

The three of us, Orlando, Jessica, and I, arrive at the Stop-N-Go convenience store on 5th and South Park. Dusk spreads dimming light over the streets, dropping a touch of coolness into the humid air.

I was right about why Hoodie Hannibal sent me a message by way of newspaper article—we've got another crime scene. Another murder victim. What I can't figure out is how Hoodie knew about the new scene, had time to go home and find the old article, get to the police station, and find a kid to give it to me. In fact, how did he know I was at the police station?

Unless he's following me.

And, he committed this murder and wanted me to come see his latest work.

I shake that thought out of my troubled head and focus on the location before me. It looks eerily familiar. There's a car parked near the handicap parking space in front of the convenience store/gas station. It's been blocked off by crime scene tape. A white blanket covers the driver's side window, meaning a dead body is probably inside. Just like a year ago.

I hope it's not someone I know.

Is this related to what happened last night? And how is Hoodie Hannibal involved? If he's not the killer then what does he want from me? To help me find the killer?

"What's going on?" Jessica asks as soon as Orlando parks, and we exit the news van.

She wasn't here last year when the original crime went down.

"Not sure yet." As I turn in a slow circle, my gaze sweeps the scene and all surrounding it. Goosies erupt over my heated skin.

Is Hoodie Hannibal spying on me from a window in the rundown, city-owned apartments across the street? I can't see in them due to the setting sun. How long until I can't see what's around me at all?

Movement to my left. A man enters a fish and bait store. I only see his back. He's too tall and not wearing black. The door slams behind him.

A child screams. A flurry of dread streaks across my back. I turn around. Exhale. It's a toddler crying, after landing hard off a slide at the city-run park next to the Stop-N-Go.

If Hoodie Hannibal is here, he doesn't want me to see him.

Yet.

But that's his MO, isn't it? I didn't even know he was following me until he told me. He obviously likes control.

The store is roped off to customers. The parking lot is full, though, with police cars and emergency vehicles. Different radio calls and crime scene chatter fills the air, along with a sense of somberness. A handful of detectives are milling around, a few taking pictures and talking to witnesses. Forensics Freddy glides around the scene.

I wait until I can catch his eye.

He nods.

I do, too, then move on.

I see García. He's leaning over the car on the other side, where I can't see in. I wish I could see what he can. So far he hasn't seen me. For the time being, I'd like to keep it that way.

"I'm going to shoot video," Orlando says.

"I'm going, too." Jessica is right behind him.

"Can you try and get García's attention?" I ask her.

Jessica can keep him from seeing me, which frees me up to talk to store employees, who at this point probably know more than anybody about what went down today. "Ask him if this is related to last night."

"Right," she says. "I'm on it." Her eyes sparkle, and determination lights up her face.

A man in jeans and a Stop-N-Go T-shirt walks with an officer out of the convenience store. They duck under the crime scene tape. The officer opens the back door to a patrol car and gestures for the young man—he has to be an employee, because who else would wear that bright orange shirt—to sit inside. The officer gets a call, looks up and walks away, leaving the employee alone in the back of the police cruiser. The guy rests his head against the divider between the front and back seat and looks down at the phone.

I look around. Good. Both Jessica and García are occupied.

The patrol car is on the legal side of the yellow crime tape. *Also good.*

I casually stroll that way, weaving around

gawkers and other officers.

The store employee sees me. He's off his phone. "Hey, I recognize you."

I've got about five minutes till some cop notices what I'm doing. If that. So I jump right into reporter mode. "I'm Mari Álvarez. You know the guy who was killed?"

The man's eyes go wide, and he shakes his head. "Hey, look, I don't know him. I mean he comes here a lot. But I don't *know* him."

Okay. Victim is a man and comes here a lot. Lives in the area?

"What a mess. Dude was beat to hell. Not much blood though. Just some on the ground outside the car." The witness's eyes are red rimmed, like he'd been crying. Or is stoned. "I think some dude beat the other dude outside the car but dumped his body in the front seat. Must have fallen over. I told the cop that's why I didn't see him when I got to work. You know, it was dark. Car was here when I opened, but I didn't call the police till some kid told me about the body. I walked out and saw the dude slumped in the driver's seat. Hey, I didn't see who beat him up. I swear. You gonna put that on TV?"

"What time did you come to work?"

"Six a.m."

The number six again. Hoodie Hannibal could have beat up this man and still had time to go home, clean up, and make it to the news conference.

"Any witnesses? Other than the kid?" I ask.

The employee rubs his eyes. "Some Uber driver who came back to the scene."

"He saw the murder?"

"Nah, man. But he may have picked up someone who did. A woman."

"Got the driver's name?"

"Nah, man. Nah. He was about to talk to some detective but took off."

A dead end. Maybe. I'll try another angle. "A lot like last year's murder?"

He nods. "Hey, freaky shit, right?"

"Any video?" I did a follow-up story about how the owner installed a surveillance system after the woman, Shantay Grimes, died here.

He nods.

"Have you seen it?"

His Adam's apple bobs, and he motions me closer.

I glance behind me. No cops are watching us. I move closer, squat next to him outside the cop car, so I'm not as noticeable.

"Someone spray painted the camera," the witness says. "There's video but you can't see anything. Hey, you hear the screams, though. Whoever did it, it didn't take long. Beat the shit out of the dude. You can hear the blows. He's like crying for his life. Then…silence. Like maybe the dude hit the guy's head on the curb or something. That's why there's blood on the curb."

"Did you hear the killer say anything?"

"Nope. But I think he left a pretty freaky-deeky message in writing."

"What do you mean?" In the shiny side of the car, I see the reflection of a cop in a patrol uniform walking toward us. The cop has his hand placed over the top of his holstered gun. *¡Ay, Dios mío!* Should I raise both hands? "I better go."

"Check out the camera," the witness says. "It's on the back corner of the store. Pointed toward the handicap spot." The clerk is looking at the approaching cop, too. "Hey, but don't tell no one you heard it from me, 'kay? And don't put my ass on TV, 'kay? I got an ex who I don't wanna find me. Like, she's looking for dollars."

"The message?" Maybe that will clue me into something important. "Where's that?"

"Trust me," the store clerk brought both hands up as if in surrender. "You won't miss the message. Something crazy about the devil and leaving one eye open."

CHAPTER FIFTEEN

I'm checking out the surveillance camera on the right side of the Stop-N-Go convenience store, careful to stay on the legal side of the yellow crime scene tape. Black spray paint coats the lens.

I'm startled when I hear, "What are you doing back here? This is a crime scene."

Detective García. He's caught me creeping around the back of the store.

"I'm not crossing any yellow lines."

"This time."

He's alone, and I wonder how he knew I was back here.

He walks up and stares at the camera. "Is this going to continue to be an issue with you?"

But he doesn't address the obvious. So I do. "No video of the crime?"

He nails me with a look that probably tames the craziest of criminals. In the right circumstances, that look might actually tame me, too. And I might even like it. But right now, I need to convince him to tell me some useful info.

"How did you find out about this crime scene so quickly?" he asks. "The scanner? We haven't put out a news release."

"I'll tell you my source, if you tell me yours." I want to know if someone called 911. Maybe I'll get to hear Hoodie Hannibal's voice. Maybe I'll recognize it.

García's eyes don't change. "Not how it works, Ms. Álvarez."

Even though I still hate the *Ms. Álvarez* title, truth is, I don't want to antagonize García anymore. I'm starting to trust him. Not a clue why, but I am. I pull the newspaper out of my pocket, gently unfold it, and hand it to him. He looks at the clipping but holds his poker face.

"It's a story about a similar crime here about a year ago," I say.

He nods but doesn't look up. "I'm familiar with it."

García wasn't in homicide a year ago.

"I covered it, obviously." I'm in the picture of the news conference at the scene a year ago. "Today at Figueroa's news conference, Hoodie"—I stop myself—"I mean Edward Jones paid a kid to give this article to me."

His poker face slips. His mouth even drops open. "You saw Jones? At the news conference?"

"I did."

He nods and concern etches in his frown lines.

"He wanted me to come here and see this." By this I mean the crime scene. I point to the camera, feeling queasy and uneasy. "But obviously, he didn't want me to see everything."

García raises one eyebrow. I'm getting used to this tic of his.

"You think *Jones* spray painted the camera?" he says.

I shrug because I don't know. "How did you find

out about the murder?"

García doesn't answer. Instead, he studies the blackened camera again as if there's something new to see.

"Off the record, Detective. I'm not covering the story anymore because I've become a part of the story—not by choice. You got me involved with that lineup. I'm trying to figure out what this guy wants with me. Is he trying to point me to the killer?" I swallow back growing fear. "Or is *he* the killer?"

"A homeless man sleeping behind the store witnessed the beating."

My shoulders relax.

"The man got spooked and ran away. Later in the day, he told another homeless friend at a local soup kitchen about what he'd seen. The other man had a phone and that second person called 911."

"So time of death still to be determined." I finish for him. No need to say Hoodie Hannibal could have done it. García and I are on the same page. I feel it.

"I don't like the fact Jones knows where you are," García says. "He has to be following you."

I see sincerity in García's eyes. "Or tracking me. Not sure how, but there's all kinds of tracking technology today."

"I don't like that he keeps articles on you, and that he's now leaving you clues to crime scenes. I also don't like the fact the witness of this latest crime said the killer was wearing a black hoodie."

My legs go noodle-like. "The killer at this scene had on a black hoodie, too?"

"According to the homeless witness, yes. Usually, I'd say he doesn't qualify as a reliable witness, but—"

"But this means it could be the same killer. Because what are the chances? The killer wants us to know he's the same person by wearing the same outfit." Heat swims up my body.

"Or a similar outfit. I agree."

"What else did that witness say?"

He doesn't answer, but his eyes narrow with concern.

"Stop looking at me like that. I'm fine."

He places his hand on my forehead. "You feel warm."

I push his hand away. "It's hot. Of course I'm warm." Suddenly, I do want to beg off—go home, eat some of Abuela Bonita's amazing chicken noodle soup. But— "I'd leave, but I rode with Jessica and Orlando, and they'll be staying to do a live shot."

García gestures for me to walk toward the front of the store and the active part of the crime scene. I scan the scene as we're walking, looking for anything else that might be a clue.

"I'm sending you home in a patrol car," he says. "I'm going to station a deputy outside your house for the night."

Normally I'd reject the offer of help, thinking it's macho Latino let-me-handle things, I'm-the-man bullshit. But after the past two days, I appreciate his concern. And his desire to protect and serve. "Are you doing this to protect me from Hoodie Hannibal?"

"Who?"

"Sorry. That's what I call Edward Jones."

"Hoodie Hannibal?" He stops. Looks at me. "Like *Silence of the Lambs*?"

I nod.

He cocks his head. "I certainly hope not."

I smile, and it surprises me. "I appreciate the protection."

"Maybe I'll drive you myself." It wasn't a question. "I need to ask you more about this Hannibal Lecter of yours."

"Who, by the way, was wearing a black hoodie when I saw him today."

"At the news conference?"

I nod.

He crooks his neck as if he needs an adjustment. "Give me a few, okay?"

"You don't need to drive me." But I actually want him to. What if Edward Jones/Hoodie Hannibal is waiting for me outside Abuela's home? García has a gun. I don't even have an azabache charm. "But if you—"

I lose my breath when I see it. The sun has dropped lower but still sends a streak of light across the bold graffiti, spray painted like black blood across the solid white wall of the Stop-N-Go. The message is facing the car that had the victim inside. The message would have been clear to the victim before he died. Perhaps it was the last thing he saw.

I can't help myself. I read it out loud. "Die well. The devil is waiting for you. Keep one eye open so you can see him coming."

If that message isn't creepy enough, it's signed

with a spray-painted crown, the signature of The West Tampa Kings.

I turn away, but my heart drops lower.

A doll sits on top of the car where the murder victim died.

The doll's right arm is broken, and I can't be sure from this distance, but I think the doll's eye is missing.

CHAPTER SIXTEEN

Detective García's department-issued vehicle looks much like his office—lived in. It wasn't dirty, but he had an empty cup, stained by what was probably espresso, in his cup holder, and two case files thrown on the passenger seat that I moved to the floor. On the dashboard next to the clock is a picture of an old man. The man wears a baseball hat that says Cuba SOS. García has his arms around the man and looks at him adoringly in the manner a man would look at a cherished father or grandfather. Next to that, I recognize a picture of the Tampa Police Memorial with a close-up of a name. In the back seat is a gym bag, fat and full.

García is driving in silence, his mind apparently miles away. He smells of outdoors and hand sanitizer, the strong kind used after picking through bloody evidence.

"You didn't have to do this." I have to break the silence. It's unnerving. If I don't, I'm going to keep staring at him because he's got a perfect jawline and serious eyes that look burdened. "I could have taken an Uber home."

He shakes his head but doesn't look my way. "No, I want to make sure you get home safely, and I want to confirm that a patrol car is already sitting outside."

I lean closer. "You're that worried about me?"

"Two murder scenes in two days." His fingers grip the wheel. They're lighter at the tips like he's applying pressure. "In both cases, you're at the scene."

"Oh." I scooch away. "So you think I'm a suspect?"

"No." He shoots me a *what are you talking about* look. "I think you're a witness." He turns his gaze back to the highway. "Edward Jones at the first scene, likely at the second. I need to prove that."

"I want to help. Maybe you find out who makes or sells those dolls. See if Mr. Jones purchased any lately. Through Amazon?"

"I can't involve you." A slight smile, and he lessens his grip on the wheel. "Although, that's a good idea. You might actually make a good detective, Ms. Álvarez."

"Ms. Álvarez." I say it at the same time he does because I felt it was coming. "You know what else I'd do right now, if I was a good detective?"

"No." His features don't give anything away.

"Is that a 'no, I don't know'?"

Now, the corner of his eyes crinkle. "It's a no to whatever you're about to suggest."

"Ha! You haven't even heard my idea, yet."

"You said you weren't feeling well. And you felt warm. I'm taking you home."

"I'm fine. And I want to prove Jones was at both scenes just as badly as you do. If I was your partner"—I get a side-eye with more of that sly smile—"I'd revisit the witness across the street of the first crime on Hesperides—the one Jessica interviewed."

We drive in silence for a moment. "Okay, I'll bite. Why?"

Anticipation bubbles in my belly like expensive champagne. "This has been bothering me." I turn in my seat to face him. "If the witness Jessica interviewed saw the man in the hoodie arguing with Natasha Rodríguez before shooting her and then watched him run away, how would the shooter have time to pose a body?"

García's eyebrows arch.

"I saw the weird angle of her leg. Her dress was pushed up. And how could he place a doll on her body and a coin on one eye? The killer staged the scene. Wouldn't the witness mention that?"

Silence. He glances at the dash, puts on the blinker, and makes a last-minute turn.

"This isn't the way to my house."

"I know." He turns left on Hillsborough, and I know he's heading for Hesperides.

I hold my tongue until we arrive, my appreciation fizzing because the detective valued my idea enough to pursue it.

The street is sadly quiet today. We pull up in front of the witness's house.

"You need to stay in the car."

"Wait. This was my idea."

He jumps out of the car.

I do, too. "I'll only listen."

García keeps walking but says, "You're pushing it—"

"Ms. Álvarez," I finish for him. I know I'm pushing it, but I don't care. I'm even willing to power through my headache to get some answers.

I follow him to the front door, stand behind him so I'm out of his peripheral vision.

A lady answers—could be the witness Jessica talked to last night. I keep my mouth shut as García introduces himself and asks the witness to recount what she saw.

It's all repetitive, until she says, "As soon as I heard the first gunshot, I ran inside and called—"

I interrupt. "So you didn't actually see the shooter after he fired his gun?"

García does a slow burn turn. "So much for just listening."

I throw up my hands and ask the witness to continue.

"As soon as I heard the shot," the witness says, "I ran inside and called 911. When I got up the courage to peek out the window, the man in black was taking off. I did see him pick up a bag. At the curb."

"A bag like a garbage bag?" García asks.

"A black bag, I think." The woman, who had to be over seventy, was wearing thick, dark-framed glasses and leaned on a cane. "The man ran behind the next-door neighbor's house, and I didn't see him no more." Her English is good, if a little hard to understand due to her accent.

"So," I ask, "you didn't see him put out any—"

"Don't lead her." García is glaring at me, and this time it's no joke.

I ignore him, thinking I have every right to be here and ask what I want. "How much time passed between when you ran inside and looked out the window?"

"Maybe a couple of minutes?" The woman is

fanning herself with a La Teresita takeout menu. "I was scared at first to go near the window," she says, fanning even faster. "What if he saw me?"

The witness rambles on and García appears to be actively listening to her, even though his gaze keeps flicking my way.

Her words fade, and all I hear in my mind is: *The killer in the hoodie did have time to pose the body and place the broken doll.*

CHAPTER SEVENTEEN

"I bet there are other witnesses," I say.

Detective García and I are driving the few streets between the witness's house on Hesperides and my abuela's home a few blocks over. I only have minutes to pick his brain before he drops me off. But interviewing him, without him catching on to my interviewing him, will be almost impossible. He's a smart guy, and he's got my number.

"Surveillance video—RING doorbell video. Right?" I ask him. It's dark now. The streetlights splash bright light across his face in a rhythmic pattern. That makes it almost impossible to assess García's mood. "There's got to be something."

We pass another street light. "Haven't had time to check the full report, but I will as soon as I can get back to the office."

It's after normal work hours, but he's not going home. Detective García is a workaholic like me. Another thing we have in common. "Was there a bag at the murder scene today? A black bag?"

The brief passage of light over his face doesn't reveal anything. "Don't remember seeing one, but that's another thing I'll check." He flicks a glance my way. "Left the scene a little early." But the light leaves his features before I can tell if he's pissed about that. Or if he's messing with me.

Heat spreads through me anyway, and I look out the window as we pass La Segunda bakery. Their front lights are still on. I can almost smell the sweet scent of sugar on my favorite guava pastries. My stomach growls. When is the last time I ate? But the open sign is off. Anyway, what I'm actually hungry for is Abuela's chicken noodle soup.

And answers.

"What do you think was in the bag?" I ask. "That the killer would stop to grab it after shooting someone six times." *Six* times. *¡Carajo!* I glance at García to see if he's picked up on the fact I know such a tiny detail he didn't tell me.

"I have no idea." He's looking at the bakery, too. Bet he hasn't eaten today, either.

"Speculate."

Side-eye. "I thought reporters don't speculate." It's dark again.

Chin up, I say, "I thought detectives do."

I get a laugh out of him before his tone goes all serious. "Serial killers like to take trophies and—"

Serial killer. "You think we've got a serial killer on our hands?" Those are the two words that got me suspended. But I was already thinking the same thing.

"I think I have two crime scenes with commonalities—the doll, the man in a hoodie fleeing the scene, surveillance cameras blacked out."

I hold back a *whaaat* and act like I knew cameras were blacked out at the Hesperides scene, too. "And the reference to eyes—one eye open, one eye shut. Keep one eye open so you can see the devil coming. Maybe an evil eye reference?" I reach out to lower the radio.

García's gaze goes to my exposed wrist.

"Do you regret giving away the azabache charm bracelet you were wearing last night?" he asks.

My cheeks flush with the warmth of his attention to this tiny detail. "No, I felt like she needed—"

"The protection," he finishes my sentence. "And now you're sick."

"I'm not sick. Just feeling a little—"

"Sick."

Again, not a question. "Feeling a little...off. A coincidence?" I ask, curious what he'll say.

"I think so." He glances at me. "You?"

I swallow. I wait until we pass another streetlight so I can see his eyes, but that doesn't relieve my dry throat or my worry. "Not sure."

"All right, let's say the evil eye is a real thing. Who do you think is giving you the evil eye?"

"Besides you?" I say before I can stop myself. I smile so he knows I'm playing with him. Give a little shrug.

He volleys back with his version of the evil eye. Or, what I picture the evil eye looking like. Furrowed brow, narrowed eyes, intensity radiating from them.

The streetlights fade away again.

"Oh, I don't know," I say to the dark. "There are about five people who could be giving me the evil eye. Let's see. At work there's Jessica, El Jefe, Orlando." I count on my fingers, but still say, "How many is that?"

"Three," García answers.

"Hoodie Hannibal, my stalker." I pause and wait

for his reaction.

He glances over at me, but I can't see his features well enough in this passing light.

I say, "And finally, you." This time I keep my tone even. "Sometimes people can wish you ill will unconsciously or unintentionally."

His eyes widen, and he pulls back a little. "I truly hope you don't believe that."

I don't answer because I'm not sure how to answer. I'm not sure what I believe. "I know I started feeling poorly after I gave the charm away."

"I turn here. Right?" So he was going to ignore my last comment.

"Right."

"Patrol car is here. Good."

"Thank you."

"You're welcome." He stops the car and turns it off.

My heart is drumming like it's holding its own Santería ceremony, and I'm not sure if it's because I'm scared or excited. "Not just for taking me home. For trusting my instincts and going back to interview the witness." Or both. "Probably not proper police protocol to take a witness with you."

"It's not."

I fill the silence that follows his admission. "Don't worry. I'm not going to report it."

He doesn't respond. Nor does he open the car door. Or get out.

We're both sitting here. In front of my house. My pulse pounding. I'd give a grand to know if his is, too.

"Why did you do it? Take me with you just

now?" I can't keep myself from asking. "If it could get you in trouble?"

"I think a snowball is starting to roll here, and you're involved in it."

My heart skips a beat. Not what I expected to hear. "You're trying to protect me from it?"

He opens the car door. "My job is to protect you and our West Tampa community." He doesn't move to get out. "But it's not just that. You have your pulse on this community."

"I do." I follow his lead and open my door, pleased at what I'm taking as a compliment. I get out and look around the simple streets. "I love this place." I love the outdoor fruit and veggie markets, the small colorful houses, with their statues of the Virgin Mary and Saint Barbara outside. I love the tricycles in the driveways and the Spanish music blaring from their backyards. I love that everyone knows each other by their first names and their family histories.

He exits the car and leans against the top, across from me. The harvest moon is bright and lights his face enough for me to see it. "Where did you disappear to last night?"

He's a good detective. "I visited a Babalawo down the street."

"Gotta admit I'm surprised you practice Santería."

"I don't. Not really." His blunt honesty surprises me, and I feel the need to explain. "Never visited a Babalawo before, but I felt drawn there. He actually did help me."

García pushes off the car and starts walking

toward my house. "I don't believe in any of that shit."

That hijacks the mood. I push off the car, too, and the aggressive movement feels good. "I know you don't. You're a I-have-to-see-it-or-I-don't-believe-it kind of guy." I hustle around the car and run to catch up with him.

He stops mid step in the middle of the stone walkway leading up to my front door and turns. I run into his chest. Full on, right into his body, and I have to fling my arms around him to stop myself from falling. I close my eyes, embarrassment rushing through me like the cool saline of an IV. I start to pull away.

His arms fall around me, and he says, "I'll tell you what kind of guy I am."

All the air leaves my body. I don't even know why—I don't even like this guy. He's bossy and a bit of a show off. He's a gym rat who's probably a hit with all the women because of those muscles and that jaw and—

"I'm the kind of guy who walks a young lady to her door to make sure she's home safely."

¡Ay, Dios mío! "Of course you're that guy." I pull away, full of shame I was actually thinking about what it would be like to kiss him. And all he's worried about is my wellbeing.

"And tells her to lock the door and don't answer it unless it's the police."

"Right, thanks." I smile and don't fight his goodness. I hand him my key and let him open the door for me.

"Do me a favor," he says as he guides me through

my front door. "Take a few Advil and get some sleep."

For some reason, that irks me. Maybe because he's proving he's a much nicer person than I am. Maybe because I'm finding myself physically attracted to him when I don't want to be. Maybe because he's pulling off that Latin machismo thing that bugs me.

In a rebellious turn, I lean against the door frame like Sofía Loren or some other *femme fatale* in a black-and-white movie classic. "First, I thought I'd visit my abuela's back room and pray to my orisha. Shall I say a prayer for you, too?" I wait for the reaction I know I'll get. Why? Because, well, I'm me. And that's not always a good thing.

He stills and eyes me with a sharp look that's not weak or joking. "Don't play with something you don't understand. Okay?"

Is he talking about Santería or this energy buzzing between us right now? I gulp, but words stick in the back of my dry-as-hell throat.

He relaxes and slips into that familiar lopsided grin of his. "If you hear from Mr. Jones, call me." He pulls out a card with his number on it.

I grab it. Energy transfers.

"My cell is—" Enough energy to halt García's words mid-sentence.

I'm conscious of how shitty I must look. My mouth tastes like dry fever, if that even has a taste, and I know I'm hot to the touch. No man wants to kiss a burning mess like me.

Why am I even assuming that's what he wants to do?

Because his eyes are glazed over, and his fingers linger, until, conscious of my own heart beating and my pulse drilling through me, I pull away.

But it takes a concentrated effort to tear my gaze off him.

His dark, knowing eyes are the last thing I see before closing the door.

CHAPTER EIGHTEEN

Abuela Bonita's house is dark, empty, and quiet, but it's the lack of smells that bothers me the most. No food bubbling on the stove, no onion and garlic sauce or hot oil for the plantains. Only the distant scent of burning candles.

The TV isn't on. No game shows in Spanish. No telenovelas. Not even the Tampa Bay Ray's baseball game with the sound turned low so she can hear the color calls by the Spanish radio host and his wife.

Just the low drumming of bongos accompanied by the claves.

I know where Abuela Bonita is. I just don't know why she's there. I head back to the private room, the one you don't show the neighbors. Unless they're Cuban, too.

Abuela is kneeling next to her altar clutching prayer beads in her hands, along with a piece of paper worn around the edges. She'll probably put that piece of paper in a glass of water after her prayer. Her short gray hair is messy as usual, but also wet, and she's in one of her comfortable lounging dresses she buys from Walmart. I bet she smells of lavender because it looks like she just got out of the shower.

That makes me smile. I love the way Abuela smells when she hugs me.

"In the holy name of God, the Father, in the holy name of the heavenly protectors, and in the name of San Luis Beltran."

I've heard her recite this prayer many times before.

Her altar table is draped in the same white cloth she washes regularly. Seven glasses of water sit on the table, circling a statue of Oshun, who is Abuela's orisha, the goddess of river waters but also of love and sexuality. Oshun represents the joy of life and is the embodiment of what makes life worth living.

I've always been a little jealous of her orisha. Who wouldn't want to embody what makes life worth living?

My orisha, Chango, always appears angry, with bolts of lightning flying from his fingers and a double-headed ax in his other hand. He's the orisha that represents passion and power, but also justice and war.

I still remember the first time Abuela Bonita told me about my personal orisha. I'd almost stumbled over a small lump of dirt and shells at the base of her old altar. It had taken me a minute to recognize the clumps of earth had been shaped into a face.

"The orisha Chango." Abuela pointed to the man-made face. "He's a warrior. You pray to him for justice."

Dark clay, with three large holes, two for the eyes and one for a mouth, gave the mask a haunting look. I was more than spooked. So spooked, I cleaned it up the next morning when she left for the Latin market. Abuela never mentioned it, but I know she knew it was me. She's sensitive to the energy people give off.

For instance, I can tell by the stiffness in her spine she knows I am here now, watching her.

"I invoke this prayer to remove the evil eye," Abuela continues, her eyes closed, her features set and serious.

I can't catch my breath; it escapes my lungs so quickly. *She can sense a fever, too?* How does she know I'm feeling a little off?

She grips her beads, pulling them to her chest, mumbling something I can't hear.

"Abuela? I'm home."

She doesn't respond, but instead says, "Amen." Then makes the sign we always made in St. Mary's Catholic Church—the sign of the Holy Trinity. "Of the Father, The Son, and The Holy Ghost."

I'm so confused about this mixture. And about how she knew to invoke this particular prayer right now, as I arrived home, before she even saw me. I shiver, despite my heated body.

"Marisol," she says. "Come here."

I walk over and kneel beside her. "Izzy home?" *Deflect. Deflect Deflect.*

She shakes her head.

My little sis is going to wonder why a cop car is parked outside. It might summon bad memories.

I shudder as Abuela's bony fingers, cold from lack of circulation, spread against my forehead. The warmth my body is putting off only makes her iciness more prominent.

"You have a fever." She clicks her tongue in that way that makes me curl up inside. "I knew it."

"It's nothing. I'm fine." I remove her hand. "It's

nothing. How did you know?"

"You know what you must do now." She rises, walking to the corner of the room. She comes back with a gallon of liquid in a clear plastic jug and places it on the ground next to me.

I exhale. This is what I was trying to avoid. I know what's in it. Water, eggshells, honey, milk, coconut, and some herbs.

"After you shower, pour it over yourself."

I want to make a smart-ass comment, because I mean, really? This is supposed to wash away the evil eye? But I don't because it's worked before. And the fact Abuela saw this coming means there's something spiritual going on.

"You do it a second time, if you need."

Here's to hoping there's not a second time. "Yes, Abuela."

She stands and shuffles around the room, stirring up the room's ashe—or energy—like it's sofrito boiling on her stove. She leans over and blows out the candle next to the picture of Oshun that sits next to a picture of my mamá.

I quake, my mamá's voice entering my head. *Santería is witchcraft.*

But Abuela explained it differently. First, when she heard my mother condemn it, the second time after I told her about an incident at my friend Sofía's house years ago, when her father was cheating and her mom and sister wrote the name of the mistress on a piece of paper, placed it in a cup of water, and prayed before their altar.

Shortly after, police arrested the mistress for stealing.

Shaken when my friend told me, concerned maybe this secret religion Abuela wanted to teach me really was witchcraft, Abuela had explained, "Marisol, people don't understand religions that don't have simple good and evil, God versus Satan. Our religion is based on intentions. Because of that, people familiar with Santería will tell you to be careful."

"What do you mean?" I'd asked.

"Sofía's mom thought her husband was cheating on her?"

"Yes," I'd said.

"What were her *intentions* when she prayed?"

"Well, I don't know. I only know what Sofía told me."

"If her goal was to harm her husband's lover, it could have been a form of *Brujería*—a dark side of Santería. If it was to have her husband fall back in love with her, or to have the orishas help her get over this lost love, it was the Santería I practice. The difference is her *intentions* when she called on the spirits."

Sofía's parents are still together today, which makes me wonder about my parents.

I grab Abuela's elbow. "Mom was cheating before she died, wasn't she?"

The room grows quiet. The energy stills. Abuela looks at her elbow, where I'm holding her. She doesn't answer.

"Do you think that guy from her work killed her?"

Abuela jerks away from me. Like my fingers are now hot irons. "You must stop this." Her voice is unrecognizable now. Harsh. Low. Urgent.

Unexpected.

"I don't understand. Abuela, don't you want to know?" The room appears to darken, like an invisible force draws the blinds shut. "Doesn't it eat you alive at night? Not knowing for sure? After all these years?"

"Someone is casting an evil eye on you. You have a fever. You ramble about the past. You worry too much about things you cannot change." She grabs my right wrist and tugs. "You must do your wash. Vamos." Her fingers dance over my skin, brushing up the inside of my arm.

I freeze.

"Where is your azabache bracelet?"

The one she gave me. The one her mother gave her. "I gave it to a young girl in need." I swallow, nervous she'll be mad. "Her mother died."

"Marisol? Regalaste la bendición?"

"I'm sorry." And I am. "I didn't think of it like giving the blessing away."

"That bracelet was blessed specifically for me." The pressure she applies on my wrist is beyond what'd you'd expect from an eighty-two-year-old. "It was blessed again for you."

I'm oddly out of my body. "If I gave it away, does the protection still work for the new person?"

My abuela's disappointment dissolves as her shoulders drop, and her lips round up into a slight smile. "The blessing and intention is carried over," she says.

I let go of the breath I'd been holding in. "Good. Good. She needs it. The blessing." I don't regret what I did. But… "I'm sorry."

"We will get you a new one." Abuela drops my wrist. "We will have it blessed."

I hear resolution in her tone. "I thought the azabache was only for babies, anyway."

She steps closer to me, so close I can smell the scent of aging on weathered, cracking skin. Her bloodshot, tired eyes lock with mine. "You need protection."

I feel her intentions right down to my bones. "Yes, Abuela. I know who can bless my new charm. The Babalawo on Hesperides." He comforts me. "The one your friend introduced me to."

"We go to the joyería tomorrow."

"For a charm and bracelet? I can order tonight. From Amazon. It will get here tomorrow. I've got Prime."

"Eh? You can't order protection from the internet."

"Why not? I mean it's the blessing on the azabache that matters, right?"

"You have no idea who makes the charm. What *their* intentions are."

"I buy everything from Amazon."

"There are some things you should not get on that computer of yours. We will do this my way."

"Okay. I'm tired." I pick up the jug. "I'm going to go do my wash."

Abuela takes my face in her hands and kisses both cheeks. Her lips are dry. "Marisol, I want so much to protect you." One more kiss on my forehead, and she leaves the room.

I'm alone now, with the picture of my dead

mother, a gallon of egg and milk wash, an unlit candle, and glasses of water.

I'm still missing something.

Something very important.

I open a four-by-six book with the word *journal* on it that was also on the table. I flip to the back, tear out a blank piece of paper. I don't have a pen on me, but there's one in a drawer. I write the name of a person on it.

Antonio García.

Why?

Because I need García's help. And it may require more than him giving me a ride home and leaving a cop in a car outside—it might require him to trust me. So that's the request I am making tonight. I want him to see me in a new light. Trust me. Work with me.

I grab the glass of water. I'll head to the kitchen. Instead of putting the glass in the freezer, I'll add sugar, along with García's name, to sweeten the attraction and feed the prayer.

There could be no one more surprised than me at what I'm doing. I've never been this kind of believer.

But I can't wait to see if my orisha Chango answers my heartfelt prayer.

Then I see it—the piece of paper my grandmother had clutched in her hand when I walked in. She'd dropped it when cradling my head in her hands.

My hands shaking, I pick it up.

I scan the handwritten note: *Come to me.*

The wrinkled piece of paper slips through my heated fingers, warmed by my pulse beating faster now than the drums still pounding in the music-filled room. Is it just a note? Or a command? Or prayer to one of the saints?

Trembling, I kneel to pick up the piece of paper, knowing instinctively this is another clue to what is happening, to the shift in the course of my life, to the bad ashe now surrounding me.

As I grab it, I notice another sheet on the ground near an envelope hidden mostly by Abuela's Santería altar, like she'd dropped both earlier and they'd slid there, forgotten.

I pick the other piece up, too, then look at it. And almost vomit.

It's a newspaper article about Mamá's murder. The picture accompanying the article is of me with Izzy, her crying on her knees next to Mamá's body. Me standing next to her, a statue standing out in our horrific garden of misery.

It's a picture of us the moment we were both broken.

I drop it and grab the envelope, my heart vibrating like an out-of-control blender. I fumble with it, dropping its contents. The first rolls as it hit the tile floor. A red candle. A love candle I recognize because I've burned them before. The second item hits the tile with a metallic-like clank. My breath halts. A gold coin? With a crown on it like the one at the Rodríguez murder scene. In my house? I try to pick it up, but my nervous fingers, combined with short nails, fail to flip it up. Finally, I grasp it and drop it onto the altar. Not a coin. It's a charm with the image of…Oshun on it? Oshun, the goddess of love.

I can't swallow.

Did Hoodie Hannibal leave this for me and Abuela found it? Is he praying I'll fall in love with him? Or did someone else leave this threatening note and article for my grandmother? Oshun is her orisha. Maybe this is the real reason she came to her hidden altar to pray to her trusted saints. What in the name of the Father, the Son, and the Holy Ghost is going on? I'll ask her but instinctively know she won't answer. If she'd wanted me to know she would have told me immediately.

I have the distinct feeling if I don't figure this out myself, someone else I love is going to die.

CHAPTER NINETEEN

My cell phone is ringing. I open my eyes, crusted from a hard sleep and Abuela's wash. I flip over in bed, drag my hand across the nightstand, tap around until I feel it.

"Hello." My voice breaks.

"His name is Eric Richardson."

Forensics Freddy. His snarky, raspy, dipped-in-sarcasm tone is unmistakable. "I'm sorry. What time is it?" I glance at the clock on my nightstand, but my eyes are still too unfocused to make out numbers.

"Seven thirty a.m. Wanted to get you before you got busy."

Work. "I'm not even up yet." *¡Carajo!* "Wasn't feeling well last night." I sit up. First thing I notice, my headache is gone and my body isn't aching. Second thing is I don't feel sticky, even though I air dried with that yucky wash on me last night. I need to get it together, get out of bed, and get to work.

It hits me.

Today is Saturday. I flop back on the bed, arms spread wide. Finally, a day off. I'm doing nothing all day. Giving the investigation a rest. *But driving myself crazy.*

"Eric Richardson," Freddy says. He goes silent.

I let the pause linger. It's our thing.

"*Think* Lois Lane." Freddy breaks first. "Does

the name sound familiar?"

"It does." I rub my temples. Sit straight up. "Holy shit. He was the boyfriend who beat up Shantay Grimes at the Stop-N-Go a year ago. I covered the story. He got off, though."

"Someone beat the life out of Eric Richardson and left him dead in his car at The Stop-N-Go yesterday."

"Holy Shit!" I shoot straight up. "So, Eric Richardson is the victim in the car."

"Head shoved against the concrete curb at his temple. That's actually what killed him. But yes, he's the guy."

"And?" There's always an *and* with Freddy.

A dramatic sigh. "I need you to pay attention, so you're able to fully appreciate my brilliance and praise my excellence."

I laugh out loud. "You enjoy this way too much."

"Think I'd risk my job if I didn't?"

His energy snakes through the phone like a lightning bolt. "Okay, I'm awake. What else?"

Another dramatic Forensics Freddy pause. "There was a lightning bolt carved into the top of our vic's right hand. Carved right into his flesh. And it was fresh."

"Give me a sec." I grab some water off the night-stand, gulp down half the cup. "There was also that graffiti on the wall. 'The devil is waiting for you. Keep one eye open so you can see him approaching.'"

"Girl, I know. We're dealing with pure evil."

I shudder. "If I remember correctly, Grimes and Richardson were fighting. The girlfriend pulled out a knife. He pushed her so hard—"

"So hard she hit her head on the curb and died. Right there in the parking lot."

"The State Attorney declined to file charges due to Florida's Stand Your Ground Law," I say. "Richardson had a right to defend himself if he felt his life was in danger."

"Even though she pulled a knife to *defend herself first.*"

It all rushes back to me now. The community protests over Richardson getting off made national news during that first week. Then died, like many other important, ground-breaking news stories. And Shantay became another victim of domestic violence. Broken, killed, and forgotten.

I jump out of bed, almost slipping on my slippers. "The killer beat up Richardson in the same place Richardson beat up Grimes—to make a point." I'm jittery, filled with new info and excitement. "We may have a vigilante killer on our hands. And I might know who it is."

"Get out of here, chica. I'm the one usually feeding you information. Do share."

"So there was this guy who approached me at the first scene. On Hesperides. Had on a black hoodie. Like the killer. I tell García and he gets his name."

"You and the German Shepherd are on a last name basis?"

I ignore his insinuation. "Hoodie's name is Edward Jones. Same guy shows up at the news conference at TPD today. I mean yesterday." I fill in the details. "If it's my stalker at both scenes, is he targeting suspects who escaped justice, or is he targeting me? Is he a caped crusader, so to speak, or a sick psycho? Or just a crime news junkie? What's his deal?"

A pause and a low growl-like sound. "Umm, girl, let's hope he thinks he's Batman. Because I surely don't want you to be his deal."

I can't even appreciate Freddy's humor. My head is too deep into the worry sandpit right now. "I've been looking for commonalities." I do sound like a detective. "I worked on both stories, although I was only on the scene the first day of the Stand-Your-Ground case. I was working another court case at the same time. But maybe Hoodie Hannibal was at the original crime scene, too."

"Hoodie Hannibal?"

The heat of embarrassment creeps up both sides of my face. "What I've named my stalker." I slap both hands over my cheeks.

"You name your stalkers?"

I've named you, too. "This is my first."

"Girl," Freddy explodes in amusement. "You going on air with that?"

"Hell no!" I'm literally getting dizzy thinking about what El Jefe would say. "You know what happened the last time I used *your* unnamed source info to tell the world a serial killer was doing his dirty work in our fine city."

"Hmmm, well my info was spot on. As spot on as those 101 Dalmatians."

This time I don't laugh. "I believe you." I shrug. "The city council member has a good attorney and friends in high places."

"So what now, Detective Álvarez?"

He's joking, of course. But I like the sound of it. "Old cold cases need to be reexamined to see if any other suspects, who got off easy or got off altogether, have recently died—suspiciously." I follow with what's been my greatest desire for years. "Including looking at the only suspect in my mom's case." My heart is thumping like an old truck barreling down a broken road. This is the link I've been waiting to find. A good enough reason for cops to reopen my mom's case. Or, if it was never closed, put it on top of the stack again. The main suspect in Mamá's murder walked because his wife gave him an alibi. *A lie.* But I could never prove it. And now, after what I found in Abuela's altar room last night, all clues are leading me to this.

Heat is rising inside me. Justice still needs to be served.

I think back to what the Babalawo recently asked me. *"Does it matter how justice is served, if it's deserved?"* I'm not sure. But I do know I'm not the only one thinking about it. "We may have more than a vigilante killer here, Freddy. If any of those old cases have an evil eye reference or broken dolls at the scene, we may have a serial killer. A serial killer with a calling card and a righteous cause. García thinks the same."

Freddy is silent.

The pause tells me everything I need to know. He agrees with me. He agrees with *us.*

Only one thing to do now. I have to convince that show-me-the-proof homicide detective our next move should be diving into cold cases before our killer strikes again. We need to look at old murders where justice went unserved. Find commonalities that might help us predict who will be next. My mother's case needs to be first on that list.

Two murders in two days.

My gut tells me our murderer is killing someone else tomorrow.

Someone who committed a crime but never paid the price.

But does that mean they deserve to die?

And am I guilty if I don't try to stop it?

The clock is ticking.

I gotta find García.

CHAPTER TWENTY

After the fourth call to García, I realize the homicide detective isn't going to call me right back, so I agree to make a run to la bodega—The Latin Fresh Market—for Abuela. It's either that or continue to listen to her gloat about how the prayer to San Luis Beltran worked.

Can't say it did.

Can't say it didn't.

But I do have to admit I feel much better today. And it only took one wash. In the middle of arguing with her over whether I need another, I grabbed her shopping list and headed to the market.

I stroll down the aisle of the grocery store, thinking how beautiful it is in here. The fresh produce bursts with vibrant colors—bright red apples, brilliant oranges, fresh yellow bananas. Next to red and green peppers, carrots, green onions, and tomatoes.

I smell pork chunks cooked with onions, probably swimming in mojo—part of the hot food items they put out. My stomach growls. I left without eating. Maybe I'll grab one of those tostones—hot and salted.

I glance at the list to see if the unripe, green plantains are on Abuela's list. They're not. Only the ripe ones used to make the sweet version of plantains. And Sazón? Seasoning. *Right.* I forgot where you find the coloring. Next to the Adobo seasoning?

Someone walks by with a Styrofoam box full of something garlicky. I inhale. It's only eleven a.m., but I moan. Out loud. Realizing what I must sound like, I glance around, hoping my lack of makeup and casual clothing will make it harder to ID me as the local TV news crime reporter. Who's been in the news herself lately. *¡Ay, Dios mío!*

The Latin Fresh Market is usually packed with people I know. This morning, there are only a few people shopping, mostly women.

Except for one fine specimen of a man standing at the meat counter.

My center warms in that delicious way I've missed. The man's back is to me, so I don't see his face, but to be honest I'm mainly focused on the buns in those tight jeans. Contrólate. Control yourself.

I'm hungry.

It's been over a year since I've been on a date. After two disastrous relationships following my mother's murder, I decided to date myself a little. Do some therapy, workout, improve me. 'Cause I'm thinking the problem isn't with the men, the problem is with me. I'm damaged, no longer West Tampa mother material. If I ever was. I'm not even fun, first-date material. Men find me intense, driven, determined to do things my way. In West Tampa, that doesn't go over so well. The only thing that saves me is I'm a reporter. People *expect* a pit bull.

They just don't want to date one. Much less marry one.

The man turns around, and my heart does one of those floor exercise runs we used to see at Le Fleur's gymnastics.

What are the chances?

Well, honestly, pretty good, if you believe in an answer to a prayer. I prayed for García's help last night, even sprinkled sugar over that request, sweetening it.

And here he is scanning the market. His gaze catches mine.

Heat runs up me as fast as local NASCAR star Aric Almirola's race car.

So, now I have a choice. Suck up the embarrassment soup and walk over and take advantage of this meeting. I can share my idea and ask him as many questions as I can before he shuts me down, which he will. Maybe even tell him about the note and the items I found last night in my home. The notes that, as I expected, Abuela refused to address. Maybe that will encourage him to at least make a professional appointment to talk with me Monday at his office.

Or I can run right out of the Latin Fresh Market and come back after he's left.

Who am I kidding? What's the purpose of a prayer to the saints if you're not willing to take advantage of it when it's granted?

An older woman walks up, stands next to García, and stares at the meat counter. She's shorter than García, obviously older, petite, but powerful, I think—it's in her elegant posture. The Louis Vuitton side purse doesn't hurt, either. She's fit for an older woman. She has to be his mother. He looks like her. Same curve to his proud nose, same refined features—same beautiful caramel skin tone. It looks like her eyes are green, his hazel.

She follows his gaze and locks in on me. She must wonder why her son and I are engaged in a slightly uncomfortable stare down, me in front of the tomatoes, him at the meat counter.

García sticks his hands in his pockets and strides my way. I know when he gets closer and opens his mouth it's going to be—

"Ms. Álvarez?"

Awkward. "I called and left a message for you." I blurt it out. My journalistic eloquence leaves me in his presence.

"You left *five* messages," García says.

I thought it was four. *¡Carajo!* Five *is* excessive. "Well, I would have only left one message if you'd returned my first call. It was urgent." Did I say that? I can't bring myself to see if his mom is still staring at us.

He doesn't move a muscle. "Any new dead bodies since yesterday, Ms. Álvarez?"

"No. But I expect one." Thanks to the ominous notes found in my grandmother's back room.

No reaction.

How does he do it? Stay so calm and in control? "Please, call me Mari." I'm not eighty. Ms. Álvarez is my abuela. "But I do have an idea of what we can do next, to narrow down who may be the next victim."

"You have a plan?" The sarcasm in his voice is thick. "To find the next victim? How about we discuss your *idea* Monday. In my office."

Exactly what I knew he'd say.

"Who is this lovely young woman?" His mother has joined us. And she called me lovely. Not intense, or thick, or exotic looking. I like her already.

"Mari Álvarez." I stick out my hand, which is weird because it's not what we do in the Latin community. We hug. We kiss. But García is so formal with me and standoffish, and I don't know what to—

"Are you Marisol's granddaughter?"

I'm surprised but shouldn't be. My abuela is popular here in West Tampa. Her rice pudding and arroz con pollo make it to most birthday parties and wakes. "Yes, ma'am. How do you know my abuela?"

"Church," she says. García's mom pulls me in for the traditional Latin greeting—a hug, followed by kisses that tickle both cheeks.

I like her warmth. "I'm shopping for my abuela, in fact."

"Bueno. You know my son?"

"I do." García is watching us. But interestingly, he says nothing. I see respect for his mother in his eyes, so he isn't going to interrupt. "We've been at two crime scenes together," I say.

"Two scenes in two days," García adds. "Ms. Álvarez has a plan for what we should do next."

His mom tilts her head. And smiles. "Let's hear it." There's no sarcasm in her tone. Nothing but sincerity. "I do enjoy following my son's work. Gives an old woman something to do."

I don't hesitate. "I think there's a serial killer at work here in West Tampa targeting former suspects who were never punished for crimes." Like the city council member. Of course I don't say that.

García makes a sound that lifts the hair on the back of my neck. His lips roll in, and I can hear what he isn't saying. *Whose reputation will you ruin today?* Instead, he says, "Ms. Álvarez, are you following me?"

I step back, taken aback. "No. What?" My body goes cold. Right down to my fingertips. "You mean like *stalking* you?"

Only slight movement in his lips, but his eyes display confusion. "You happen to be at the same Latin market on Saturday morning, at the same time? On a morning you've called me five times?"

I can't tell him Chango may have something to do with the timing. But I can remind him, "I'm shopping for my abuela at her request. Remember? This is the most popular Latin market in West Tampa. The fruit is always fresh and doesn't go bad in two days."

Out of my peripheral vision I see García's mom nod.

"And your police escort?"

I hesitate. "He was an escort? Thought it was only for one night. Didn't see anyone there this morning."

His eyebrows dive. I bet someone is going to hear about this.

"Abuela is cooking today. I have her shopping list." I show it to him and point to the word Sazón. "I forgot where to find this."

"Sazón is near the rest of the seasoning. She's making yellow rice?" García asks.

He knows Sazón makes the rice yellow? "Thank you." *Impressive.* "Yes. Yellow rice and chicken."

"I'll show you." His mom, who still hasn't told me her name, puts her manicured nails on my upper arm, to guide me a little forcefully, I think. She's a strong woman.

"Mamá," he calls after us.

The detective calls his mom the same thing I used to call mine. Again, I feel an unwanted connection to this man.

García's mom ignores him. She puts her arm around me and squeezes. "You think a serial killer is on the loose?" She pushes me forward, and we walk down the aisle. "That must be weighing heavily on you."

"It is." I'm following her blindly.

She leans in, too close for someone I just met, Cuban or not, and whispers, "I needed to get you away from Antonio for a moment. He wouldn't approve."

"Approve of what?" I'm getting a weird feeling, but I also want to take this chance to gain favor with his mom. And hopefully, eventually him, too.

García is following behind us, but not close enough to hear. Still, I can feel the heat of his impatience with every flap of his feet on the tile floor.

I stop and look back at him, hoping he'll jump into the conversation.

He doesn't. He keeps drilling me with a look that might land him in the county jail for assault with a deadly weapon.

His mother tugs me forward, and says, "The Babalawo visiting from Cuba tells me I need to get to know you."

I stumble.

She turns me so we're facing each other and looks me straight in both eyes. "He thinks you're in trouble. You show up here. You mention a serial killer. And you're working with my son. Now, I am concerned."

I have no idea what to say, but I know, instinctively, this is a woman I can trust. We're all connected. I want to tell her about the threatening note and items I found. How now my abuela might be a victim of a stalker, too. How it all might be related. I just need time to figure out how. And why.

García is a few steps away. He's glaring at me like I'm intruding on family time.

"I'm sorry." I direct that to his mom. She'll know what I mean. "I'm sorry for bothering you all on Saturday." That sorry is for García. I spot the Sazón seasoning on the shelf and point to it. "Thank you for your help."

But she stops in the center of the aisle, blocking my exit, and drills me with a look. Now I know where García gets his from.

I grab the Sazón and turn to face García. He appears to be in full defense mode, arms crossed, legs spread, brows furrowed. "I'll call you Monday," I say to him.

He doesn't respond.

I don't move.

I don't know what it is about him that makes me want to stand up and prove myself.

I don't know what it is about him that makes me feel a hundred conflicting emotions all at once.

"Are you expected at dinner with Marisol

tonight?" García's mom interrupts my moment of indecision and self-reflection. It takes me a minute to digest what she's saying. Marisol? Oh, right. My abuela, Marisol. "No, she's cooking for a gathering at church." I'm not invited, nor would I want to go.

"Perfecto! You'll come to dinner at my house tonight. I want to continue our…" She pauses. "Our conversation."

"I can."

"She can't." García and I say at the same time.

His mom looks directly at her son. "I don't need your approval to invite the granddaughter of a dear friend to *my* house."

I may not know García well, but I know him well enough to tell he won't disrespect his mother. And it hits me like pungent cigar smoke—I'm getting my wish! My goal last night was to get his time and attention today. A door opened, and I didn't even have to push it. The most unexpected person granted my request at Abuela's altar.

García's mom.

Divine intervention? Or luck? I can't say for sure.

But I notice she's wearing a necklace with the face of a saint on the front.

And it looks like the face of Saint Barbara. Also known, by those who follow Santería, as my orisha, Chango.

I can't help but smile as I leave the Latin Market, a small victory skip in my step. Chango is on my side. I feel it.

But just as quickly as that feeling of confidence washes over me, it's erased by a wave of warning.

I have no idea why.

Until I see it.

Or him, rather.

When our eyes meet, the man in the parking lot instantly whips around and jumps back into a flashy red and black Mustang. But not before I see it.

A tattoo on the back of his neck.

A crown, just like the graffiti I've seen numerous times in our West Tampa neighborhood. A crown, like the one left on our door after my mother's murder. It's the symbol of the West Tampa Kings. Just like the crown on the coin on the deputy's closed eye.

It's a symbol Izzy warned me about many years ago.

My heart drops with such force I actually grab my chest. My breath stalls and I wobble, the world fading at the edges.

There's only one person I know who wears the crown tattoo on the back of his neck instead of the typical place, on a shoulder or an arm or even across a shaven chest. There's only one way to prove whether it's that asshole gangbanger. I jump in my car, but the Mustang is gone, disappeared into the crooks and narrows of our Old West Tampa neighborhood.

Doesn't matter. I know these streets well. I know exactly where I must go.

CHAPTER TWENTY-ONE

I pull up to the corner house on Hesperides, parking across the street, just south of Deputy Rodríguez's house. My stomach is speaking to me, not with hunger, but with concern—I'm probably not welcome in either of the homes across from each other. I grab a quick drink of water then set my water bottle in the cup holder, twisting it so the label faces me. *Inhale. Exhale slowly. Don't forget to breathe.* And I'm out of the car before I can change my mind. I'm going to see if Izzy's ex-boyfriend Raúl is still alive and now back in West Tampa. If so, I need to find out if he's still a member of the West Tampa Kings and not the dead narc I believed him to be. Could the gang have had something to do with the deputy's murder? Maybe she busted one of them recently and this is revenge? Or maybe one of the gangbangers left the note at my house, as a new warning to remain silent now that Raúl is back.

This is what a reporter does, I say to myself, nodding away any misgivings about stirring up old memories that could sicken me like toxic dust.

Outside my car, I glance around the street. A couple of kids play bocce ball in the front yard, throwing the colored balls to see which rolls closer to the pallino, a smaller ball used as a target. A dominoes game is underway on the front porch of the pharmacist's house. Do they ever stop playing? Retired life, I guess.

The deputy's house is quiet, though. No lights on inside. No cars in the driveway. No signs of life. Just a scrap of crime scene tape fluttering because part of it is lodged in a row of bushes near the front door. The girls are probably with family or foster care, so no one is likely home to care that I've parked close to the driveway.

Across the street, the driveway leading to Raúl's childhood home is also empty. His old Ford Mustang isn't parked outside, neither is the new one I saw the night of the deputy's murder. *And then again at the Latin Market,* I think. In fact, it looks like no one is home here, either. Maybe his mom's car is in the garage?

At the front door, I pause. What exactly am I going to say to Mr. or Mrs. Martínez? Am I here as a reporter on a crime story or an old friend concerned about their son? Right. They'd never believe that one.

I knock twice. The door creaks open. It wasn't shut, much less locked? I'm covering my heart with my right hand because my reporter's intuition just kicked in, and I know something isn't right. The Martínezes, like most families in this West Tampa neighborhood, have iron bars across most of their windows and a locked gate leading to the backyard. Yet they don't shut and lock their front door. After a murder took place right across the street?

I step to the right and glance through a front window.

"You are trespassing. You are trespassing."

I jump and spin around to see who's talking in

that mechanical voice. *¡Carajo!* It's just a motion sensor above the door detecting my movement. Well, that should get Mrs. Martínez's attention. I allow myself a second to recover. Even laugh at myself. *Ridiculous.*

I wait in front of the partially open door. It's almost one p.m. and the sweat isn't only beading on my forehead, it's rolling down my back. I'm not sure the sweat stains are entirely due to the August heat, though. More like my fear I'm walking into an Alfred Hitchcock moment. There are quite literally birds gathering on the power wire above the Martínez home, as if watching in anticipation of what I will do next. Squawking among themselves, smaller vultures wait to swoop down on yet another murder scene— Whoa, I'm letting my mind get away from me.

"Mrs. Martínez?" I knock again and the door creaks open a few more inches, enough to see into the living room now. Pretty typical tile floor, leather sectional, a cigar burning in an ash tray on the coffee table. There's no smoke rising from the tip, but I see the red glow, and the aroma drifts up my nose, telling me someone recently lit this cigar and it's not a cheap smoke. "Mr. Martínez? It's Mari Álvarez. Everything okay?"

No response. I calm myself, including my now thudding heart, and listen. The low buzz of a dryer running, sounds of a Spanish TV novella in a back room, but nothing else.

Suddenly, the phone rings.

I gasp. Not because I'm scared, but because I've been trying to make out even the slightest sounds my body has a visceral reaction to the brash, shrill ring.

Three times.

Four.

No one answers and the phone goes silent.

My pulse rocks in the center of my ears.

Now I'm concerned. Someone is here. Are they hiding from me? Or hurt? A murder took place across the street. The killer is still out there. And someone left a smoldering cigar in an ashtray as if they needed to leave in a hurry.

I push open the door, thinking oddly about the fingerprints I might be leaving behind. *¡Ay, Dios mío!*, the crime beat is getting to me. That, and murder too close to home.

"Mr. and Mrs. Álvarez. Are you okay? I'm coming in to check on you."

I tiptoe into the living room, careful not to—I'm not even sure. Like most women in this neighborhood, Mrs. Martínez has family photos covering the walls of her family room. They're everywhere. A timeline of the annual Nochebuena, Raúl's high school graduation, church confirmation at St. Lawrence. Raúl used to have a talking parrot. What was his name? Don Francisco. His mom named the bird after the popular Univision host of *Sábado Gigante*. Izzy used to joke how much Raúl hated that name, how he'd mock it and in return, Don Francisco, the talking African Grey, would mock him back in a voice that sounded like his mother's.

A half-finished puzzle takes up much of the kitchen table.

A pot on the stove has oil still in it. Probably will be reused to fry plantains.

And in the back right corner, an altar is built into

the wall. Not a big one like Abuela's. Mrs. Martínez probably has her own hidden room as well. But this one has a statue of Saint Barbara. A ceramic bowl with a stone in it is surrounded by objects: a bell, a few candles, a statue of Jesus, and multicolored rosary-style beads.

Among the candles is a red one similar to the one left at my house. It also says "Come to Me" on the glass casing. Ven a mí. It's definitely a love candle, which surprises me. It's not that they are unusual in this neighborhood, they aren't. But why would a married couple need one? Then I think of my mother and her lover, and my father's angst over losing her. The surface picture isn't always the same one you see when you dig deeper. Maybe this candle means something in relation to the note at my house. Maybe it means nothing at all. I'm still nowhere.

Except for the cigar. I pick it up and roll it until I see the label.

My breath catches, and not from the residual smell of smoke.

The label reads El Reloj. The clock.

"What are you doing?"

I flip around like a kid caught behaving badly.

"I'm calling the police."

Mrs. Martínez is standing in front of me with both hands holding onto a very large kitchen knife. The kind you use to cut the tough pork into eatable chunks. The kind you use to eviscerate someone.

Instantly, I raise my hands. The cigar hits the tile and rolls.

She stops it with her slippered foot. Doesn't even look down. *Damn.*

"Mrs. Martínez, it's me, Mari." I can't assume she recognizes me, although she has to, right? "Mari Álvarez, Izzy's sister."

Her gray hair is matted on one side like she'd been sleeping. At this hour? Maybe she's a night owl, up all night, sleeps much of the day.

"What are you doing here?" Her eyes narrow. While I do see recognition, I don't see trust. "Why do you just walk into my house?"

I swallow but there's no saliva to wet my mouth. "I knocked. Set off your motion detector, too."

"You're spying." At least she lowers the knife.

"Spying? Why would I—" I don't finish my sentence. "The door was partially open. I was worried."

Her grayish eyebrows remain in a deep dive.

"Ms. Rodríguez was murdered just across the street, and I thought—"

"You thought what, eh?"

I shouldn't go here, but, "It's eerily familiar, don't you think?"

Now her eyebrows hike up. Her mouth moves into a thin line.

"To my mother's murder."

She shakes her head. "I don't remember." Her cheeks flush, and I know she's lying. So I do what any good reporter would do when someone is caught lying intentionally. I dig for more. Poking at her with, "You don't remember my mother's murder? Shot in her doorway—crumpling at the entranceway like the woman across the street." Minus the broken dolls and gold coin, but with the same crown symbol left behind—the symbol of the gang your son used to hang with, I want to say, but

don't. I hate the heated tears pressing at the back of
my eyes. I blink to hold them in check.

Mrs. Martínez cocks her head. Maybe she notices
the emotions stirring in my wet gaze? Maybe she—

"You think they are related?"

I exhale. I've got her curious and talking. "I don't
know."

"I thought your mother's lover killed her."

Holy shit. She knows about that? The edges of
the room get fuzzy, and I widen my stance to keep
my head from spinning.

"Wasn't he questioned?"

"He was." I'm answering on autopilot.

She walks to the kitchen and lays the knife on
the counter. Her back is to me. Her shoulders drop.
"Family lawyers got him off."

"And his wife."

Mrs. Martínez turns.

I can't read her features. It's like a poker player
right before they fold or lay out a winning hand. So I
continue. "His wife gave him an alibi." That had
been in the newspapers and on TV. Surely she
remembered. "But I've never believed it."

She picks up the dropped cigar and grinds it out
in the ash tray. "Isabella told Raúl about the affair,
the threats, the fights between your father and your
mother's lover."

Freaking Izzy sharing family secrets. I bite my lip
until I taste blood.

"Raúl had to intervene once," she says, studying
me now.

Am I blushing? Why do I feel like this interview
has turned, and she's the one digging for information?

"Did you know that Marisol? That my son had to stop your father from killing Barbara's lover?"

She spits out the word "lover." And no, I did not know. I was away at college during that time. "Is Raúl still alive?" Mrs. Martínez has now opened the door for me to ask about her missing son. "Izzy told me our mother was killed in retaliation for Raúl narcing on his West Tampa King buddies. And that the gang killed him for it. But I saw him today at the Latin Markct." Or at lcast I think I did. "And I know this because of the tat—"

"Impossible," she cuts me off.

I stare at her. I'm still. Remain silent.

She drops her gaze. "Impossible, because he's still living in Cuba."

My breath stalls. "Living in Cuba? Since when?"

"Ever since your mother forbade him to see Isabella again and shamed him into thinking he needed to leave and become a better man." She spits out the words, shaping them into bullets. "Ever since his gang friends gave him an ultimatum: leave now or we kill you."

¡Carajo! Raúl is still alive. Does Izzy know? Abuela?

"I blame your mother for my son's banishment."

She's blaming my mother? This conversation isn't going as I'd hoped. And I should shut up and walk out the door. Process this new information before I speak. But I can't. So I don't. "My mamá didn't want your twenty-five-year-old gangbanger sleeping with my fifteen-year-old sister."

CHAPTER TWENTY-TWO

TEN YEARS EARLIER

I know they are trying to be quiet. But my bedroom bumps up to Izzy's, my headboard literally flat against the same wall as hers. And tonight, I hear the consistent thumping of her headboard against our shared wall. Again. And again. And again.

Usually I just cover my ears with my big headphones and blare music to drown out the fact that my fifteen-year-old sister knows the joys of sex before I do. I'm not a tattler, even though my heart aches to feel what's she's feeling. Sometimes envy urges me to wake Mamá. Sometimes resentment roars louder than common sense. I've gotten up out of bed, tiptoed to Mamá and Papi's room, but I've never been able to open their door. I can't betray my baby sister.

Tonight, her moans are like nothing I've heard. Or made. She giggles and then yells. Raúl, who's ten years older than her, does something that makes her yelp. Izzy's a strong girl. I imagine she's done something back because they fight. At least that's what it sounds like, but then the headboard rocks against my wall again, and I slink lower beneath my sheets wondering how Izzy has the cojones to bring this street thug into Mamá and Papi's home.

Papi will shoot him if he sees what Raúl's doing to the baby of the family. She's lucky he's working the night shift tonight.

I roll over and smash a pillow over my head, my heart bumping against the mattress. I'm so awkward around men, I can't imagine sneaking one into my room. And letting them do things— Why is she yelling again? Is he smacking her? Is she liking this? Maybe I should go over there and knock. They're making so much noise. It's…it's…it's…my stomach is knotting.

I kick the mattress.

Earlier tonight, I'd warned Izzy about hanging out at a house party with kids who were of age and able to do anything—like sell weed and stronger stuff. She told me the cops busted through the door and started making Raúl's friends lay on the floor. Izzy ran to the bathroom, called me, and I rescued her. Like I always do, this time with my bike. She jumped through the bathroom window and ran down Raúl's street until I met her. I pedaled so hard all the way home I thought my heart would rocket out of my chest. My legs are still wobbly. She laughed the whole time like it was all a grand adventure. Like she was high on that stupid shit Raúl sold. I'm not sure what had my blood pressure higher, the exertion of getting to her in time, or the fact she didn't even appreciate it.

Mamá slept through it all, as did Abuela. Like they always did.

I left Izzy in her room at ten so she could take a shower. She stunk of smoke and body odor and other stuff I couldn't put a name to.

I'm not sure when Raúl arrived. Izzy said he'd been arrested and taken to jail, but maybe he'd just been questioned, and the police had let him go.

If he did get arrested, who bonded him out of jail? Probably his mother. That makes bile rush into my throat. His mother thinks Raúl can do no wrong, cause he brings her money and gifts and bought her a car. A fancy sports car. She's too old to drive a Mustang. He's twenty-five. How does she think he gets the money to buy her a car like that?

I just know it's two a.m. and they're still going at it. How is that possible?

I roll over, pull the pillow over my head, and scream, partly because I'm so conflicted. Do I go rescue my kid sister again? She doesn't really sound like she needs help. Do I kick the door down and yell at them both for keeping me up, cause it's just rude.

Do I ask her how the hell her drug dealer lover bonded out so quickly?

Do I warn them Papi is coming home at four a.m. Maybe earlier.

Do I—

"Isabella Álvarez!"

I pull myself up, throw my legs over the side of my bed. *¡Carajo!* Mamá's up and at Izzy's room. I stand.

"¡Carajo!"

Mamá doesn't cuss.

"What is he doing here?"

Furniture moves, or something heavy. Feet slap the floor. I'm out of breath trying to throw my clothes on and get to Izzy's room.

"Isabella," my mamá's voice drops a register. "Put your clothes on. ¡Ay, Dios mío!, I'm calling your father."

I'm out my door; I'm not missing this. And despite thinking Mamá is right to be so upset, I don't want her to call Papi. He gets so—

"Mrs. Álvarez, please." Raúl is pleading. Never heard him sound so scared. His tone actually makes my pulse pick up. "I'm sorry, I—"

"Don't speak to me." Mamá's voice is gravelly from sleep, and yet sharp as a sword. "You don't speak to me."

"Mother," Izzy's voice stretches toward the ceiling. "I love him."

"He's a—"

I'm thinking exactly what Mamá is vocalizing. A loser and a drug—

"Stop!" I can see Izzy's hand shoot up even though I'm not in the room. Her eyebrows are likely raised, and she's drilling Mamá with a look that brands her with guilt. "I love him."

"You are fifteen years old, Isabella."

"I am—"

"He is twenty-five!"

"I love her, Mrs. Álvarez, and I want to apologize—"

"For what? Taking my baby's virginity? Do you plan to marry her?"

"I do. I will."

"I do not give you my blessing."

"What's going on?" I reach the room, breathless.

"You know about this, Marisol?"

"I—"

"You are right next door. Why did you not warn me?"

"I—"

"Tell me the truth, Marisol."

"His party was busted tonight. The police came."

"Mari!" My sister's cheeks heat up. I can see the glow across the room, and her eyes blaze like she'd like to burn me.

But it's about time I told Mamá the truth. For Izzy's own good. "Arrested for selling drugs at a party Izzy was at while you thought she was in here doing homework."

"You little bitch." Each word from my sister is enunciated as if being sharpened on a whetstone.

"I am trying to protect you. You almost got arrested, too."

"Mrs. Álvarez—"

"What is that?" She runs up to Raúl and turns him around. "You're bleeding."

"A fresh tattoo," I say. Maybe to celebrate getting out of jail? Or not being charged?

"A crown," Mamá hisses. "You are a member of that gang?"

She knows what the crown means. So do I. Anger rushes up my body, exiting my lips. "You get out of jail and the first thing you do is get a tattoo?" I'm so pissed at Izzy for never appreciating my advice or my help. "Then you come over here to screw my sister. What's wrong with you?"

"Marisol!" Abuela has joined us. "Watch your tongue!"

"I speak the truth. I always speak the truth. It's just no one wants to listen, because sometimes the truth hurts. But I speak the truth, Abuela."

Abuela Bonita stands behind me, a wrinkled robe thrown over her skinny, bony body. Her arms are folded around her like they're part of the belt holding up the robe.

"What's the truth, Marisol?" Mamá asks.

"The truth is…" The truth is I'm ready for Mamá to know the whole truth. Finally. "This has been going on for a while."

"I hate you, Mari!" Izzy's hands are fisted, but she doesn't come after me. "I hate you, and I will never forgive you." My little sister holds her ground, standing between Mamá and her lover. Choosing her lover over family.

"I'm calling the police." I see all the torment on my mamá's tired face. She has to get up in an hour. Go work all day so we all can eat. Now she knows she's not going back to bed. She has to tell Papi about Izzy's boyfriend being arrested, getting a tattoo and being a West Tampa King, and screwing his baby. The one he thought was still a virgin. Then, she has to talk to Izzy about why sleeping with a twenty-five-year-old bad boy is not a good idea or a healthy decision. I see it all etched in her furrowed brows and tight lips.

The room falls silent. Raúl's short breaths, the floorboards creaking as my grandmother moves past me is all I hear.

Then, the garage door opens.

"Your father is home."

Like Mamá had to tell us.

Raúl's gaze darts across the room to the window. "I'm leaving, Mrs. Álvarez. I won't come back until I can prove to you I'm a better man, worthy of your daughter. All I ask is for you to give me that chance." His eyes are wide as dinner plates and his bronze skin looks lighter, like he might throw up. Doesn't look like much of a gangster now. "Let me leave through the window. I promise you when you see me again, I'll be a different man."

"Please, Mamá." Izzy moves across the room and throws herself at our mother. "If not for him, do it for me. Just give him a chance to change." She hugs her like she hasn't in a long time. In that instant, I feel her puppy love for Raúl.

Abuela puts her hand on Mamá's shoulder. "Give the young man a chance. None of us are perfect. We all do things we regret, mi niña, no?"

Those words stall my mother. Maybe she's thinking about all the things she's done wrong over her lifetime. Maybe she's thinking how love conquers all. I don't know. But Mamá turns and leaves Izzy's room as Papi opens the door leading from the garage to the kitchen and the alert chimes. Abuela follows.

I stand there watching as Izzy helps Raúl escape another judgment.

Mamá never told Papi what happened that night. And true to his word, Raúl stopped coming to the house. Izzy no longer talked about him. Until the crown showed up on our door. Spray painted in black. That's when Izzy told me The West Tampa Kings probably killed Raúl and were warning us to stay quiet.

Even though I didn't like Raúl, I grieved for him. And I felt sorry for Izzy. Raúl might have gone to make himself a better man, or maybe the gang really did kill him. Either way he was gone, and he'd left Izzy alone during the worst days of her life. Grieving our mother's murder then our father's death. She withdrew into a shell of herself, dating and probably screwing guys, but never giving her heart like she'd given it to Raúl. And to this day our relationship has never been the same, either. It's like our tight sister bond died that night, a creepy foreshadowing of our family's fractured future.

CHAPTER TWENTY-THREE

"Raúl is a better man now." Mrs. Martínez busies herself with cleaning up ashes on the floor, left as the cigar rolled. "He is working full time at the family store outside of Havana. In Playa Hermosa. It is beautiful there." She's using the same kind of mop my grandmother uses, a Cuban wood mop stick with a rag on the end. "He has a girlfriend. I no longer need to send him money." The way she pushes the mop, in long, strong strokes, tells me she's proud of her son and wants me to know it. "He's turned his life around. He's no threat to Izzy or to you anymore."

"Why is he back, then? If his life in Cuba is so perfect? If his old gang gave him an ultimatum?"

The mopping stops. "He can't come back."

We're locked into a stare.

"But would you deny a son the chance to visit his mother?"

I drop my gaze. I'd like to visit my mother, too. But I can't.

"I can't go visit when I want. I can send medicine and money to the family. Clothes." She shuffles the mop toward the back of the kitchen, disappearing for a moment. When she returns, her hands are free. "You know." She waves like I do know.

And I do. But I'm not here to talk about helping

family in Cuba or how difficult it is to actually go visit yourself. "Does Raúl still have that tattoo on the back of his neck?"

Raúl's mother straightens her spine, my words, no doubt, the rod pulling her tall with indignation. "He has many tattoos."

"I thought I saw him here. That tattoo placement is unique."

"I told you. Impossible. Is that what this is about? A tattoo? And you think—"

"Call him." I cross my arms. I can't leave here without confirmation. She might just have to call the police to get me out of her house, because when I set my mind on something, I dig in like a thirsty tick. I need to know if Raúl is here, because if he is, my family is in danger. If the West Tampa Kings warned him and warned us. What the hell is going on?

She moves back into the kitchen. I follow, hoping that she isn't going to offer me something to eat or drink. I can't right now. I just need the truth. That's what feeds me.

"You know how the internet and cell service is in Cuba. You don't just call or FaceTime." Instead, she clangs about, making noise as she puts dishes, washed and on the counter not in the dishwasher, away. "Our family is not rich. They are servants of the government, they don't—"

"If they serve the government, they'll have internet and cell service. Call him." I haven't moved an inch. Ballsy, because I came into her house uninvited, and she could actually call the police. "I know you can." I inhale and hold.

She stops banging dishes, but she still won't look

at me. "Why is it so important to you?"

"I think…" *No, be strong with her.* "No, I saw Raúl at the Latin market, today. I want to know why he's back and if he's been in touch with Izzy. If he's still part of that gang. I found a note that said—"

She pushed away from the counter. "I will call him. To prove to you he is a changed man." Her voice level rises, and her words are forceful, like she's had enough. She grabs her cell phone and points it at me. "But you do not talk to him. I do not want to upset him. I do not want him to know you are here. It took him a long time to get over your sister."

I hesitate but then agree. If I don't, she won't call him. And I need to know he's in Cuba, not in Tampa, stirring up trouble for my family again.

She picks up her phone and dials.

Raúl answers almost immediately. "Dígame."

Mrs. Martínez jumps into routine conversation with a tighter voice than she'd just been using. She asks where Raúl is.

"At the beach. With my girlfriend."

I recognize his voice. The last time I heard it, he'd been pleading, so it was higher pitched. But he has the same lilt to his tone and the sound of arrogance has returned full force.

"I need to see him."

She turns and shoots me the iciest stare.

"Who is that?" Raúl asks.

"I told you not to speak!"

I can tell she's about to hang up, so I rush around her and look at the cell screen.

"Who is it?" Raúl asks again. And then he sees

me. His face falls. Resentment enters his eyes like his gaze is loaded with ammunition and preparing to fire. "What do you want?" It's almost a growl.

"I want proof you're in Cuba."

"I owe you nothing." And he hangs up. Her cell screen goes back to home.

But not before I saw it. A sign behind him that said Playa Hermosa. A beach definitely in Cuba.

"My son is no longer a West Tampa King," Mrs. Martínez says, not addressing her son's rudeness. Or mine. "But you know who is?"

I shrug, because I don't know. I don't hang out with the local West Tampa Kings.

"Sebastián Figueroa."

"Sebastián?" I'm trying to place the name. I know it. But—

"Thomas Figueroa's son."

"Sofía's brother." The realization rushes out of me in those two breathy words.

"Yes, he was at Deputy Rodríguez's home when his little sister was shot. He witnessed it. Natasha told me the kid never got over it. His parents divorced. His father started using."

"What are you saying?" But I'm beginning to see it.

"I'm saying, if you are looking for who killed Natasha, maybe you should look at who had a reason to killer her. Sofía's father—"

"Already on my list."

"*And* Sofía's brother."

"That I didn't think of." I'll have to tell García.

"Natasha and I were not friends, but we were neighbors. She told me she feared Sebastián and his gang friends. She busted a few, but she never arrested Sebastián, although he's risen to the top of the gang here. I think she stayed away from him because she feared what he might do in retaliation. It was her gun that killed his sister. An eye for an eye, you understand?"

I nod. Boy, do I.

"But another cop picked Sebastián up in a sweep of gang members not too long ago. He never served a day. Walked because of his attorney." She hesitates and says, "He'd probably have a mug shot, no?"

I google his name. Sure enough, not only is there a picture of Sebastián being booked, but video, too. Chills rush over my skin like a rash. As Sebastián Figueroa is being walked into police headquarters in handcuffs, the camera man falls behind him. Sebastián sports a crown tattoo, not on his shoulder or his arms but on the back of his neck. *Bingo*! Maybe that's who I saw at the Latin Market. I have to get home and get ready to go over to García's moms for dinner. I can't wait to tell the homicide detective what I've learned. I have another viable suspect. At least for the Natasha Rodríguez's murder. Maybe it isn't Thomas Figueroa, but his son. He could be the one seeking revenge for his sister. The gang thing ties him to my mom's murder, too. I don't know what Sebastián's tie would be to the second murder at The Stop-N-Go, but that doesn't mean there isn't one. I just have to keep digging. All I know is that every murder investigation I've ever covered started with me asking this one simple question.

Who has a motive strong enough to kill?

CHAPTER TWENTY-FOUR

I make it to the Garcías twenty minutes late. García's mom's, Beatriz, doesn't make a big deal of it, saying she expects people to arrive on Cuban time.

I'm sitting at her formal, antique dining room table with half a dozen family members I've just been introduced to. Beatriz has a china cabinet for her good dishes, some of which we're now using, which surprises me. Many Cuban families use paper plates for informal dinners. Less to wash. And we rarely use the dishwasher.

Maybe having me over is a big deal?

Concentrate on what you came here for. First, win over García's mother. Then, enlist García's help with moving forward on the plan to revisit cold cases. Tell him about Sebastián Figueroa's ties to the West Tampa Kings. Maybe he already knows. Finally, find out why the visiting Babalawo thinks I'm in trouble, and what I can do about it. No pressure. Easy. Breezy.

"Beatriz, I love what you've done with the pictures."

Almost every wall is full of family memories, a lifetime of them, and much like the walls of Mrs. Martínez's house, they tell a lovely story. Easter outside the church, baseball games, and graduations. Wedding pictures and first babies. In the middle of that family wall, a picture of Jesus.

On a white lace-draped table at the opposite end of the room, a statue of St. Barbara sits. Various candles surround a picture of an older man in uniform, a police officer for the Tampa Police Department. *García's father.* Killed in the line of duty a year before I got my job reporting. But once I saw his face, I remembered his story. The officer pulled over a driver for speeding, not knowing the person was high on meth and wanted on warrants. The driver had a gun and a death sentence waiting for Juan García. The murder shocked the community, the funeral moved it. I hadn't put that García with my García until tonight.

Another connection between us. We share the pain of losing a parent to murder.

There are chairs around the table, García's mom at one end. The other end is empty. I wonder if it's held open out of respect for García's father, who probably used to sit there. The thought makes my whole body flush with sadness. The meth driver who'd killed García's dad died of an overdose that same day in the hospital. Some said he got what he deserved. Many said his death was too easy of a sentence, that justice wasn't really served.

I agree with the latter.

I wonder what García thinks?

I'm doing my best not to look at the empty chair next to me. Or glance up into the living room where García is.

He hasn't joined us for dinner because he's in the living room feeding his grandfather, a rail-thin man with sunken cheeks that make his face look haunted.

His eyes track movement, but he can no longer speak. Antonio García, the first, is ninety years old. He has dementia and can no longer walk.

García feeds his grandfather with a gentle persistence and a loving manner.

I find myself staring. My eyes water.

My heart catches when García discovers me watching them.

I look away, heat slapping my cheeks, embarrassment drying my throat.

"Would you like some more black beans, Marisol?" García's mom asks.

I'm grateful for her interruption. "Yes, please. These are the most delicious black beans I've ever tasted." I put a finger to my lips. "Don't tell my abuela."

Laughter at the table as I expected. García's family is educated and polite. They also seem happy.

I chance a look at García again.

He is not looking at me. He's wiping his grandfather's chin, patting it gently as if it was the most important assignment of his life.

"My mom won the Goya competition in Ybor City last year for best black beans recipe," García's oldest brother says to me. "She won a trip to Spain."

"She couldn't take it because…" The older brother's wife pauses.

In the silence that follows, we all *don't* look at Antonio García, the first. Or the second, absent from the table, but present, I imagine, in every way that counts for this family.

I break the awkward silence. "I'd love the recipe to surprise my abuela."

"Oh," daughter-in-law number one says. "Beatriz doesn't give out the recipe to anyone. Trust me. I've begged."

More laughter, this time, a bit too polite.

I glance at García's mom to see how she's taking all this.

"My secret recipe." She winks at me. "Who knows? I might win another trip."

I smile back. I like her—she's a cool combination of my abuela's old school beliefs and my mom's new world sophistication. When I first arrived, Beatriz had warned me not to put my purse on the ground, or my money would run away. That's a Cuban legend. I also noticed Beatriz had a glass of water in a corner on top of the refrigerator to counter any negative energy and bring good luck.

I wonder if she put that there tonight, specifically because I was coming to dinner. Because the Babalawo told her trouble might follow me in.

Conversation continues, but I'm watching García puree more food in a blender in the kitchen. He hasn't eaten a morsel of food, while we at the table have feasted on Beatriz's black beans and rice and bistec de palomilla. The pan-fried sirloin is one of my favorites, and she cooks it super thin with sautéed yellow onions on top. The food melts in my mouth, the buttery soft onions igniting my taste buds. But, because Beatriz has placed me in a seat facing the living room and kitchen, I'm not focusing solely on her meal. Instead, I devour García's actions with his grandfather. I can't help but think what I'm witnessing is the true definition of love. And it has set off a reaction in me I'm fighting, but

I'm not sure why. It's okay to see García as a man, as a good son, and even better grandson. Right? Even if I don't like professional García, the sarcastic, by-the-books cop?

"You keep looking at Antonio and his grandfather," Beatriz says.

"I just…I'm sorry." Heat prickles all over me. "It's just…I've never seen a grown man so tender with another grown man." *Tender*. That's the word sticking with me, like the flavor of strong Cuban coffee hanging onto your breath.

"We named Antonio after my father," she says. "I knew they'd have a bond that was inseparable." She glances at her son with tears in her eyes.

"What happened to him? Your father. I know what happened to your husband." I reach out and take hold of her hand. "I'm sorry."

Her eyes continue to water, and she doesn't bother to hide it. "We both have suffered great losses." She continues to hold my hand as her gaze slides to her father. "It's why I feel a connection between us."

Her skin is warm. Comforting.

"My father is ninety, so age has withered him away, but he's also lived a hard life."

"In Cuba." It's not a question.

"In a Cuban prison," the oldest brother says.

García stalls, a spoon in hand halfway to his grandfather's mouth. He looks first at his older brother, then at me. The look in his eyes I can't decipher, but it makes something deep inside me shift.

"A story for another day," he finally says.

I think he's uncomfortable with me entering his deeply personal world and seeing him vulnerable with his grandfather. I want him to see I appreciate what his family has been through. "I can't imagine the horror your father endured." I speak to both Beatriz and García.

"My mother died in Cuba waiting for my father to escape that prison. My father came back to us eventually, but a part of him broke while in captivity. He was never the same man. He had physical illnesses and mental battles we could never fully understand."

I sense injustice makes García mad. "Is that why he became a cop?" I ask Beatriz.

"Please don't talk about me like I'm not here." García's attention is no longer on his grandfather.

"I'm sorry." But I'm not. Not really. "But is it? Is it why you became a detective?"

"My mother may want to share personal family stories with you." He lowers the spoon. "But I do not."

An awkward silence follows. I shift in my seat, not sure what to say.

"I'm sorry, Marisol. My son is being rude."

The last thing I want to do is cause a rift between this awesome mother and her, well, awesome son. "It's okay. I have to go." I've failed my mission.

She grabs my hand again. This time it's like she's grabbing on to something else—something I can't quite put my finger on. "Tell me about *your* family," she says.

I glance around the table. Juan, Jr, the oldest brother, and his wife are busy with their two kids.

Another brother and his wife are deep in their own conversation. One of the kids jumps up on Beatriz's lap, throwing her arms around her grandmother, burying her nose in her abuela's neck. These are the things a happy, blessed family does. They interact. They take care of each other.

They love each other.

I wish I didn't feel it. This envy. Burning like hot stones on my heart, pressing down until a darkness rises. I see it in my mind's eye, but I ignore it. I won't let it win. "We were once a happy family."

García is helping his grandfather up, lifting him to move him into a wheelchair.

His grandfather moans, a sound that is unmistakably from pain.

It can't be easy. But García isn't struggling.

Why am I?

CHAPTER TWENTY-FIVE

"Your father," Beatriz asks. "What does he do?"

The question stuns me.

We're still at the family dining room table, despite me deciding it's time to leave while I still have my pride. But García's mother isn't ready to let me go. "My father is dead." My blunt, tell-it-like-it-is reporter comes out. It always does. I thought Beatriz might know that already, considering how our family's past made the news.

Another awkward pause.

Lately, I seem to be the queen of instigating them. I hear the clock on the wall ticking. *Wanna get away?*

"I'm sorry, Marisol." Color fills Beatriz's cheeks. "I remember now."

"Let me make coffee." The oldest brother's wife jumps up from her seat. "Any takers?" She's probably thrilled to get away.

"Yes," I say, even though I'm supposed to be getting out of here before I do more damage.

"I'll get the rice pudding," the other daughter-in-law says, pushing her chair back and making her escape.

Beatriz reaches out for my hand again. "Do not feel embarrassed." This time my fingers are like ice. "Many young people do not understand how to handle grief. I asked you here tonight because I can feel yours." With her other hand, she encases my fingers, rubbing them warm. "You have such heaviness about you."

García is now pushing his grandfather out of the living room, heading toward a hallway. Antonio García the first is still moaning, an awful wail that makes me cringe. But the family doesn't recoil like I do—this must be a sound they've grown accustomed to. Both brothers jump up and come to García's aid. I guess they'll all help get their grandad into bed.

"You remind me of Antonio." Beatriz is also watching her sons. "He bears the weight of his grandfather's stories on his shoulders."

And the weight of his grandfather's body and pain.

"Antonio thinks if he can solve our city's problems, he can make up for the atrocities his grandfather and father suffered."

He believes in justice. But by the book. The brothers disappear, back to their grandfather's bedroom, I think.

"It's better to concentrate on solving current problems," his mom says, her focus back on me.

I swallow, lick my lips. "You want to solve mine?" It's been so long since someone other than close family tried to break through my wall and get in. I usually don't trust people. The reporter in me is a natural skeptic. But my heart is stretching, like fingers, reaching out to connect with this woman.

"The Babalawo says I can help you," she says. "But he wasn't able to tell me how."

"Or how I'm in trouble?"

She shakes her head.

Then what's the point? Do I speak the truth? Open my wounds for this woman I barely know? At least García is no longer listening.

It's only Beatriz and me.

Tonight, I feel blessed to have someone willing to listen and hopefully not judge. So I decide to tell her the awful family secret I've held close for so long. "My mother was having an affair with a coworker. For years. I think my father knew. When I was out of college, working my first job at a TV station in Fort Myers, I came home one weekend and my sister filled me in. I should have known, but I was so busy trying to survive on my own. We didn't have a lot of money, so I was working my way through school."

Beatriz squeezed my hand. "You don't have to justify why you didn't know, Marisol. I know already what happened was not your fault, and you could not have stopped it."

My fingers are warm now, and I don't pull them away. "I came home because I wanted to check on the family. Mamá promised me she'd broken off the affair, but the tension was higher than normal. Izzy, my sister, was always in her bedroom, door shut and locked. Abuela was always in her…bedroom, too." I don't say backroom closet with the saints, but Beatriz understands, because she's nodding. "On the night it happened, I was helping Izzy with homework. There was a knock at the door. Mamá answered." I squeeze my eyes shut and it all comes rushing back. I haven't talked about that night since the time I had to go over what happened at police headquarters. Reliving the worst moment of my life had made me vomit in the detective's office.

Tonight, I'm only a little nauseous. The wound is still with me, even if it's not quite as raw. "Mamá seemed so at peace that night, happy at the stove." I picture her dancing, twirling before tasting the food. "Papi was working, but on his way home. It seemed so normal."

I can still hear the knock followed by the loud pop. The thud of my mother's body hitting the floor. The sound of footsteps pounding down the pathway. My sister's scream.

My own heart pounding my ribs like a jackhammer.

I tell Beatriz what happened next, sparing no details. Her eyes fill with tears. "I was the first to see her at the front door. So much blood. I didn't know how to help her. I froze. I didn't know where to begin. I couldn't even scream."

The house had gone quiet. The only thing I hear now is the pounding of blood as it rushes to my head.

"I couldn't see the gunshot wound. I didn't know how to stop the blood. All I could think of was 'how will I live without her? What will I do without my beautiful mother?'" A hand on my shoulder makes me jump.

"I'm sorry." It's one of the daughters-in-law returning. She puts a white, porcelain cup of Cuban coffee in front of me.

The smell of robust espresso wafts up my nose. "Thank you." I untangle my hand and sip it. It's very strong and sweet. Enough to make me react. "Oh!"

"I hope you like sugar," the younger daughter-in-law says.

"All Cubans like sugar. Azucar!" I say it like the Cuban salsa queen Celia Cruz used to.

That breaks the tension. Even Beatriz laughs.

Conversation starts again.

Thank God.

I rub my wrist—still no protection on it. Beatriz watches me, and I stop rubbing. I don't want her to ask about my missing bracelet. So I break the stare and look to the hallway.

My heart jumps.

García is leaning against the wall, arms crossed. But I see compassion in his sad, drawn eyes.

He's been listening? For how long?

My stomach flip-flops. My emotions are a regular CrossFit workout these past two days.

I'm embarrassed, but also realize I have his attention, which is exactly what I wanted when I came here tonight. So, despite my reluctance to share sordid details of my family's past, despite my abhorrence at looking vulnerable, I continue. "My father was so devastated when he came home. Mamá was still in the doorway…but now with police officers walking around her body. I thought he was going to drop right there and die of a broken heart." I'm looking right at García. I want to look away, because this vulnerability is a coat I don't like to wear. It's hot and uncomfortable. But something magnetic is holding our gazes together. "Turned out his heart did break. It gave out less than two weeks later. A week after Mamá's funeral."

García's jaw moves, and he blinks, looking away.

"I think he just didn't want to live without her. And then, we were alone. Izzy, Abuela, and me." I'm a bit breathless and need water, not coffee, but I continue because this is the part of the story I need García to hear. "Police thought gang members killed my mom because of our connection to a member who'd become a confidential police informant. But I never bought that. When I first saw my mom's body, I also saw a car I recognized parked down the street. It looked like my mamá's lover's car. At my insistence, police brought the man in for questioning. Andreas Santiago. I'm sure you recognize the name. But his wife"—I rip my gaze away from García and turn toward Beatriz—"yes, he was married. His *wife* gave him an alibi. I think it was a lie."

"Why would your mother's lover shoot her?" Beatriz asks.

"Because Mamá had broken it off with him." I hope García is still listening. I've never vocalized what I'm about to say next. I believe in manifestation, so I've kept it buried deep. "But now I think if I hadn't interfered, my mamá would still be alive. My papi, too." I exhale. It's out there now. "Maybe they wouldn't still be married, but maybe they'd both still be alive and part of our lives."

Beatriz reaches out to hug me.

"It's guilt that's driving you," García says. "I wondered what could drive a young woman so hard."

A little hurt by his words, I pull back. I'm not a kid. He can only be six or seven years older than me. "Yes, I do feel guilty."

"You didn't kill your mother," he says.

"I know that. But I may have instigated her lover's anger by forcing her to break it off." García starts to speak but I stop him. "The reason I'm here sharing personal details of my life is because the person who killed my mamá is still out there, living a great life after destroying *our* great life."

"You want revenge," García says, his tone flat.

That statement brings me to my feet. I rise so quickly I almost knock over the coffee. "I want justice."

"Do you even know the difference?"

My hands find my hips. "Do you?"

"I do. I've learned it the hard way."

"It's not just for myself." Anger fuels my feet as I stride over to him. "I want justice for those two young, broken girls, who are without a mother now. Who will help them?" My voice is skyrocketing, and I need to control it. I turn to García's mother. "This isn't just about me." She's standing now, too. "I want my life to be about justice for victims' families. But I can't lie. I want to start with justice for my own family." I flip back around and face García eye to eye. "You should understand that."

He doesn't answer but grabs my wrist.

He pulls me closer, gently.

My wrist is bare. His fingers chill my thin flesh.

"She gave her azabache charm bracelet to the oldest girl at the murder scene." He's talking to his mother. "The 'broken girl' she's referring to."

"Not *my* bracelet." I correct him. "My abuela's." I turn to his mother. "Her mom gave it to her."

"And your mother passed it on to you?" Beatriz has walked over and is next to us now.

"No, my mamá was not a believer." I pull my wrist out of García's grip. "And she wouldn't wear the azabache. Ever."

"Giving that bracelet away was a selfless thing to do," Beatriz says. She's looking at García. "Antonio, you two should work together. I feel it." Her voice is breathy.

García pushes off the wall with a grunt. "Mamá, don't start with *the feelings* tonight." He shakes his head as he passes into the kitchen. "I can't."

But I see the way he looks at me as he walks by. Something has shifted. I think it's that he finally sees me as a person, not a reporter. Not an ambitious woman. Not a pit bull with a problem. I hope he now sees me as a person who aches for those I love and have lost. A person who wants justice. The same damn thing he wants for his grandfather and his victims' families.

"Okay, Marisol, I give in," García says. "I can't fight you both."

I'm so in my own head I almost miss his words. "What?" He called me Marisol. Not Ms. Álvarez. "What does that mean, Detective García?"

"Tony," he says as he dishes out some of his mom's black beans and rice onto a paper plate. "If we're going to work together, you can call me Tony." He's moving again to the high bar counter in the center of the kitchen.

So, García—Tony—doesn't eat on china and prefers the kitchen to the formal dining room.

I hand out my own olive branch. "And you can call me Mari. I dislike Marisol." I blush, realizing I might be disparaging my Abuela Bonita. "I mean, I like the name but it's my grandmother's."

We look at each other. He at the counter about to take his first bite. Me in the middle of the kitchen, while the rest of the family moves around us as if we aren't even there. And I feel it again. The connection.

Tony takes a bite, chews slowly. I watch him eat and imagine the wheels in his head churning.

Two kids fly by me, brushing me into a complete circle. They hit the door and head outside. Their bubbly laughter makes me smile.

"I'll call the head of cold cases Monday and set up a meeting. Hanks—you met him at the Hesperides scene—remember? He can go over your mom's case, and we can do a check on the whereabouts and safety of your mom's ex-lover."

I want to tap dance my excitement, like I did as a kid. "I know his address."

"Please don't go there alone." He lays down his fork. "In fact, don't go there at all. We need to do this the right way, Mari. The legal way."

He said we! He called me Mari!

I'm on my tiptoes but manage to restrain myself from jumping up and down. "And we can ask the detective if there are other cold cases where suspects may have—"

He holds up a hand. With a fork in it. "Yes, Mari. I'm on board. I'll pursue your theory. It actually makes sense. Meet me at my office Monday morning at ten a.m."

I want to run over and hug him. Throw my arms around him and squeeze him until his breath is gone and he's empty, except for my gratitude. But hugging him would be, well, awkward. Instead, I turn and run to his mother and hug her. Because make no mistake, Tony's mom made all the difference tonight.

Beatriz whispers to me, "Now I know what the

Babalawo wants me to do. I know how I can help you. And I will."

García jumps in. "But my help is contingent on one thing."

My heart drops. I move out of his mom's arms and turn back to him, my attention diverted by his *I'm not kidding* tone of voice.

"My help is off the record. You don't report what we learn until I give you permission to release it."

And there it is. The ultimatum.

What if we do have a serial killer loose in the community, and now that I have García's help, I can prove it? If I hold that information from the public for my family's personal gain? Or my own personal satisfaction? My own revenge? What kind of reporter would that make me? What kind of person?

I've finally gotten what I want.

Now, I'm not sure I want his help.

Because it comes with a big price I'm not sure I can pay.

Who am I kidding?

I must find out if Hoodie Hannibal is the killer we're looking for, if he's stalking me for a deadly reason, and if any of this is related to my mamá's death. I have to tell García what I've learned about Sebastián Figueroa. I have to find out if any other cold cases are related and if someone else is targeted for death. I don't want more blood on my hands. Or on my doorstep.

What could possibly go wrong if I'm under the watchful eye and protection of a straight arrow, do-everything-right, homicide detective?

I look at Tony and say, "Deal."

CHAPTER TWENTY-SIX

It's dark when I get home and I'm so excited about Tony accepting my theories and agreeing to work with me I don't even notice the slaughtered animal perched up against our front door like an unwelcome mat—until I step on it.

My foot, in open-toed sandals, slips on something fleshy and sticky. The wetness creeps up between my toes. Busy digging into my purse for the house keys, I'm distracted. I step off whatever it is, kicking my foot, thinking it's a dead bird or something, maybe a mouse, because I feel feathers. Possibly fur. I finally find the key and look down.

¡Carajo! Shit. Shit. Acid rolls up my esophagus, burning as it pushes my disgust upward. I've stepped on the head of a rooster! There's no body. Just a bloody, dismembered, feathered head.

Animal sacrifices are common in Santería, performed for life events like birth, marriage, and death. Also for healing. The animals are killed by cutting the carotid arteries with a single, swift knife stroke. The intent is not to hurt the animals. In most cases, the animals are cooked and eaten following a ritual, but I know in my gut this animal wasn't used in hopes of bringing anyone in my home health or healing. Because right now all I'm feeling is bad ashe.

A paper sticks out of the dead bird's bloody beak. That's another giveaway. I glance around for an unusual car, a person out of place in my neighborhood. Hoodie? Sebastián Figueroa? A different gang member? Maybe whoever left this here wants to watch me freak out.

I'm not going to give them the satisfaction.

After the initial shock, I still myself. I won't vomit, nor will I run. I am, however, deeply concerned that the notes are being left at our home.

The paper is in a plastic baggie, probably to protect the message from blood or rain. I put my purse down on the porch and tear open the bloody baggie, careful to wipe my hands on the grass before taking the message out. It reads: *You did not meet me at El Reloj. The Clock.*

NOW YOU WILL HAVE 30 DAYS OF BAD LUCK.

Oh shit.

I do my best not to react. That includes turning my face away from the street and biting the inside of my cheek.

I keep a poker face, just in case someone like Hoodie Hannibal can see my features under the porch light. Whoever is screwing with me, and my family, knows the dark side of an Old-World religion.

This is not Santería, it's Brujería and it's not something Abuela Bonita ever practiced. In fact, no one I know would delve into the dark side.

And what is with the clock reference? The only place I know of with a clock, known by its Spanish name, is in Ybor City. Why there? There's no time listed. No name on the note. Maybe the messages aren't for Abuela. Maybe for Izzy? But if not Raúl, then maybe a new boyfriend left them? Or a new gang member?

Or is a rooster's severed head meant for me?

Who else might be giving me the evil eye, lacing it with Brujería? Well, now I have both notes to show García. Maybe he has a handwriting sample from Hoodie Hannibal? Should I preserve the rooster head? Would there be evidence on it? Should I call the police now? Whoever did this could be charged with animal cruelty.

No. No. This would make the news, and I can't call any negative attention to myself right now. I'm already on probation. I can just imagine what crime reporter wannabe would say about this.

I'll just take pictures and clean this shit up. I can tell García tomorrow, but life experience tells me whoever left this message doesn't really care about the police. Their religion is protected by the U.S. Constitution. While I support that protection, I grab my wrist, wishing for some of my own. Because this isn't the first time I've felt the power of a curse.

Five years ago, I accidentally ran into an elderly woman while dashing through the West Tampa Wal-Mart parking lot during a typical summer afternoon downpour. Her bag of groceries ripped, and her food hit the asphalt, rolling in all different directions. Not only did I get soaked by rain, but the stranger whacked me with a whammy, wishing thirty days of bad luck on me. Even after I helped her pick up every single item.

Nonbelievers might scoff at the thought a person

could toss bad luck at you like it's a rock off the road, but what had happened over the next thirty days left a lasting impression.

My work-assigned laptop slipped out of my hands and the screen shattered. The cost of the repair had to be taken out of my paycheck.

Police ticketed me for speeding—a $150 fine!

A rotting oak tree fell on top of my car during another afternoon thunderstorm two days after our car insurance ran out because Abuela Bonita forgot to pay the premium.

A woman from Palm Harbor emailed El Jefe and told him I might be the worst reporter in the state of Florida, one day before my annual review.

And the dog I'd recently adopted from The Humane Society died after licking one of those toxic bufo toads, an invasive species introduced to Florida.

So, I believe.

And this note, left in the beak of a rooster on my front doorstep, scares the Jesus, Mary, and Joseph out of me. We've been jinxed.

CHAPTER TWENTY-SEVEN

First thing Monday morning, García—no, wait, I have to get used to calling him Tony—keeps his word to me. He takes Orlando and me to meet up with Detective John Hanks, of the black hat and City Council Killer nickname. We come to his office in the cold case unit of the Tampa Police Department. Unlike Tony's messy office, which was filled with folders and family pictures, Detective Hanks's office is remarkably uncluttered, especially for a man in charge of numerous old cases. A lot like his neat appearance the first time I met him at the Hesperides scene. Detective Hanks is, in my opinion, organized. Put together. I hope that works in my favor.

The detective sits behind his Ikea desk, with a single row of files stacked neatly on top, pushed perfectly into the right corner. Instead of leaning back in his X-chair, he's sitting straight, as if his spine is made of metal. The only sign of any nervous energy is the handful of shiny objects in one hand. He's shaking them as if they are dice. Maybe that's his version of an azabache bracelet?

My phone *dings* with a text. Orlando is sitting right next to me. We began this texting thing a while back, when we were at a crime scene, and we didn't want the victim's family to know what we were thinking.

*You know the boss will be pissed if he finds out
we are here. He told you to stay off the crime beat.*

I don't bother texting back.

Orlando is texting off steam—he's here because
El Jefe assigned us to do a story on a local lady who
makes gnomes to honor local veterans. Another
feature. *Internal eye roll.* I set up the interview for
one p.m., and it's now ten a.m. That gives me plenty
of time to convince Detective Hanks there might be
a vigilante serial killer at work. One who is taunting
me with notes and newspaper articles. And one
bloody, severed rooster head. One who might be
targeting former suspects in his old cases. Including
my mamá's.

Easy. Breezy. Right?

"Thanks for seeing us on such short notice," Tony
says. Since there are only two chairs in front of
Detective Hanks's desk, Tony's leaning against the
doorframe.

Hanks shrugs. "I must admit your call intrigued
me, García. It's rare you bring both a reporter and
photographer up to see me." He nods at Orlando
and me. "Good to see you again, Ms. Álvarez."

He didn't call me City Council Killer. That's an
improvement. He's a smart guy, despite his sarcastic
comments and frat boy lingo. It's in his eyes, which
simmer like fire burns right underneath his corneas.

"I'm usually begging your types to give me a
little airtime for old pictures or new evidence." He
stops shaking whatever it is he's got in his hands.
"Maybe we can help each other." And tosses them
on his desk.

I'm a little surprised by his action. Even more

shocked when I see what they are.

I glance back at Tony, but he's got his poker face working.

The shells rattle and fall silent. Four shells. Sandy in color, with one side open—like a half open eye. All four land with the open side faceup. As if they're staring at me with suspicion.

"Well, I guess that's a yes," I say. And wait for a reaction.

Hanks doesn't answer, but his eyes blaze again with a fervor that doesn't match the rest of his pasty complexion or don't-give-two-shits composure.

Tony stays silent, and I force myself not to look back at him. "If I'm right," I say, "our conversation today will benefit all of us."

"Well, goodie," Hanks says. "I defer to you."

I open with my blunt, journalistic honesty. "We think there's a serial killer at work in our community."

Hanks reacts like I expect—both eyebrows shoot up, and a sneer takes over his face. "A serial killer?" He leans back, gathers the shells, and shakes them again. Looking at me, he says, "Another one?"

I'm pretty sure he's referring to the city council member I did a story on. "Funny. You should be a comedian." Too many girls with ties to the politician had disappeared. One found recently, barely alive. She'd pointed the finger at the city council member. Called him a serial killer. At least during police questioning. But she was a street girl with a drug habit and a history of lying. "I still stand by my story."

Didn't Hanks agree with me about the city

council member's guilt at the Hesperides scene? I can't remember.

"Isn't that your department, García?" Hanks says. "Or better yet, the FBI's?"

Tony pushes off the door and stands next to me. "Ms. Álvarez believes the killer is targeting former suspects in criminal cases that got off—"

"Or were never charged," I jump in. "The mom murdered two days ago—a former deputy who got off easy, despite her gun being used during an accidental shooting."

"I was there."

"Right. Next, a killer beats a man to death in a convenience store parking lot a year after the victim beat up and caused the death of his girlfriend in the same spot. The guy got off on Florida's Stand Your Ground defense because his girlfriend came at him with a knife. But I think she was the one protecting herself from repeated abuse by him."

"Seems like a stretch." Hanks looks at Tony. "You believe this, too?"

"Not sure."

I glance at Tony.

He meets my gaze. "We do have a suspect, similar in size and demeanor, seen at both scenes." *He said we.* My pulse picks up. "The man was wearing similar clothing at both scenes," Tony adds. "A black hoodie."

Hanks snorts. "Who would be stupid enough to wear the same outfit to different crime scenes?"

"Someone who's doing it to make a statement." I can't help myself. I don't like it when my ideas are ridiculed. "Someone who wants us to know it's the same person." I forge ahead, determined to make Hanks see. "What if someone is coming back to deliver justice unserved?" I explain how both recent victims died in a way similar to how their suspected victims were killed. "I don't think that's a coincidence." Then I fill Hanks in on the newspaper article Hoodie left me directing me to the Stop-N-Go scene. And I tell them both about the new notes I've received at my home. "I think my stalker is screwing with me. He's dropping clues for me to find. I just need to figure out why. Maybe he wants to lead me to a killer. Maybe he wants to get me alone so he can kill me. And I'm still not sure how it's all tied to this idea of justice unserved and that's why I'm—"

"When were you going to tell me about these notes at your home?"

Tony is pissed. "I just did." And I decide right then and there to skip the part about the rooster head. I'm so close to getting Detective Hanks on board. I don't want him to think I'm unhinged. A message in a dead rooster's beak sounds crazy.

"Other commonalties in the cases?" Detective Hanks asks, breaking the tension, his eyebrows scrunched, but his posture still rigid. "Other than the clothing. And these notes?"

"The method of murder being similar to past crimes." I go for my azabache charm and remember it's not there. Maybe I should wear a hair band temporarily, so I can snap it six times, or something. "Kind of an eye-for-an-eye thing."

I see a spark of something different in Hanks's eyes. Appreciation?

"And there are the broken dolls," I add.

"Yes, the broken girls," Hanks says.

"What?"

"The dolls. They were both female dolls."

"Yes."

"Probably a clue." Hanks starts shaking the shells again.

I stare at his hand.

"Sorry." He opens a drawer and puts them away. "Nervous habit."

Is it? I was beginning to think there's more to Detective Hanks than meets the eye. But my eye sees what others can't. I'm curious about his past.

"Any idea who this suspect is?" Hanks asks. I assume he's asking Tony. "Might narrow down which cold cases I look into first."

I exhale. Well, he's onboard. It takes all my effort not to bounce up and down in my seat or glare at Orlando with an *I told you this would work* look.

"We don't even know if it's the same person at both scenes. Or if the person in the black hoodie is our murderer," Tony says. "But we do know one suspect wearing the hoodie at the first scene is stalking Mari." He clears his throat. "Ms. Álvarez. And, as she mentioned, he's the one who told her about the second murder scene."

"Interesting. And you think he's also leaving you notes?" The cold case detective sits up.

I nod.

"Got a name on this guy?"

Tony tells him. "Edward Jones."

"Pretty common name," Hanks says.

"Not in West Tampa," Orlando jumps in.

Hanks writes the name down. "I'll cross-check to

see if he was ever listed as a suspect in any cold cases."

"Thanks," I say, rubbing my arms to clear static electricity.

"While I wait for that info, do you have any particular cold case you'd like me to look into first?" Hanks directs this question at me. He is smiling, but only with those flaming eyes, and that makes me think he already knows where I'm going with this.

"Her mother's case," Tony says it for me. Which surprises me.

"Barbara Álvarez," I say. "That's my mother's name."

He nods, and barely pauses before saying, "That's a very cold case."

His words hit like ice water. "A cold case with a tie to these current cases."

Hanks leans forward. "Do share."

"A couple of days after my mother was murdered, someone spray-painted a crown on our door. Street cops, first on the scene, thought it was a warning from the West Tampa Kings." I explain my sister's connection. "The same crown was found on the coin on the deputy's eye. Also spray-painted on the wall at the Stop-N-Go."

Hanks's eyes go wide. He glances at Tony. "You think the West Tampa Kings are involved?"

I answer. "I don't know. The gang is still active. Maybe my stalker is a gang member. Thomas Figueroa and his son Sebastián are current members and they both had motive to kill Natasha Rodríguez." I leave out Raúl's name on purpose. He's in Cuba.

Silence hangs heavy in the room. Hanks breaks it with, "You've created a list of suspects."

"I guess I have."

"Impressive."

O's stare heats me like a stove coil. I want to see if Tony is impressed, too, but turning around to look might appear needy. So I continue, "If you look through cold cases for any ties to the West Tampa Kings, or where a crown symbol was found at the scene, or where there was evidence of a revenge killing   "

"I do remember reading that investigators thought your mother's death might have been a killing–"

"For my sister dating a man who turned informant. They couldn't prove it, though. Izzy's boyfriend disappeared. The gang didn't cooperate. Imagine that. But it is their MO—to seek an eye for an eye."

Hanks's cocks his head, that weird smile of his looking even more crooked. "Wasn't there another suspect in your mother's murder?"

I think he already knows the answer to the question, but I reply anyway. "Andreas Santiago."

Hanks whistles. "Of the Ybor City Cigar Santiago family?"

I nod, wondering why if he knew about my mamá's case, he didn't know about the other prime suspect. Or maybe he did. He's just testing me. "Last time I checked on Santiago, he was still living in Tampa. But he's been out of the media for years."

"I remember some details of your mother's case." Hanks leans over and reaches for something in a drawer in his desk. Those shells he was shaking?

"My mom was having an affair with Santiago."

Hanks stops and looks up. Guess he didn't remember that detail.

"She'd broken it off with him, which gave him motive."

"But his wife gave him an alibi," Tony counters.

Hanks straightens. "Which I'm sure our colleagues checked out." He has a file in his hand.

I get a chill looking at it. "People lie, Detective."

"They sure do," Hanks says, flipping open the file. "All the time. Okay, Ms. Álvarez."

"Just Mari."

"All righty, Just Mari." He's flipping through pages and pictures. "Rhymes with sorry."

Is he making jokes while flipping through pictures of my mamá's murder scene? He's moving through the pictures so quickly and so casually. Doesn't grimace at the blood. Squint at the gory details. Cry at the horror of a life shed on the front doorsteps of a place the victim called home.

But—it is his job. I once interviewed a surgeon cracking jokes while operating on a man's brain. While he was awake.

"I'll run down Mr. Santiago and see what he's up to, or if your *killer* has already served up some *vigilante justice*. But my gut tells me no one's getting close to Santiago to do a revenge killing."

Why are some cops so damn cocky?

"But"—Hanks looks up at me—"I do think the West Tampa Kings theory is a plausible one."

My heart high jumps.

"I'll start with your mom's case."

"Is that her file?" My mouth is as dry as a James Bond martini. Which is exactly what I'd like right now.

"It is." His face is still blank.

I'm both shaken and stirred. "May I look at it?"

He closes the file. Picks it up.

I lean forward. Reach out for it. My hand trembles.

He pulls it back. "How about over lunch?"

I sit back.

The energy in the room shifts, a tremor we all feel.

Unexpected offer. Even inappropriate. But, why not? "I am hungry."

Orlando's text: *We gotta go.*

Answer: *I can meet you there.*

Orlando: *I'm not covering for you again.*

I text back. *What is your deal?*

Orlando: *You're gonna get us fired.*

Me: *Not if you don't tell.*

"Ms. Álvarez?"

I look up at Hanks. My mom's file is in his outstretched hand.

Like bait.

"I'd like to take a look at that file, first," Tony says.

Hanks hesitates.

I flip around and drill García with a look.

He drills me with his own.

I can't fight Tony. Especially when he's agreed to help me.

Hanks's chair squeaks—he's making his way around his desk.

Orlando also gets up. "We have to go. We have another interview to get to."

They all move toward the door.

But something catches my eye. A picture. Perhaps the only personal thing in Hanks's otherwise all-business office.

On one of the bookshelves, back right corner, almost hidden, sits a picture of him with a group of people. Family? They're dressed for the beach. He's on the far left, in swim trunks. The group is standing in front of a huge house that looks more like a giant piece of art. I recognize it immediately. Abuela Bonita told me about it. The Babalawo on Hesperides talked about it. An infamous house in a little beach town. *In Cuba.* That would explain how Hanks knew about the spiritual energy ashe.

With everyone's back to me, I swing up my phone, zoom in, and take a picture of the picture, making sure I get the tattoo on Detective Hanks's left shoulder. I'll have to look better when I get home, but that looks like a unique weapon with an even more unique history.

A history I know well.

CHAPTER TWENTY-EIGHT

It's Tuesday. Finally, I enter the daily news meeting early. I'm riding in on the confidence Orlando and I pulled off a touching and well-received feature story yesterday on the woman who honors veterans in a unique way. I managed to get through this morning without texting Freddy or Tony, even though I've been bursting with eagerness to share a couple of clues I've tracked down since talking to either. The anticipation is racing up my spine like a kid on a new Christmas scooter. Should I tell Orlando when I see him? Or wait until I can tell Tony, too?

First things first. I'll pitch a feature on a new school opening at the Rotary Camp in Brandon that caters to children with cancer—the nonprofit running the school has a fundraiser coming up. My story will help kids who are sick, feeding my journalist's soul. It will also leave time to work on my personal investigation.

I also intend to request new photographer, Chris Jensen, so I can meet up with Tony or Hanks without involving Orlando, another *Mr. By-The-Book*.

Right before the meeting, Detective Hanks texted me, asking me to call. I almost called back right away, but I'm determined not to do anything else to make El Jefe angry.

I need this job.

Ding. A text alert. *¡Ay, Dios mío!* My coworkers are still arriving, and Mr. Payton isn't here yet. I sneak a glance at my phone and smile. Forensics Freddy. No telling what info he wants to share. Maybe I'll blow him away by sharing what I've learned this morning. After all the off-the-record tips he's shared with me over the years, he deserved a tip from me this time.

I pick a seat at the back of the conference room, on a chair behind the spot where Mr. Payton always sits. That way I can text Freddy without my boss nailing me with that disapproving stare.

Freddy's text reads: *No DNA in the car at the Stop-N-Go scene. Killer is a pro.*

My spine straightens as if he'd inserted a rod into it. I flip my phone so no one around me can read his text. I knew it!

More reporters and producers and photographers are piling in, but no one is sitting next to me. Kinda weird. I don't see Orlando yet. Que Bueno.

I text back: *You cool with texting?*
Burner phone, remember.
Ah, right.

Finally, Chris Jensen sits next to me. I want to ask him if he's interested in shooting a feature with me today. I want to get everything lined up. No room for mistakes. But he won't make eye contact. The room is now full.

Another *ding.*
Can you talk?
Tony! My pulse flutters. *Tony.* Texting me.
Freddy: *Did you get my first text? No DNA at second scene.*

I can't stop myself. I have to share. I text Freddy: *I did. I've got news, too. Will share in a minute. In a meeting.*

I want to share what I've learned with Tony first. So I text the detective: *In a news meeting. But I can text.* My news is bubbling up and threatening to pour out in molten words. *I got a tip from an employee I met at the Stop-N-Go.* My fingers tap the phone as fast as fire spreading. *He said an Uber driver picked someone up near the scene. After the driver heard about the murder he came back to the scene to tell police about it. But chickened out. I tracked the Uber driver down. Guess what he told me?*

Tony: *I'd like to talk about this in person.*

He's so careful. Me, not so much. So I text: *He picked up a woman near the Stop-N-Go scene around six thirty a.m. the morning of the murder. Thought it was strange, cause the woman was out before sun-up—standing out of sight in the parking lot of a closed store. Woman was carrying a bag. A black garbage bag.*

I hold my breath, wishing I'd waited to tell him in person. I wanted to see the surprise spread across his face like syrup rolling off hot pancakes. I wanted to see his eyebrows raise and that slow smile lift his face, proving to me he's impressed with my find. Because it's big—in both recent murders someone collected a bag.

I text: *We need to know what's in the bag.*

Tony: *A woman? There's been no mention of a woman as a suspect.*

He's right.

A sports photographer walks by me. I shift in my chair, moving my legs to let him pass. I text: *Know where she wanted to go?*

Tony sends an emoji. The one with the blank face and straight line for a mouth. The one that says: *What do you think?*

I like him even more now that I know he uses emojis. So I text: *St. Mary's Catholic Church.*

Another emoji. The one that is shrugging to ask: *So?*

My church. Before mom's murder.

But he doesn't reply.

My shoulders drop. Finally, I text: *Someone's screwing with my head.*

Another *ding*.

Can you come to my office, please?

Tony wants me to leave and come now? My breath catches. That's not Tony.

I look around the news meeting. El Jefe isn't sitting in his usual chair, but I've been so busy texting, I didn't even notice. Jessica's absent, too.

Heat slithers into my cheeks, creeping up the back of my neck. Where's Orlando?

El Jefe: *Mari, I would like to talk with you now. Please come to my office.*

I stand. The blood rushes from my head, and the room spins like I'm in one of those damn deceptive Disney teacups. Is this why no one will look at me? Am I about to be suspended? Again?

CHAPTER TWENTY-NINE

Orlando is entering the news conference room as I'm leaving. We bump shoulders but don't make eye contact. Which is weird. I twirl around to see if he stopped, wanting to make a connection.

He keeps walking into the meeting, his back to me.

My heart hurts. And my reporter's instinct knows this is NOT good.

"Let's get started," the assistant news director says. "Álvarez, can you shut the door?"

I freeze. "Okay." Does everybody but me know what's about to happen? My stomach is trying out for the Olympic gymnastics team. I shut the door, careful not to make it sound like I'm slamming it.

What is El Jefe going to suspend me for this time?

Staying on the first murder scene? Walking under the crime scene tape? Staying at the news conference. Going to the second crime scene without his permission. A giant lump of fear jams my throat.

His door is open, and Jessica walks out. *Right on cue.* I pause and drill her with a questioning look. At least she makes eye contact.

"I'm so sorry," she says. She's shaking her head and pulling her lips inward.

I hurry past her, praying I find the air to speak,

because frankly, the adrenaline dump hitting me is making it difficult to do anything but slurp in shallow amounts of oxygen. Why do women do this to each other? We should be supporting each other, not turning each other in.

"Mr. Payton." His name comes out breathy, and it's obvious I'm nervous.

"Please shut the door and sit down."

Another shut the door request. Never, ever good to hear that.

And the Human Resources director is here.

¡Ay, Dios mío! My heart dives off the Sunshine Skyway Bridge as I slide into a chair in front of his desk. I decide to take the offensive because I can't stop myself. It's who I am. "I don't know what Jessica told you—"

"Jessica actually came to your defense," Mr. Payton interrupts me. "She says female coworkers should be supporting each other, not stabbing each other in the back. She declined to answer my questions or give me any details, saying it wasn't her business."

I'm stunned. My cheeks flame like meat on the grill, and I'm ashamed of my small-minded assumptions.

"Orlando, on the other hand, is worried about you."

Worried about me? "I'm fine." He sure didn't look worried, he looked like he didn't care. "I'm fine."

Mr. Payton leans forward, his elbows on his desk, hands clasping in front of him. "He says your judgment is off."

"I'm fine," I say with more emphasis on the word *fine*. I look at the H.R. director. She's taking notes. Not looking at me.

Mr. Payton starts with the pen tapping. "You stayed at a murder scene when I told you to leave."

Jessica didn't know, so that had to be O. "Orlando told you that?" *Didn't peg him as a snitch.*

"He didn't have to. I saw you on footage another TV station aired, talking to a detective, it looked like."

I have to make him understand how personal this is to me. "The murder scene looked like my mother's—"

El Jefe raises a hand, stopping her. "I'm sorry, Mari."

My whole body goes still. Lake water on a windless night.

"This is what Orlando is worried about. You're making judgment calls based on your grief. And while I've had compassion for your situation"—he clears his throat—"I've already suspended you once for an error in reporting—"

"I haven't made an error since."

"And now, you are blatantly ignoring my requests. And your coworkers—"

"Coworker. Just one. Right?"

"Are concerned about working with you. Worried you're crossing the line."

"Orlando said that?" The hurt in my heart stretches into something large and lonely. A big, black hole I'm about to fall into. Head first.

"There's no easy way to say this."

So don't.

"I'm going to have to let you go."

"What?" The lump erupts and exits in a water-works display I can't control. I shake my head, but nothing is stopping the tears. It's an afternoon thunderstorm raining down my face. I love this job. I need this job. What will I tell Abuela?

"You've violated company policy, disobeyed my orders, endangered fellow coworkers—"

His voice fades, and all I hear is white noise. A buzzing—the kind you hear right before you pass out. Here we go again. The curse has begun. It feels like a tornado landing right on top of me.

I've lost the job I need to pay the family bills. I've lost my professional title that opens doors and allows me to continue investigating. I've lost a partner and a friend. And I don't think I deserve this. And twenty some more days of this just might kill me.

I gasp.

Maybe that's what the bearer of that last note intended.

"Effective immediately."

The HR director says something about my badge and parking tag.

I get up, but it's a total out-of-body experience. I know I'm standing, but I can't feel a thing. I hear myself say the right words. "Yes sir. Yes ma'am. Yes sir." Over and over. But I don't feel my lips moving. My tears, though, they are warm. My fingertips cold. I feel all of that.

Now I know who's been giving me the evil eye. *Orlando!*

I can't believe it. Betrayal is the house I'm now

living in and it's imploding.

Cursed by someone I considered a friend. That's the worst kind of betrayal. Even worse than being cursed by a stranger.

I drag myself out of El Jefe's office. I think the HR director is still talking.

My iPhone *dings*.

I've forgotten about Freddie. And Tony.

It's not Freddie's number.

It's not Tony's, either.

It's Izzy—she never calls me anymore.

I stall outside El Jefe's door and read the last incoming text: *Abuela had a heart attack.*

An ambulance is taking her to Tampa General Hospital.

CHAPTER THIRTY

I stand beside the doorway of my abuela's ER room, my heart shredding. Because—I know. I'm sweating, even though the ER isn't hot. In fact, it's downright chilling, both in temperature and mood.

I haven't gone into the room yet. The nurse left me standing here outside ER Room 3 with the door half open. I'll push it open in a second. I'm not ready for this. Not if entering the ER room tonight means viewing death in the eyes of a loved one. Again.

I swallow. Close my eyes. The drumming of my heart vibrates all the way up to my temples.

I know I won't see the abuela I remember. I won't see the strong woman who stood between a bully and me on the playground when my middle school principal refused to act. Or the smart woman who taught me about money after Mamá died. Or the fun woman who teased me about my lack of domestic skills as she taught me how to make chicken fricassee. Or the brave woman who gathered Izzy and me together and guided us through prayer, giving us the strength to survive our mother's murder and our father's death.

When I walk into this room, I won't see any versions of that woman.

My heart ignites like a July Fourth fireworks show, minus the vibrant, lively colors. This eruption is all black and white.

I long to feel her boney arms around me.

I want to hear her weary but wise voice tell me it will be okay. I want to ask her what we'll do for money now that I've blown it and gotten myself fired. How we'll pay these medical bills. How *I'll* pay these medical bills. How I can wash away this new curse. How Izzy and I can protect ourselves.

As I enter, I hear Izzy, bent over Abuela's bed, whispering, "I'm sorry, Abuela. I'll keep the secret. I promise. I won't say a thing. Not ever. I won't say a thing."

"What are you talking about?"

Izzy flips around so fast, *I* feel dizzy. "Mari! You scared me."

"How is Abuela?"

"Unconscious." Izzy's gaze hits the floor.

She lied to Abuela using our secret sister code. Say one thing twice—it means the opposite. "You were talking to her." Now Izzy is lying to me.

She shrugs. "Telling her I love her." She doesn't look up.

"That's not what you said."

"I'm so glad you're here." Izzy glances at me. Her eyes are red-rimmed and weepy. I can't remember the last time I saw her show this much emotion. Maybe the night Raúl left her bedroom for the last time.

"What happened?" I move a few steps closer to the bed.

"She collapsed. Hit her head." Izzy's hands are flapping. "I couldn't wake her up."

"That's why you called 911?" I can see Abuela's

head now. Her eyes are closed.

"She had another heart attack. Mari—she's dying."

"Stop!" I hold onto the wall to keep the room from spinning. "Don't say that." Izzy knows how I feel about manifesting ideas. "Don't put those words out into the universe."

She's shaking her head. "The ER doctor told me."

"I don't believe you."

"Her heart." Izzy covers her heart with one hand. "It's giving out."

"No. She has the strongest heart I know." I choke on the word "strongest."

Izzy moves away from the bed. "I'm going to call the priest. The one from St. Mary's. She'd want last rites given."

The word *no* is stuck in my chest like a barbed ball. As her health care advocate, I know this *is* what Abuela would want. So I don't stop Izzy from leaving the room to make the call. She drops something into the trash can as she leaves. Probably a Kleenex. At least I know now that Izzy still has feelings.

It's only Abuela and me now.

Shaking, I walk to the side of the bed.

When did she get *this* thin? The blue lines of her blood streak through her hands, her skin like see-through parchment paper. Her closed eyes have sunken into her face, leaving bony cheeks peeking out from the oxygen mask.

Her chest rises and falls, but only slightly. And only every so often. Her heart is being monitored. Her blood pressure is low. But the routine beeping assures me her heart is still working. Weak, but still pumping.

I blink tears away. "Please, please Abuela, don't leave me. You know how much I hate to be alone. Izzy can't wait to leave. Go live her own life. What will I do? Please, Abuela. You can pull through. I'll take care of you." The image of Tony with his grandfather fills my head. "I'll take better care of you. Please, please, don't die. I can't imagine life without you."

"Mi princesa."

Energy whips up my spine, straightening me. Mi princesa. Only Mamá called me that.

My gaze shoots to Abuela Bonita's face. Her eyes are open now, but they look unfocused, and she's not actually looking at me.

I reach for her hand.

Her flesh is dry and ice-cold. Her hand's so thin, I can roll her bones between my fingers.

"Mi princesa, someone is giving you the evil eye."

My abuela's mouth is moving, but her words are not connecting with her facial expression or her eyes. "Stop looking for my killer, and the evil eye will stop, too."

The air in my lungs stalls. I grip the bed to keep from falling. "Mamá?"

Embarrassment flames my cheeks. I look around to make sure Izzy isn't listening or watching—she'd think I'm crazy, hearing things. Talking to Mamá as if she's here. Maybe I did hear incorrectly.

Maybe I'm manifesting Mamá.

I lean over, gripping the bed rails, and place my ear right next to Abuela's mouth.

"Don't trust those closest to you."

I spring straight up. That sounds like Abuela Bonita.

Those words I hear clear as a fire alarm.

Beep. Beep. Beep.

One long, continuous *beep*.

That I hear, too.

That is the sound of my beautiful abuela's heart beating no more. That is the sound of my support system dying. I run from the room, unable, unwilling to see death in the eyes of someone I love again.

But something stops me from sprinting toward the exit. I back into the room, as nurses run in calling a code.

I reach into the trash can and pull out the crumpled piece of paper Izzy dropped on her way out. It's not a Kleenex. It's a newspaper article. Two things hit me as the paddles of a defibrillator hit my grandmother's bony chest.

Number one—words are written in black magic marker across the article: *Say a word and I'll kill someone you love. And I'll blame it on this murderer.*

"Clear!" someone yells, followed by the sound of brittle bones rocked by electricity.

Secondly, it becomes clear my Abuela Bonita's death may not be due to her heart giving out.

I'll blame it on *this* is referring to the picture of the crime scene from the Stop-N-Go the other day. Circled in the crime scene picture—a broken doll. But this time I look closer.

The doll's eye isn't gouged out.

It's her heart.

CHAPTER THIRTY-ONE

As soon as I get home from the hospital, I strip off my work clothes. They smell of disinfectant, recently-got-fired sweat, and death.

Or, maybe…murder?

I can't think about that right now, because I can't change it.

I slip into old, comfortable sweat pants, twist my hair up into a sloppy bun, and slip my bare feet into Abuela Bonita's house shoes.

I want to feel her with me.

It's three a.m., and the house is unusually quiet. Abuela's favorite standing clock still ticks. My own pulse zips, but that's it. Izzy's TV isn't blaring from her room. Her car isn't in the driveway. Not surprised—she's never around when I need her.

I need her to help me plan Abuela's funeral.

Who am I kidding? I need Izzy home, so I don't fall apart. Emptiness rushes through me, and it burns like my blood is on fire. I need her home to ask her about the notes. Are they directed to her? Or did she find the last note in Abuela's hand when she found her unconscious? Is she aware of who would want to curse us? Has she heard from Raúl? Have any crazy things happened to her besides Abuela dying? I need her to stay home. Stay safe. Stay with me, even if she doesn't want to talk to me.

I try her cell again. No answer.

I won't be able to sleep until I hear from her, and I make plans for Abuela. Should she be buried in her white dress given to her when she was initiated into Santería? Or her favorite light blue outfit worn during Sunday Mass? Should I invite her close friends only? Or open the service to anyone? Wait. Abuela didn't want a funeral. Now I remember why. Should she be cremated? Her ashes spread over her homestead in Cuba? How much would that cost? Where will I get the money now that I'm not working? These thoughts swirl—a vortex in my overtaxed brain.

I'm hanging over the edge of the tallest roller coaster at Busch Gardens, strapped in, facing the ground, with no way to get out or change course.

I still. Take a breath. Exhale slowly. A chill hits my flesh.

Change course. That's it! Change the course I'm on.

I have to get my job back. There's only one way to do that, by proving I've been right all along.

That won't be easy. Perhaps, impossible.

Propelled by a strong sense of urgency, I sweep into Abuela's back room.

This is where I'll find Abuela. Her spirit will come here. She'll help me. I know it like I know what I have to do next.

It's her voice in my head: *Do not cry for me, mi niña. Get to work.*

I almost cry at the inspiration.

Instead, I search for matches and light a candle on her altar. The one next to my mamá's picture.

Smoke and a mix of lavender and orange scent waft from the wick, the smell comforting.

I'm going to put the pieces of this puzzle together. Map out clues that will lead me to the serial killer who's hurting my West Tampa neighborhood. And taunting my family, it seems, while he's doing it.

I can't wait for someone else to die. And someone else *is* going to die. I feel it.

The clock in my head is all I hear.

I kneel and say a quick prayer to both Abuela's orisha Oshun and mine, Chango. I pull from my memories, from watching her over the years, with both fear and interest.

"I kneel before your image. I admire your power, strength, and knowledge, and I ask for your benevolence. In the name of God, and the Holy Spirit, protect me from all evil influences and evil thoughts and intentions of my enemies."

Crazy to think I have enemies. But clearly, I do.

I add, "And lead me to the answers I seek. I will use this room, and your guidance, to lay down the map and track the killer."

Someone's gaze heats the back of my neck. The hair all over my body rises and sizzles as if singed.

But I know no one is here.

Izzy left the hospital before the last rites were even given, distraught after a phone call. Perhaps the current boyfriend who never bothered to show up for her during challenging times. Perhaps someone else. Izzy always did pick bad boys, with no morals and questionable hearts.

I spend the next five hours a human cyclone, swirling around my computer, printing pictures off the internet. I write thoughts on note cards or anything I find and throw down ideas like darts.

I begin hanging up my corridor of clues on an empty wall next to Abuela's altar. The first picture I pin up, one I took of the crime scene at the deputy's house. Next to it, I tape up a picture of Deputy Natasha Rodríguez in uniform. I pin up a note card and write the number six in black magic marker.

Next to that, I post a picture of the little girl Sofía Figueroa, the victim shot in Rodríguez's home.

Under the number six I write: *Rodríguez shot six times at six p.m. The first victim was six when killed.* "So many sixes. Coincidence?"

I don't think so. I add in red, erasable marker: *What if six references something else?*

Next up, a picture of an anonymous person I found on Pinterest—the woman had one eye open, and one eye shut. I draw a circle over the closed eye, representing the coin, and sketch a crown inside, like the one I saw on the police war room wall. Then, I draw a line from the number 6 to this picture.

I originally thought Natasha Rodríguez's killer could be the six-year-old victim's dad, Thomas Figueroa. I'd seen him at the scene. He had motive. I pin his picture next to the Pinterest picture. Raúl's mom told me Figueroa's son is now a leader of the West Tampa Kings. I write Sebastián's name on a Post-it note and paste it next to his father's picture. I circle the coin with the crown and write West Tampa Kings. I put a question mark by that and add, *But could it be a reference to a king, who is also a queen?*

Surveillance video showed Figueroa busy during the time the murder took place.

But Orlando and I saw him in the street. Can't rule Figueroa out, yet. His son is still very much a viable suspect, too. *Gotta check on his whereabouts during the murder. And see if Izzy knows him. Sebastián would be just her type.*

Next to the Figueroas, I tape up the first note I found in our home. The one that reads: *I'm back and I'm watching you. You know why.* This note was for Abuela? Or for Izzy? Or for me?

Hoodie Hannibal, aka Edward Jones, called me "queen of TV crime news." *Weird.* And worth noting, I hang his picture next to Figueroa's because his comment fits in with the crown on the coin.

Next up, a picture of a necklace made of red and white beads similar to the one I saw at Natasha Rodríguez's crime scene. I pin up a picture of a doll, like the ones at both crime scenes. The picture came from Amazon. I write: *BEADS AND BROKEN DOLLS.* The serial killer's calling card? I have to ask Tony if he's had time to track sales or shipment of such dolls to either Jones or Figueroa.

I step back from the wall and scan it.

Time for Scene Two.

Up goes a picture of the Stop-N-Go scene. Next to it, a picture I found of Edward Jones, aka Hoodie Hannibal, from Facebook. I found out he's a member of a national real-crime lovers' group that connects online to try and solve cold case murders. They especially love cases tied to serial killers. He also works for an online magazine devoted to unsolved crime stories. Hoodie is a murder junkie.

Hoodie knew about the Stop-N-Go murder

before Tony did. I walk up to his picture and write with red marker: *HOW DID HOODIE KNOW FIRST?*

Hoodie had a year-old newspaper article, a copy of which goes up next to his Facebook picture with me in it. I write in red: *IS HE STALKING ME? WHY? OR IS HE STALKING THE KILLER? OR IS HE THE KILLER?*

Next, I pin up the second note I found in our door. The one that says: *You did not meet me at El Reloj. NOW YOU WILL HAVE 30 DAYS OF BAD LUCK.*

I write on it; *GET A HANDWRITING SAMPLE FROM HOODIE. WILL IT MATCH? OR IS THIS SOMEONE ELSE?*

Next, I pin up a pic I snapped of the graffiti on the wall of the Stop-N-Go. "*Die well. The devil is waiting for you. Keep one eye open so you can see him coming.*" Those words are like cold fingernails shimmying over my sensitive skin. Creepy. *But it's the crown spray-painted next to it that ties together past and present murders.*

Our killer is obsessed with crowns, broken dolls, and evil eyes. Notes and newspaper articles.

I shake off the sense of doom that sits on my shoulders like weights.

Concentrate.

What else do the two scenes have in common? With each other or with my mother's murder?

I grab a piece of paper and write in red:

1-both present day victims are involved in past crimes but never convicted or sentenced for their part in the crime. JUSTICE NOT SERVED.

2-both victims killed in a similar fashion as their previous victims were killed. On purpose? REVENGE?

3-Both crimes witnessed, but killer still got away. HOW?

4-Hoodie Hannibal at both scenes. HOW TO PROVE BOTH TIMES IT WAS JONES? HOW DOES THIS TIE TO ME? DOES HOODIE HAVE ANY TIES TO THE CITY COUNCIL MEMBER? OR TO MY MOTHER?

5 Check FIGUEROA'S ALIBI for Thursday night into Friday morning, when second murder occurred. If he has one, that rules him out. BUT WHAT ABOUT HIS SON? SAME MOTIVE.

6-No DNA left by suspect at either scene. A PRO. DONE THIS BEFORE.

7-Killer at both scenes holds garbage bag. WHAT'S IN IT?

8-Killer has time to move or pose the body. TIMING IS GOOD. STALKED VICTIMS FIRST?

9 No working surveillance video at either scene. COOL PRECISION OVER CRIME OF PASSION.

10-Notes left at my house. IS SOMEONE IN MY HOUSE THE NEXT TARGET?

I step away. Turn in a slow circle. Shake my whole body like one of those Magic Eight Balls, hoping to erase what's already in my head. I'm starting to visualize a potential new suspect. Like I'm some FBI profiler, except I know no one will believe me. They'll think I'm crazy for even suggesting it.

The first thing that struck me early on: *lightning.*

I write:

1-Stop-N-Go victim has a lightning bolt carved in

his hand. WHY?

I close my eyes. In my mind's eye, I see a light-ning bolt on a hat. The same man was wearing it. Twice.

It's a coincidence. It must be.

But, what about the other things that are making me nervous? I don't understand how a person who is not Cuban can be connected to so many of our cultural things.

I write on a new piece of paper and stick it up: *DOUBLE-EDGED HAMMER.*
CUBAN BEACH TOWN
COWRIE SHELLS
The only thing I can't fit in yet is the notes left at home. I will have to ask Izzy about those. When she answers her phone!

I drop to my knees in front of Abuela's altar, because I realize this killer may be playing on a level few know about.

I'm beginning to understand.

I may have much in common with my suspected killer.

Which means, if he's a bad guy, I may be the only one who can see it.

I may be the only one who can stop him.

I know exactly where I need to go next. On a little history mission. But I'm not going alone. I pick up my phone and dial.

CHAPTER THIRTY-TWO

Wednesday, close to eleven a.m., Orlando and I pull up to the address I dug up during my espresso-energized murder wall session. The sky is gray, much like my current mood. A light drizzle keeps the windshield wipers wiping.

It's a steamy, midmorning served with a late-summer side of humidity. And humility.

"I'm sorry."

"O, for the fourth time—it's okay."

"I didn't betray you."

I shrug. "You kinda did."

"I just told Mr. Payton I was worried about you." His fingers grip the wheel of his personal car so tightly his fingertips pale. "I may have suggested he give you a few days off."

"Well, I've got more than a few days—"

"I talked to him again and told him he misinterpreted my words."

I leave it there, thinking maybe this is why Orlando showed up for me this morning even though this could get him in trouble at work. Associating with the enemy. He feels guilty.

I feel guilty I'm willing to take advantage of that.

The modest one-story home with a two-car garage is in the working-class area of Brandon, a suburb of Tampa. A plastic kiddie pool, full to the top, sits in the front yard. A dirt bike, decorated with Mortal Kombat stickers, sits next to it.

We both comment that the style and size of homes here are probably as different as the people who live in this transitional neighborhood, but I wonder what it was like when John Hanks grew up here. A white kid in a diverse, lower socioeconomic part of town.

"Okay, we found the address," Orlando says. "What now?"

I unclick the seat belt, thankful we've fallen back into our routine without too much drama over my firing. It happened. I believe he wasn't the sole reason behind it. He couldn't stop it. Didn't want to get fired himself. He's helping me now. And I need him.

We both jump out, me with an umbrella, O without. He doesn't have any hair to worry about getting wet. We're in his personal car, so it's not marked as TV, and he doesn't have his camera or equipment with him. I wouldn't ask him to take a chance like that, and I don't want to spook this family.

"Who are we looking for?" he asks.

I realize he came with me without knowing the answer to that question—he followed me blindly. *That is trust.* "We're looking for the family that raised Detective John Hanks."

Orlando whistles and then asks why.

I tell him about the office picture of Hanks in Cuba. His tattoo of a double-edged hammer. Remind O how Hanks was playing with cowrie shells while we were there. "All of which led me to dig into Hanks's past last night—to figure out how an all-American boy from Tampa learned about these Cuban American cultural things. I found an article in the Times about how Hanks was adopted after his family was killed. *Killed*, O. His whole family. In a car accident. And I thought a visit to his adoptive family might answer some questions that keep coming up in the back of my mind." Like red flags warning of dangerous riptides.

"You gonna just walk up and start asking questions?"

"Like I always do." I've always been an intuitive person. I follow my gut. Push when I feel I can, retreat when necessary.

I knock on the door.

It takes a second before a deep, raspy, just-woke-up voice answers. "Who is it?" The door creaks open enough for the person to look out.

"Hi, sorry to bother you." I have to crane to look him in the eye. "I'm Marisol Álvarez. And this is Orlando Moore."

The door opens wider. "The TV reporter?"

I don't want to lie, silly as that might sound. A journalist isn't supposed to lie. Am I a TV reporter anymore? "Glad you watch." *Not a lie.*

The man looks like he's in his forties, tall and big boned, with bleached hair and dark roots that haven't been touched up in a while. He's wearing jeans, ripped at the knees, and a faded, stretched-from-wear T-shirt with the name of a Latin group on it. His complexion is sallow, his eyes tired. He looks to me like a man who drank too much Jack Daniels last night. Or, by the look of his protruding belly, consumed too much Miller. Not Lite.

"You investigating someone?" he asks.

"I'm looking for someone. Someone who used to live here."

"Well, my family's been here near forever."

He's closing the door when I say, "I'm looking for Patricia Lopez."

The door stalls. The man's formerly fierce face falls, and he blinks back what looks like tears. "Ma passed years ago."

He calls her "Ma". Many reporters would apologize, embarrassed they didn't know that important detail, and leave, thinking they can't get what they want now, or they're too scared to push this angry, agitated man when he looks like he's about to slam the door in your face.

I don't budge. "I'm so sorry. I didn't know."

"You're investigating Ma?"

"Actually, her son."

He pulls the door open. Stands taller. "I'm her only son." The pupils in the man's cloudy blue eyes widen.

"John Hanks didn't grow up here?" Orlando asks.

"John." The man draws his name out like it's a nasty taste he's trying to brush off his tongue.

Interesting reaction. "He's your brother?" I push.

He snorts. "Not by blood."

"May we come in?" I ask, gesturing to my umbrella. "It's raining."

He hesitates, his energy almost as charged as the air.

Time for action. "I'm sorry. I forgot to ask your name." I hold out my hand.

"Nando." He shakes my hand, shakes Orlando's, too, and looks behind him.

I bet the house is a mess.

"Well, the kids have been playing," Nando says. "And the wife is working."

I throw up a hand like I totally get it, which I do. "We won't take pictures, and we'll be quick and quiet." I move through the door before he can say no. "It's starting to pour and who knows—" Thunder rolls past. Right on cue. Gracias. "Lightning usually follows," I say.

The move pays off. Nando, the beer drinker in the *Gente de Zona* T-shirt, allows us room to enter.

Tall, colored candles, covered with stickers of the Virgin Mary, are on a table in one corner, but in full view. Family pictures are everywhere, some black and white, most with layers of dust on them. There's a mop with a rag wrapped around the bottom, propped up in the corner of the room, like Mrs. Martínez's mop. My abuela's, too. Old school Cuban way to mop the tile. I also spot a cross on the wall next to a Cuban flag. My heart begins to beat faster. I'm on to something. John Hanks was raised by a Cuban American mother. That explains away some of my concerns. But raises others.

I walk past a bookshelf. I don't have time to stop and read titles, but I do spot plastic party favors that say Katie's Quinceañera, with a date five years ago. I smile. It reminds me of Abuela Bonita, who hated to throw away anything that had emotional value. She has party favors stacked on shelves I'll now have to clean. My heart flutters with that realization.

Nando is going on about how long it's been since

he's seen John, when I realize John isn't in any of the family pictures. At least not that I recognize. "No pictures of John?"

That stops Nando.

In the pause that follows, Orlando clears his throat and gives me a questioning look.

"I took them down after Ma passed," Nando says, his gaze darting across the main living room wall where many family pictures hang. He drops his gaze.

My reporter's red flag is rising. "Why?"

"We had our issues." No pause this time.

This living room is in sharp contrast to García's. García and his siblings appeared in almost every picture. I wonder if John ever came back to visit. And if he noticed, too, that someone erased him from this family's history. By an evil adopted brother? Interesting, too, that Hanks never changed his last name to Lopez. "Did your mother have issues with John, too?" I intentionally poke Nando to get him angry enough to spill secrets.

"Hell no. Ma doted on him." As he says this, a young boy, looking to be about ten, walks in and puts his arms around Nando's fat middle. "She treated John like he was a rescue puppy, or some damn orphan thing."

Some damn orphan thing. So he was jealous of John. *Envy.* It's a powerful emotion. I know this firsthand.

"I'm hungry," the boy whines.

"Grab some croquetas. Your ma left them on the counter." Nando unwinds the young boy, forcing his arms off his waist.

The boy's shoulders drop, and he slinks off into

the kitchen.

"I gotta get something for my son," Nando says, gaze already on the kitchen.

My stomach fizzes like a shaken soda pop can, but I know how to keep him here. "Nando, I came here because I thought something was up with your brother. Something I couldn't explain. Not sure it's anything now. But—"

His body stiffens. "Like what? What was up?"

"Did you ever observe any unusual behavior with John?"

Orlando side-eyes me.

"I knew it!" Nando claps his hands against his thick thighs. "From the first day Ma brought him home, I knew he was different."

"Different? How?"

"When he was a kid, he couldn't make friends. Used to pull the tail off lizards out back. Stayed in his room a lot. Weird shit."

This kid didn't sound like the John Hanks I've met. The adult John Hanks is charming, cocky, definitely comfortable around people. "Your ma was okay with that behavior?"

He shrugs. "For some reason, Ma connected to the kid. Brought him home after one particularly bad beating in an institute where they'd placed him. I'll never forgot what he looked like. Missing a front tooth. A black eye. Scratch marks on his face. The kid was a mess from day one, but he loved my ma loyally. Like he replaced his dead ma with mine. She loved to be loved. She used to say she never met a good man till John came. He acted like he was *the man* of our house."

The heated resentment in his voice penetrates me, even half a room away. "Your mom gave John a loving home. He would have done anything for her?"

He snorts again. "And did."

"What do you mean?" I ask, but at the same time Orlando asks, "How did your mother die?"

"Her fucking boyfriend killed her."

And that answer erases all that came before it. I almost fall over, I'm so shocked by this.

"You didn't know that either?" Nando sneers at me. "What the fuck kind of reporter are you?"

My cheeks heat as if slapped. "The kind who came here looking for these kinds of answers. Please tells us more."

"Bastard ran over Ma with his truck when they were fighting and she wouldn't get in and go with him. I wasn't home, but John saw it. Went crazy. He was seventeen at the time. Chased down the car like he was going to kill that man. I think he would have, if he'd caught up with him."

Hanks also watched his mother die. What are the chances? "So, what happened to the boyfriend?" My pulse is zigzagging like it's drunk on the potential of this lead. I knew my instincts were right. Something is off about Hanks.

"Served ten years for involuntary manslaughter. Bastard said it was an accident. He didn't see her. The jury believed it. The court system is fucked up, if you ask me. I think that's why John's a cop. He never did get over Ma's death, or the fact her killer got off lightly. He wanted the man to get fucking life. A life for a life, he used to say."

"A life for a life," I whisper. *Or an eye for an eye.*

"Where is he now?" Orlando and I ask at the same time.

"John?" He grunts and scrunches his face. "Still a cop, I guess. We don't break bread on Sundays."

"No, we mean your mom's boyfriend—the one convicted. Is he still in prison?" I ask, impatient, because I'm desperate to interview that man next. Today, in fact.

"A couple months after he got out of prison— five years ago I think—he was hit and killed while walking home from a bar not too far from his home. He was drunk. Always did love his hard liquor. The fucker."

He was killed in the same way he killed. Chills sweep over my skin like cold waves.

"They ever find the driver?" Orlando asks in a breathy voice I've never heard from him. He's catching on.

"The guy who hit the bastard? No. No." Nando glances into the kitchen. His son is pulling something out of the pantry. "No. Shit. Not that."

I sense this interview is about to end. "Any video of the accident?" I can look it up. Trace the vehicle.

"Fuck if I know. Ask John. I reckon if there was any way to find the driver back then, he would've found him. Or her. He was a cop by then. Even more obsessed than when he was a kid."

"John Hanks investigated your mother's killer's death?"

Nando shrugs. "Like I said, we don't do dinner."

Orlando grabs my upper arm. It's the first time I've seen him excited about information in a long time. I feel like fist pumping, but instead I bite the inside of my lip and squeeze my legs together, holding back my excitement.

"Look," Nando says, moving toward the front door. "I gotta feed my kid before he eats the shit that makes him breakout. My wife will beat my ass. I don't know what this is all about, but if it's about my ma's case, if you ask me, the driver did us all a big favor that night. If you ask me, justice was served. Look, I never much liked John, but I do agree with him on this one thing. You should take a life for a life. That monster killed my mother because she wouldn't sleep with his ass anymore. Fuck him. He deserves to be dead. And I don't care who killed him."

But I do.

As we walk out the door, I thank him for his time, but in my head all I hear is: *The boyfriend didn't just die.*

Someone murdered him.

The man who killed Hanks's adopted mother might be victim number one.

CHAPTER THIRTY-THREE

As soon as we're back in Orlando's car, I flip to face him. "What if John Hanks is seeking revenge for the woman who adopted him and gave him a good life? What if he liked it so much—"

"Killing?" O's voice takes on that incredulous tone that always irks me.

I try to explain. "What if he liked *killing* so much he began looking for other victims of crimes gone unpunished?"

He slams the car into reverse and whips out of Nando's driveway before he says, "That accusation is gonna get your ass sued."

"Only a theory, at this point," I reply. "He could have killed his mom's boyfriend, and because he was the homicide detective investigating it, covered it up."

Orlando's gripping the steering wheel, maneuvering the car through Nando's back street neighborhood. He isn't looking at me or acting excited we may have uncovered a dirty cop. Which surprises me, considering what he said cops did to him when he was younger. Pulled him over—racial profiling. Instead, he says, "I don't think TPD would let John Hanks investigate his own mom's murder."

"Easy enough to check. But even if he didn't head up that case, he'd have access to evidence, etc.

He could have—"

Orlando hits the brakes. "He could have what?"

Damn. My body lurches forward. He almost drove right through a red light. "I'm not accusing an innocent man. It's a hypothesis to explore. Nothing more at this point. Not airing anything, okay? I don't even have a TV news platform anymore. Remember?"

He takes a deep breath and says, "You have to do more to convince me of his guilt." The light turns green, and he moves forward. "What do you have on John Hanks, except a gut feeling? And his adopted brother, who hates him, telling you he's weird?"

"He pulled tails off lizards."

"Boys do that."

"Did you?"

Orlando blows out air. I know he's on board. He just doesn't realize it yet. "Can you connect Hanks to other murders?" he asks.

His words are like wasps stinging me, because O went from following me blindly to Nando's house to doubting my intuition. More than intuition. Clues winding like individual threads to form a rope that might hang Hanks. "Yes, I think I can." I'll show him my murder wall. And explain how Hanks's connections to the Cuban American world are leading me to wonder if he, too, could be a suspect. "Let's head to my house. I've got something to show you." My phone rings. "It's Tony."

"Tony?"

"I mean, Detective García."

Orlando takes his eyes off the road long enough to stare at me. "Answer it."

I do. "Mari Álvarez." My heart's thumping, because if Tony's calling, it's something important. I put the phone on speaker so O can also hear.

"It's Detective García."

We're both being so formal. "I'm so glad you called. I have a new theory—"

"We executed a warrant on Edward Jones's home this morning." Tony's words are taut, his energy fast, like rapids after the rain.

"Jones?" I wish I had my azabache charm. I want the comfort of an old habit.

"Your stalker."

Hoodie Hannibal. "What did you find?" I brace myself.

"We found pictures of you—articles about you. He's been stalking you. At least for a couple of years. We have so much evidence, we arrested him on the spot and charged him with aggravated stalking. In all the years I've been a detective, I've never seen anyone as obsessed."

Did Hoodie want me to meet him at El Reloj? Why? To woo me or to kill me? Why there? I lean my head back on the passenger's side headrest. "He's in jail?"

"Yes. He'll make a first appearance tomorrow."

"Bond?"

"The District Attorney is going to ask for no bond."

I exhale. "Okay, thanks for letting me know."

"Detective García," Orlando is talking. "We have something else we need to talk to you about. You're not going to believe where we were today and why."

"Come to my office." Tony sounds stressed.

"Now?" I ask.

"We also found enough evidence to charge Jones with the murder of three people."

"Murder? Wait." I lean forward. "Three people?"

"Natasha Rodríguez. The man at the Stop-N-Go." He pauses.

I wait.

García clears his throat.

Enough of this. "Who else?"

"Your mother."

My muscles are so locked, it hurts like bad spasms.

"We found something. I need you to come to my office as soon as you can for the official ID."

CHAPTER THIRTY-FOUR

I'm sitting in Tony's cramped office again, Orlando on my right side, our knees almost touching. This time my leg is bouncing, and I can't stop my physical reaction to the pictures of photos spread out across Detective García's desk. Tony couldn't show me the actual pictures he took from Edward Jones's home, because they're now in evidence. So, instead he took photographs of what detectives had collected and spread the copies out across his desk.

I'm staring at them but haven't touched one.

I'm numb.

And on fire.

All at the same damn time.

I wanted to come to Tony's office to identify the item he said he'd found and anything else he wanted to show me. Then I wanted to get him alone so I could talk to him about Detective Hanks's past.

But Hanks is here.

Hanks is freaking here, standing right freaking behind me. His breathing is audible. Quick and uneven, like he knows where O and I have been. How could he know? His weird-ass brother could have called him, silly. Even though my back is to him, I can feel him watching me like *I'm* the suspect.

Tony pushes one photo toward me. "Edward Jones had one entire wall dedicated to you."

One. Entire. Wall.

A wall covered with snapshots, newspaper articles, magazine spreads, even Polaroids, assembled in a creative, clean way, like it's a special display in a modern art museum. Much neater than my murder wall. I look for any examples of his handwriting, but don't see anything that could help match writing examples with the notes left at my house. Not that it matters now.

I move my gaze across Tony's desktop and point to one individual photograph. "This is from me at the news conference." *¡Ay, Dios mío!* "And he takes pictures of me at murder scenes." I didn't mean to say that out loud.

Tony slides another picture toward me. "He dedicated another wall to local unsolved murders."

The picture is of a different wall. It's similar in that it's covered with photos, newspaper clippings, magazine articles. It's different in that they're all pasted on top of each other, as if it was some paper-mache project for school. One made with gruesome scenes of death and human destruction.

"Revolting," I say. "Where the hell did he get all of these photos of crime scenes?"

"Some pictures become public record when released to the defense," Tony says. "I was able to track a number to articles Jones wrote for his online magazine for crime junkies. Many are from either newspapers or other internet sources."

"When you asked Hoodie, I mean Jones, about these photos, what did he say?"

"Jones says he made your wall as homage to your great work." Tony shrugs. "Says he's a fan. That's not breaking the law. I informed him he was wrong. All the pictures are proof of aggravated stalking."

I nod, thankful García had enough evidence to jail Hoodie for a while. How did I not see him at all those different places on all those different days? Because he's good at hiding in plain sight.

"The murder scene wall was part of his job. We confirmed he does write for an online crime junkie website. They have tens of thousands of followers, all people trying to help solve open crimes in their communities. Jones denies killing anyone."

"Of course he does," Hanks says from the doorway.

"Any proof that he actually did kill someone?" Orlando asks.

"Off the record?" Tony is looking at both of us. O nods.

"I got fired," I say. "Remember?"

Tony keeps a detective's poker face. "Serial killers usually take something of their victim's. While they can be creative with their methods of killing, most hide their souvenirs in simple places. Places they won't forget. Like a shoebox in a bedroom closet."

"You're kidding?" I sit straighter. "What did you find in that shoebox in Jones's closet?"

"We found a ring belonging to the deputy killed on Hesperides and an ID badge from the guy killed at the Stop-N-Go."

That ties Jones to both murders. If you'd hit me over the head with a double-edged hammer, I wouldn't be any more stunned. I was so sure it might be Hanks. I was so sure I had it figured out.

Tony slides a baggie my way, labeled with today's date and a number. Inside is a simple wooden rosary made of dark beads and a wooden cross. He flips the bag over.

The word *Barbara* is etched into the back of the cross, like I remember. I close my eyes. Squeeze all the tears back. I can't breathe. I can't breathe. The room spins and I open my eyes to steady it. This isn't the closure I'd expected—in fact, this opens a whole new can full of questions.

"Do you recognize this rosary?" he asks. He's so gentle in his tone. *The good cop. The kind cop.*

"You okay?" Orlando shakes me by leaning his shoulder into mine.

"Yes. Looks like my mamá's." I look up at Tony.

His eyes are warm with regret. "I'm sorry."

"I wanted closure." I just can't believe this is how I'm getting it.

"García says you had something to share with us?" Hanks leaves his perch at the door and walks around so he is now looking right at me. "Some new theory?"

"It's nothing." I shoot a wide-eyed look at Orlando and say, "What I've seen today wipes away any new ideas we may have had. Right, Orlando?" He doesn't like to lie. Neither do I.

"Right," O says, but he's looking at Detective Hanks in a way that will totally give that lie away.

Damnit, Orlando, put on a poker face.

"You sure?" Hanks says, moving closer to me. "I'd love to hear it anyway." He parks himself on the side of García's desk. Like he's not going away till I tell him.

"Were you at the scene today?" I ask. "When García arrested Jones?"

He sits taller on the desk's edge. His eyes narrow. He reminds me of a snake about to strike, but it could be my paranoia.

"I was."

"Why?" I ask.

"Jones might be tied to some of my cold cases."

After all the pictures I saw, that does make sense.

"Like your mother's," Tony adds.

This is exactly what I'd been hoping to find out. Tony knows that. Hanks does, too. I ask him, "You also believe Edward Jones killed my mother?"

"You don't?" Hanks arches both brows and gestures to the desktop behind him. "Given the proof you've seen?"

"The rosary— It's my mamá's, b-best as I can tell," I stammer.

"It's a good thing Hanks went to the scene." Tony leans back in his chair.

"Why?" I can smell the faintest scent of after shave waft by. Hanks, I'm sure. But I can't place it.

The corners of Hanks's mouth lift, but I wouldn't call it a smile. Then, he says, "Because I'm the one who found the shoebox."

I'm processing all this information at once, but questions keep interrupting my thoughts.

Maybe Edward Jones did kill my mother. I mean, there's no doubt about his obsession with me and his obsession with killing and crime scenes. That wall of his points to a serious mental health issue. "If he killed my mother"—I'm thinking out loud—"he's been stalking me for a long time."

Tony nods. "Exactly what I was thinking."

"Before I was even a reporter? That doesn't make sense to me. And why would he have wanted to kill my mother?"

"Maybe that's where and when his obsession with you started?" Hanks is focused on his phone as he speaks.

"Way back then?" Something isn't sitting well in my stomach.

Hanks shakes his head and gives a low throat growl. "All questions I'm going to ask Mr. Jones when I accompany him to Tampa General."

Tony sits taller. "He's sick? Looked fine when I cuffed him."

Hanks shows us the face of his cellphone. "Just informed by text he's having chest pains."

Tony flops back in his chair. "Oh, here we go."

"He can't get treated at the jail?" O asks.

Hanks shakes his head. "Chest pains gets you a ride by ambulance to TGH. Anyway, I'm out. Gonna hitch a ride with the paramedics right now, see what I can gather from Mr. Jones about a couple of cold cases I've singled out before our guy lawyers up. If he's smart enough to cry chest pains, he's getting a lawyer."

Tony nods. "I'll join you at the hospital after I

finish up here."

I should be elated. Celebrating. My shoulders shouldn't feel so weighted. "I guess this means Santiago, my mother's lover, didn't do it." I turn to O because he's heard this story so many times before. "I saw his car there that night. I was so sure."

"Sometimes our desire for revenge blinds us to the real evil." Typical O response. I squeeze his hand.

Hanks, heading out the door, pauses at that comment. He turns and says, "Does it matter, as long as justice is served?"

CHAPTER THIRTY-FIVE

I'm down on my knees in front of Abuela's altar. The lights are off, and a couple of small candles are lit. Paralyzed by indecision, I've opened a bottle of cheap Yellow Tail Cabernet, and right now the wine is the only thing relaxing my muscles.

I sent Orlando home so I could think.

I left Tony's office earlier without saying anything to him about my suspicions that Detective Hanks is another suspect. Tony had hard evidence against Hoodie. All I have is some odd connections between Hanks and clues I've seen at the scenes. They feel like dropped clues left especially for me. But maybe I've been wrong.

The red wine warms my scratchy throat. I may have a headache tomorrow, but tonight, I want to drown the devil that's hijacked my tongue and kept me silent. I close my eyes, sway enough to know I should stop, then drop my butt onto the back of my ankles so I don't tip over. I don't want to spill red wine on abuela's perfectly white lace. She'd kill me.

I stop breathing.

¡Carajo! Abuela is dead.

Dead.

I put the bottle down. This is not how she'd want me to handle her death. And it's not me.

I phone Izzy, but it goes right to her voicemail.

What if Hoodie killed Izzy before he was arrested? What if she's dead? A rooster's head is a strong gift to the saints. That would be the ultimate punishment to me—kill those I love, strip me of my whole family.

How do the notes figure into all of this? Maybe they were for Izzy? Maybe she's at El Reloj? I could head to Ybor City.

I look at the wine bottle. Or I could just get drunk.

Shame showers over me like Abuela's wash, which I really wish I had more of now. I'd soak in it to wash away more days of bad luck. Drinking is not what Abuela would want me to do in her back room. She'd want me to pray. To which saint?

Chango.

My orisha.

What is it Tony's mother and the Babalawo said? *Turn to your orisha, and you'll find the answers.*

I get up on my knees again and face the altar.

"Chango, I pray if you are here with me, send me a sign." I light the candle next to the image of Saint Barbara.

"Abuela, if you are here with me, or Mamá, if you are here with me, send me a sign please." I light the candle next to Mamá's picture. Tomorrow, I'll add a picture of Abuela Bonita.

"Jesus, if you are with me right now, please send me a sign." I make the sign of the Holy Trinity.

"What should I do next?" I ask them all.

Ding.

A text message coming in. It's from Tony: *Edward Jones escaped from the ambulance a half hour ago. Hanks was shot.*

My heart spasms. *He's gone?* I text back. *As in missing?*

Yes.

A knock on my door.

No. I'm imagining it. I close my eyes, force my lids tight.

Another knock, this time louder, followed by the doorbell.

Oh God, Oh God, Oh God.

I have no doubt the person knocking on my door is Hoodie Hannibal.

CHAPTER THIRTY-SIX

My heart races as I reach to make sure the deadbolt on the front door is engaged. The room is spinning around me, and I'm tightening my muscles to keep standing straight.

"Mari, it's me." His voice comes through the wood door. "It's Tony. Open the door."

Tony.

My breathing slows. I press my forehead against the door in relief.

It's Tony. He's here to protect me. My hand is shaking, but I manage to undo the dead bolt and open the door. Only a crack, just to make sure it's him. He's casual, in jeans, no badge, hands in pocket, shrugging like a little boy. But it *is* Tony. And he's still packing his gun.

"I came over as soon as I found out," he says.

I open the door, gesture for him to come in.

"And you were acting a little, I don't know, nervous at the office today. When I heard Edward Jones escaped, I knew I needed to check on you."

Tony's curly hair, usually so in-place with gel, is messy. He has a five o'clock shadow, and his shirt needs to be pressed. All this imperfection looks perfect to me, though. I didn't want to be alone tonight. And that's before I found out my stalker fled the coop.

He steps inside, looking around. "You alone?"

But I'm not ready to admit my fear to him. "Always the detective."

He raises both eyebrows but says nothing. "Where's your sister?"

He's checking me out. Do I have a red wine ring around my lips? "I don't know." My tongue is probably red.

"What do you mean?"

He's definitely staring at something. "I mean, I've texted her." *Aw, ¡Carajo!* I'm in yoga pants and a tank top and I'm not wearing a bra. I'm a big ole mess. "She's been gone since she got a call at the hospital. I'm really worried about her. What if Hoodie got to her?"

I'm holding onto the door for support, but it's not because I'm drunk. "I've tried calling and calling." I put my back on the now closed front door and cross my arms over my chest. I don't tell him that Izzy hates me. She could be avoiding me just to worry or piss me off.

"I'm sorry," he says.

"Me, too."

He walks into my kitchen, and I notice his hand is on his gun belt.

"You think he might be here?" I follow behind him.

He stops. Turns around. Takes his hand off the top of his gun and stares at me. "Habit. Sorry. Mind if I check the house out?"

"I'd appreciate it." I follow close behind as he does. Not taking a chance.

Finally, we're in the kitchen, house secured. He

puts his gun back into his holster and his shoulders drop.

Our eyes meet.

I smile, surprised by butterfly wings of nervousness. "Thank you for coming to check on me. I am a little—"

"I brought you something."

I pause. He's saving me from admitting my fear. Once again, I'm thankful for his actions. Is Tony the sign? I'm so wrapped in that thought I don't even see him move. But I feel him when he gets to me. He's got something in his hands.

It's a new azabache charm bracelet.

"It's been blessed by the local Babalawo. The one you went to visit."

That brings up my eyebrows. "Want to tell me why you brought me an azabache charm bracelet when you clearly are not a believer?"

"You don't know me as well as you think."

"Your mom sent it?"

He smiles.

I hold out my hand so he can slip the bracelet on me.

Static electricity jumps from his skin to mine with a sharp sting like a snapping band. I pull back, embarrassed.

"Let's try that again."

I laugh and let him anchor the bracelet on my wrist. It's beautiful. Looks to be real gold, with three charms, one a black gem like the charm on my old bracelet and two new ones. The first one is an evil eye charm, the eye blue with a black dot in the middle. The last charm, a black fist with a red charm at the bottom. "Thank you." All different versions of the same thing. Charms to ward off the evil eye. "I feel better with this on."

"I know you do."

"Especially now."

His fingers hesitate on the thin skin at the base of my wrist. "And that's what matters."

He must know how much this gesture means to me. He must know how glad I am he's with me here right now. I want to hug him—it's how we say thank you in the Cuban American community, and I wouldn't hesitate at all if it was anybody else. It's like Tony checking out my kitchen with his hand on his gun. It's habit. You hug and kiss those who bring you a gift. But I hesitate because…because he's not just anybody.

"You okay?"

¡Ay, Dios mío! Snap the hell out of it, Marisol. "Yes. I, well, I wanted to hug you to say thank you and—"

He pulls me into his arms, and I fold into him. Naturally. He smells good. Clean and masculine but without trying. I'm not even sure he has on aftershave.

I exhale again, and this time I feel his goodness fly into my soul. I hope all that goodness fills me up. I need it.

We stay like this—my face finding the crook of his neck, his arms securely around my waist, our breaths intermingling. We stay this way for a moment until he gently breaks our bond and says, "I wish we could—"

He doesn't finish. "Right. Right. I mean—" I swallow, unsure of what to say next.

Tony takes a step back.

The heat he leaves fills up the empty space. I want to tell him that I'm really scared. That Hoodie knows where I live, I'm sure.

"I need to show you something," he says.

"Another gift?"

He drops his gaze. "I'm hoping you can help." He pulls a picture out of his back pocket. "You're not the only person in danger. Time may be of the essence."

García, head of homicide, is confirming I'm in danger. I can't even respond. The words are lost in my suddenly parched throat.

He shoves a picture at me, and it hits me all at once. The blood. The savage way the words were finger-painted in a hurried message on the side of an ambulance.

"Read the message, Marisol."

My eyes are blurring. It's all the blood. I remember the smell of it stuck in my nose for days after Mamá's murder. Panic is rising like a flood. "How could this happen?"

This time it's Tony who has difficulty forming words. "We have a team looking for him. But my focus is on saving the next victim."

"Me?" I whisper.

His shoulders drop, but his hand doesn't waver. "Read the message. Por favor."

I read it out loud:

Look into the mirror,
A reflection you will see.
Look behind the cracks,
For the truth you must set free.

I am a guilty man,
And more broken girls will die.
You have a chance to save them.
Marisol, give it a try.

CHAPTER THIRTY-SEVEN

I can't draw in enough air. It's like an asthma attack. "Why is he screwing with me?" The room is blurring around the edges. "He's been dropping these clues, and now he's literally putting lives in my hands."

I hold the picture Tony brought. The picture of the message Edward Jones, aka Hoodie Hannibal, painted across the back window of the ambulance he escaped from. In Hanks's blood. With *my* name in it. He had to be the one leaving messages at my home. Makes sense now.

Tony places his hands around mine, stilling the shake in my fingers. "We need to find and save these broken girls."

I notice how red his eyes are, the lines creasing his forehead. "You believe these girls exist?" He's kind of a mess, too.

"Given the broken dolls left at the recent murders scenes?" He shrugs. "Regardless, it's my job to act like they do. I can't risk any more girls dying. Anyone dying. Including you."

"And my sister." My heart expands about one hundred inches at his words. "Any idea where to begin looking for these girls? I can't even find my own sister."

Tony shakes his head, his weary gaze locking with mine.

Now may be the time to tell him my theories. It's not like we have any other clues to follow right now. "Maybe I can help."

"How?"

"I've been brainstorming. Putting pieces together on a wall. Like you did at the department downtown. I know the clock is ticking, but if you have a few minutes—"

"Let's see it. You've got good instincts. I have patrol at Jones's house, but I have no other idea where Hoodie might go. So—"

You've got good instincts. Oddly, that response makes my heart skip a few beats. I grab my new charm and twist it three times to the left, three to the right. My heart rate is slowing. And I have two more charms if I need them.

But I don't.

I know what we have to do.

We have to save the broken girls.

"Follow me, Tony. I'd like to show you my war room."

CHAPTER THIRTY-EIGHT

Detective García stands in my Abuela Bonita's altar room. He's staring at the statue of Saint Barbara. Then his gaze moves to the cross, the candles, and finally the picture of Mamá. "Your mother?"

I nod, turning away before the dreaded lump jams my throat. "Barbara Álvarez."

"Of the rosary."

Not sure why he said that. Maybe he's simply trying to fill the silence.

I have this moment to persuade a veteran police officer that *my* working theory is a plausible one. But once he sees where I'm going with this murder wall, he's going to push back. He's going to try to convince me the killer is *his* main suspect, Edward Jones, the man he arrested. The man who apparently collected souvenirs from crime scenes. The man who is on the run. Hoodie is the logical solution. But, I know what it's like to believe something wholeheartedly...and be wrong.

And be crucified for it.

City Council Killer. Detective Hanks's words roll around in my head.

García exhales slowly and turns to face my murder wall. He strokes his chin, eyes narrowing as he scans the wall. It's quite a mess, my murder wall, much like me.

He's silent for a few more minutes. Finally, he says, "Walk me through your train of thought here. I'm a little, I don't know, confused?"

I love his honesty. Hate it, too. It makes me feel less of a perfect human.

I start at the beginning of my corridor of clues, at the picture of the first recent crime scene, Deputy Natasha Rodríguez's murder. I point to what I've posted on the wall, explaining why, all the way up to the big number six.

"At first I thought six was important because the original victim was six when the kid shot her. The deputy—shot six times, at six p.m. Six keeps showing up."

"Why did you write 'what if six references something else'?" he asks.

I'm not sure he's going to like the answer. "Promise you'll stay with me before passing judgment."

"I'm here, aren't I?"

I glance at the picture of Saint Barbara on Abuela's altar. "Six is the number associated with Chango."

He nods. He doesn't ask who Chango is, or why Chango has a number. He's Cuban American. He knows Chango is a mighty orisha in the Santería religion. He may not like it, he may not believe it, but he knows it. And he doesn't judge it.

"And what does this line lead to?" He drags his finger across the red marker and points to the picture of an anonymous person with one eye open and one eye shut. "What...who is this?"

"A picture from a magazine to illustrate the one

eye closed of Deputy Rodríguez. It's the crown on
the coin that's important."

"Chango wears a crown."

Not a question. *He's catching on.*

García walks next to a picture of red and white
beads, like the ones I saw at the first scene.
"Chango also wears red and white beads." He's
shaking his head, and I think I see a slight smile.

"Deputy Rodríguez's eldest daughter told me
the doll didn't belong to her or her sister. Did you
ever check if Edward Jones ordered dolls off
Amazon?"

"Hanks is working on that angle."

I pause and look at Tony but say nothing about
that. "The dolls, they're the killer's calling card.
Maybe they represent Chango, too."

He scrunches his eyebrows together.

"I'll get to why in a second." I inch closer to
him. "And the beads, I'm sure they represent
Chango. Red and white are his colors. I made the
connection, because they looked like the green and
yellow beads worn by the Babalawo I met the same
night."

"Okay, let's go to the Stop-N-Go." He stops in
front of the note I found in our home: *I'm back. I'm
watching you. You know why.* "Related?" Tony asks.

"Not sure yet." I lead him to the pictures of the
crime scene I got from the newspaper. "So, at the
Stop-N-Go, we have the graffiti on the wall with
another evil-eye reference. One eye open. One eye
shut. We have another spray-painted crown. We
also have another victim who got off without being
punished. Another doll at the scene...broken.

But"—my heart is fluttering. I can't believe how much I'm enjoying this. Maybe I've been in the wrong profession—"this is the key." I point to a picture I found online of a painting of Chango, my Santería Orisha, holding a lightning bolt like a weapon. "This new victim had a lightning bolt carved into his hand."

"Lighting is another symbol of Chango."

I nod.

Tony has his fingers on his chin, rubbing it. "The killer thinks he's Chango?"

He's not really asking me. He's thinking out loud. So I help him. "You call upon Chango when you need justice."

"The killer is seeking vengeance for all the broken girls."

Tony has followed my clues and come up with the same conclusion. And I'm not sure vengeance is such a bad thing in these cases, since I consider myself a broken girl.

But García's brand of justice is black and white. Nothing like Santería, with its good and bad intentions, and its orisha named Chango. "Thus the broken dolls left at each scene."

"Wow. I see the connection." García drags himself to a sticky post next to the picture of Hoodie Hannibal. He reads out loud what I wrote in all caps. "*How did he know first*? Jones? How did he know what?"

"I don't think Edward Jones is the killer but I can't figure out how he knew about the crime scene at the Stop-N-Go before you did."

Tony's shoulders rise. "We found a police

scanner in Jones's home. It's full of local first
responder frequencies."

"How did he—"

"I don't know how he got the scanner or the
frequencies. We're working on it. But he was a paid
crime writer and an unsolved-case junkie. Likely,
he spent his days listening to dispatch calls and 911
send outs."

I grab the red marker and X that question out.

"I still think Jones may be our man," García
says.

"I know you do."

"You did, too." He starts reading the list I wrote
after Abuela died—I pinned the list to the end of
my corridor of clues. He stops in front of number
three and reads it out loud. "*Three: Both crimes
witnessed, but killer still got away. HOW?*" He turns
to face me. Candlelight warms the angles in his
face, and the light flickers in his dark eyes. "Got a
theory?"

"I do. A source told me that an Uber driver
came by after the Stop-N-Go murder. I located the
driver and talked to him myself. The driver
reported a woman called for a ride. Remember, I
told you that."

"And I've had a chance to confirm that. What's
that got to do with Chango?"

"Chango is both a king and a queen."

Tony's shoulders drop. "You've lost me."

"Chango, the male orisha, is also Saint Barbara,
the female Catholic saint. He's both a king and a
queen. Cuban slaves gave their orishas the face of
Catholic Saints in order to practice their religion in

plain sight. Many Cubans still pray to both the male Chango and the female Saint Barbara today."

He doesn't respond, but I see realization slide across his face.

"Legend has it, Chango often escaped his enemies by dressing in woman's clothing." I pause to let that sink in. "So maybe the killer hid a bag of women's clothing in the woods near the Stop-N-Go. And maybe the killer had a change of clothes waiting for him at the first scene as well. Change out of the bloody black hoodie, reenter the scene and fit right in?"

His Adam's apple drops and rises. "You've been spending too many hours in this room." He blows out a candle. The one right in front of Saint Barbara. That's disrespectful, and he knows it.

I grab a lighter and relight it. "Chango is my orisha, too. The Babalawo I met told me to look to my orisha to find answers. All the clues point to my orisha. They point to Chango."

"Like. I. Said." He heads for the door.

I grab his wrist. "You don't have to be a believer like your own mother is. Just don't be a skeptic, until you hear me out."

He looks down at the intersection of our hands. I know he sees the azabache charm bracelet.

"Okay, as long as you also hear me out." He pulls out of my hold and walks to my messy murder wall. He doesn't break stride or speak a word. He points to number four on the list of questions I wrote. He reads, "*Hoodie Hannibal at both scenes. HOW TO PROVE BOTH WERE JONES?*" He flips to face me. "You saw Jones yourself at the first scene, right?"

I nod. "I did."

"He was at the second murder scene, too."

"You have proof?"

"Am I a homicide detective?"

I smile. I mean, that's so García. "And I'm a reporter. So I have to ask." I close my eyes. ¡Carajo! *Used* to be a reporter. My pride takes a direct hit. *Don't think about that. Don't think about that.* I reach for my azabache charm. *Six times.*

Tony clamps his hand over mine, putting a stop to my ritual. "You don't need that."

"Why did you give it to me?"

He lets go and steps back, his gaze still glued into mine. "We have Edward Jones's DNA on a can of soda from the Stop-N-Go scene."

The candle flames are dancing in his dark eyes.

"A homeless man pointed it out, for ten bucks and a cigarette."

I scoff. "A man down on his luck would probably do or say anything for ten bucks and a free cigarette."

"It tested out. Jones was there, Mari."

"But Jones is on the lam now, so you can't ask him why. Detective John Hanks was there, too," I mumble.

The energy in the room shifts.

I glance at Tony. The look of confusion on his face morphs into what looks much like rage. His body goes rigid. His fingers fist.

I wish I could press rewind.

"You think the killer is Detective John Hanks?" He says each word slowly and precisely. "A cop?"

"I do." I don't hesitate.

"An honored police man?"

"A vigilante killer with a safe platform from which to work. Where no one would suspect him."

García starts to laugh. It starts as a small chuckle under his breath, hot with disbelief, but it escalates into real disdain, bouncing off the walls until I shout, "Stop!"

The room falls quiet.

His eyes seem to darken. "Detective Hanks was at the police station with me the day of the Stop-N-Go murder." His clipped words reflect his attitude.

"What was the approximate time of death for the vic at The Stop-N-Go?"

"Six a.m." Tony's eyes widen as he answers. His jaw sets, and he drills me with a look that tells me I don't even have to say, *"There's the number six again."*

"Hanks would have had time to get there, kill the man, and get to work."

"Edward Jones would have had time to do the same," García says.

"Agreed." I shrug. "But Jones didn't do it."

"What other proof do you have it's Hanks?"

"The lightning bolt carved into the second victim's hand." I close my eyes. In my mind's eye, I see the lightning bolt on his baseball cap. "Hanks was wearing a hat with a lightning bolt on it the first time I met him."

"Maybe he's a hockey fan?"

"I asked him if he liked hockey. He said he's not a hockey fan, Tony. Lighting is another symbol of—"

"What else?"

"In Hanks's office, there was a picture of him with no shirt on. He has a tattoo on his shoulder of a double-edged hammer."

"I think it's a double-edged battle ax."

"Whatever! Both lightning and the double-edged ax are unusual weapons of Chango."

García snorts. "That's all you've got?"

"Do you know what cowrie shells are?"

"Santería again, right?"

"The shells are supposed to be a doorway to access your spirits. Some believe the magic comes from their resemblance to a half open eye. Did you notice Hanks was playing with them when we first went to his office?"

"I noticed he was tossing shells onto the table. Maybe in a nervous habit?"

"Maybe." I walk over to my abuela's altar. I grab four cowrie shells and show them to Tony. "Or maybe he is reading them. He asked, if you recall, maybe we can work together. He wasn't talking about you. You already work with him. He was talking about working with Orlando and me. He was asking Chango a question." I toss the shells onto the altar. "Then he threw the shells onto his desk. Remember?"

Tony nods. But is unusually still.

"All four shells landed face up." I point to the shells on abuela's altar. "Like this, with the open eye, so to speak, looking at him. That's a yes. It's the most blessed of responses."

Now he's shaking his head, and a strange sound comes out, a little like a laugh, more like he's ridiculing me. "You think Hanks decided to work with you—"

"And trust me, too."

"Based on the throw of four shells?"

"You're a homicide detective. Surely you've seen people do stranger things." When he doesn't react, I keep talking. "There was a picture of him on a beach in a town I recognize as being in Cuba. Playa Hermosa. What's his connection to Cuba? Do you know?" I don't mean it as a challenge—I truly want to know how much he knows about Hanks.

"I'm sure you do. Please, share."

He doesn't sound pissed or envious. Simply resigned. "His adoptive mom was Cuban American."

Tony's silent, his shoulders down.

"What if she taught him Santería? All the clues lead to his orisha being Chango. I know the signs because he's my orisha, too. Chango can be called on to seek both vengeance and justice."

I fill him in on Orlando's and my trip to visit Hanks's family. "Hanks may be seeking vengeance for his murdered mother and other victims of crimes unpunished. His motive is vigilante justice. When you can't get the killer the legal way, he finds another way. And his calling card: the broken dolls, Chango's crown, and the evil eye. He's seeking vengeance for all the girls the law didn't get justice for."

"And the evil eye?"

"I'm not sure yet. Maybe he's trying to open our eyes to justice not served? But Hanks believes in an eye for an eye. Think about it, Tony. Did Hanks *ask* to join the cold case unit? Or was he moved there for a reason?"

He shifts his weight and looks away. "If I remember correctly, he did ask. I mean, it's unusual to ask to leave homicide."

"He wanted access to old unsolved cases that have been pushed aside as new cases happen, along with the locker room where the evidence of those crimes is stored. He figures he'll fix what homicide can't solve."

García's gorgeous caramel skin has gone pale. His eyes look haunted, and he's rubbing them as if tired.

I think he's close to believing me, and it scares him. "I think Hanks is on to me being on to him."

"You're not afraid you'll be next?"

I smile at him. "You're here."

"I'm serious," he says, walking toward me. "I can't protect you 24/7. From either man."

I break first. Moving to him. "Can you see it?" I put my hands on his shoulders. "Please tell me you see it, too."

He removes my hands, but says, "I'm impressed with how you put all of this together."

I see in his eyes that his words are true. He's looking at me in a way he's never looked at me before, as if he's seeing me with a new appreciation.

A ringtone blares.

We both jump.

Not mine.

Tony grabs his phone off his belt hook, looks at the number, and groans. He turns away from me and answers it.

I exhale in disappointment. I liked the look of appreciation in his eyes.

"Got it. Text me the address."

An awful feeling chills me. "What?"

"Another murder scene."

"Related?"

"How could it be?" he asks.

"Couldn't it be?" I counter.

He turns back to me.

Will he shut me out now?

"Let's go see."

CHAPTER THIRTY-NINE

We arrive at the murder scene in record time. That's because Tony used lights and sirens on his unmarked car. I think he let me ride along because he feared leaving me alone in my house. Feared who might come try to find me. During the ride, Tony confirmed Hoodie was still missing, and Hanks checked himself out of the hospital after getting stitches.

We have no idea where either man is.

A thought rips through my head as quickly as the flash of lightning filling the sky, so close to Tony's car it's blinding. Do I really know where Raúl is, either?

I jump as thunder breaks so close, the windows in Tony's Ford Fusion rattle. I take a couple of deep breaths. Everything about this day has been *stormy*. Thunder and lightning bolts zipping to the ground hard, like they're being thrown by Zeus from the mountaintop. Or Chango, from the ground. The driving rain leaves pools of water on low-lying streets deep enough to form wakes when you drive through it.

The windshield wipers whip back and forth at Olympic speed. The sound is hypnotic. *Wish. Wash. Wish. Wash. Wish. Wash.* The wipers do little to let us see the road ahead of us.

I take advantage of the drive and our isolation to run another thought by him.

"Here's another thing I can't get out of my head."

"Not on the wall in your war room?"

"Not yet. My mother's rosary. Was it checked into evidence after her murder?" I feel him tense. Can't see it, cause it's dark. "It had to be. She was wearing it the night she died. I saw it on her."

Another flash of light. I hold my breath and count. One thousand one. One thousand two. One thousand—

The rolling crack of thunder rattles me further.

"I'd have to check," García says after the thunder dissipates.

"Because if admitted into evidence, Detective Hanks would have had access to it, right?"

An audible sigh. "Hanks is able to check out the evidence, but there are procedures. Security measures are in place. With cameras."

"Fine." *Doubt me if you must.* "Will you check it out, please, when you can. Maybe he planted it in Jones's house. He did find the shoebox."

Wish. Wash. Wish. Wash. Wish. Wash. The wipers are my only answer.

Tony pulls onto a street in Drew Park, an industrial area near Tampa International Airport. About six blocks of car shops, and low-income housing with laundromats and a few bottom-of-the-barrel strip clubs. Not the flashy ones on Dale Mabry that make all the news stories when events like the Super Bowl come to town. No, these clubs have parking lots hidden by well-placed landscaping so no one can see who's freaky enough to frequent these dives.

He pulls up to a gray building with a flashing

pink and gold sign. I'm too embarrassed to even read the name out loud. *The Pretty Pussy. ¡Ay, Dios mío!* Who would actually come to a place with a name like that? "What's the victim's name?"

He throws the car into park. "Brace yourself."

"For what?" The Pretty Pussy? With the power off, and windshield wipers falling silent, we get the full blast of rain beating the windows. I raise my voice. "I've been to a strip club before." Well, kind of of. Did a live shot outside of one once.

In the flash of light from above, I see Tony's arched eyebrow. But he isn't smiling. "But you've never seen a murder victim in a strip club before."

"True," I say. "So, who is it and how was this person killed?"

Tony is pulling one of those thin, plastic rain slickers out of the glove compartment. "Here." He hands it to me. "These places don't open up until after ten p.m. Late night crowd."

"I'm sure." I pull out the clear blob and struggle with trying to figure it out and put it on over my clothes in this confined space.

"When the manager came to work a couple hours ago"—Tony has taken out a second slicker and is fighting to find the opening—"he found the victim hanging from a stripper's pole."

"How is that possible?" I'm trying for a visual.

"There!" He's got the rain jacket on "We're about to find out. Ouch!"

"I'm coming in?"

"Don't you want to?"

"Of course, I just—" I'm not used to anyone letting a reporter enter a crime scene. "I just remember the last two crime scenes."

"There's an umbrella in the back. Grab it if you want. Not sure it will even help but—"

"I'm good. Let's make a run for it." I try to locate the door, but the rain is too thick to see through. *Great.*

"I'll tell them you are no longer a working reporter—"

Ouch!

"Now you're a consultant on these cases."

A consultant. Wow.

"Let me do the talking, okay."

"Oh yeah, I'm supposed to brace myself. You never said why."

"The victim—shit!" Tony's struggling to stuff his phone and keys into his pants pocket.

"Is...?" I've got my hand on the door handle. "Let's do this on the count of three."

"Pedro Viaga."

My body goes ice-cold.

Pedro Viaga is the city council member I accused of being a serial killer.

And now Pedro Viaga is dead.

CHAPTER FORTY

Inside *The Pretty Pussy,* the smell hits me first. Baby powder and dirty feet. Or something else I don't want to think about. My stomach turns as I see the body. Just like Tony said. Long and thin, like Pedro Viaga, but in silhouette, thanks to the obnoxiously bright pink neon lights on the wall behind the poles.

The body is broken at the neck.

This time not a broken girl.

A broken guy.

First sign this crime scene will be different.

"You okay?"

"I'm fine." Tony is standing at the entrance, me beside him. "I'm fine." *If being cursed is fine.* He's talking to a uniformed officer, with a clipboard and a list or something. The young cop takes down our names. "I saw the body." I turn away. No need to take everything in at once.

"Breathe." Tony's hand is on my back. "And if it becomes too much, step outside. Otherwise, stick with me. Okay?"

Like I'd leave your side. "Yes sir, Detective."

"García, that was fast." One of the women I met in homicide walks up to us. She's in a professional black suit, hair pulled back, facial features—all straight lines for business.

"What we got?" Tony asks her.

"Pedro Viaga, city council member, fancy strip club owner, apparently owns this shit hole, too. His club manager found him hanging by his own belt from the top of the biggest pole on the main stage."

The main attraction of his own shit show. Ironic.

"Any witnesses?" he asks Detective Smith, the one who helped me during the police line-up.

She shakes her head. "Club never opened it. Manager came in early—found his body. Still warm. About nine p.m."

When we were going over my murder wall. But where was—

"Hanks here?" Tony asks.

The air stalls in my lungs. *It's like we share the same brain.*

"No," Detective Smith says. "Why would he be? Wasn't he shot earlier?"

"Checked himself out. This case might be tied to a couple of his old cases."

"Haven't seen him." Detective Smith flicks a wary gaze my way. "What's with her being here?" She lowers her voice.

I'm standing right here.

"Isn't she the—"

I can't help myself. I finish for her. "Ex-reporter." I throw Tony a shoulder shrug.

He frowns but says, "She's consulting with me now."

"Consulting?"

I hear what the female detective isn't saying. *Didn't I do a lineup with you picking out a suspect in a homicide? Yep.* I feel like raising my hand. *That's me right here.* I stand taller. I'm not getting booted.

I'm not getting—

"If you've got a problem with Ms. Álvarez being here, you can go above my head as your supervisor and take it to the chief."

My heart stretches about a hundred miles. Because no one has ever defended me like Tony just did. If we weren't knee-deep in stinky strip club smell, wet from a monsoon, with all eyes on us from the working detective crew, I'd thank him.

"Got no problem." The detective smooths back a string of hair that's fallen out of her perfect bun. "I need her to check in like everyone else, so we know who's at the crime scene. Read her the rules, García."

"Yep."

After the formalities, he takes me to the center of the room and asks me to describe the scene. I prefer to not state the obvious. I see an empty strip club— except for the working forensic team minus Freddy. That's too bad. I see a dead man hanging from a pole center stage. So, instead, as I walk in a tight circle, looking at the room from every angle, I describe what's *not* here. "I don't see any broken dolls. No evil eye references. No beads. No spray-painted crown. Nothing so far to tie it to the other recent crime scenes." *Or Santería.*

"Except you," Tony says.

Way to make me shiver. "What do you mean?"

"Take a wider walk around the room."

He's standing right behind me. His breath is on my neck. And despite the room buzzing with forensic activity, flashing camera lights, a low hum of conversation, I'm focused on what's different.

"Tell me what stands out to you."

I don't want to disappoint him.

"Take your time."

So I stroll around the room. Weave around those working to document the scene and preserve evidence. I brush past the detective with the bun, who's eyeing me with suspicion. Can't say I blame her. What am I doing here? I'm not a detective.

Then I see it.

A dominoes table set up to the side of that big mirror with the flashing pink strobe lights that blink the name of the business I'll never forget. "Well, this is odd."

"What?" Tony walks my way.

"Don't imagine too many men come here to play dominoes." Five dominoes are in a straight line in the middle of the table. "There's only one seat. No dominoes in the holders. The rest of the dominoes are in the box. Doesn't look like they're set up to play a game."

"It's almost as if someone set up the dominoes in this pattern on purpose." Tony's voice vibrates with excitement.

For me. But I don't say it. I sit in the only chair around the table.

"What do you see now?" he asks, coming up behind me. I feel as if he's about to put his hands on my shoulders as reassurance, but the female detective clears her throat. He stops.

"I see the mirror on the wall. In front of it, the main room of the strip club."

"What's behind the mirror?" he asks.

"Good question." The room doesn't end with the

mirror. There's a side wall, maybe ten feet long, that meets the back wall of the building. "Maybe a storage room for brooms and mops and such."

"Maybe an office?" Tony asks.

"Maybe an exit?" Detective Smith chimes in.

"Does anyone know?" I ask, looking around for the man Tony ID'd as the manager. Didn't see him. "Can't be an exit," I say out loud, but really to myself. "There's no door. Can I touch it? The mirror or the wall?"

"Gloves." Tony hands them to me over my shoulder.

I put them on as I'm walking toward the mirror. I stand in front of it first, because I keep hearing a verse in my head. The poem Edward Jones allegedly left for me.

Look into the mirror.
A reflection you will see.

"If you look into the mirror, you do see your own reflection." I'm breathless when I see mine. Hair damp and blown up like a Brillo pad. Makeup smudged under my eyes. Lips naked, skin pale. I look more wet dog than TV star tonight. But I don't care. Because behind me, the body of Pedro Viaga is being lowered down from the pole. "You can also see what is going on behind you." I flip around. "And you have a front row seat to the show."

Front row seat.
To the show.

An idea is fertilizing. I turn back around and scan the wall-length mirror. "I don't see any cracks."

"I'll check, too," Tony says, walking the length of the mirror behind me. "You're thinking of the poem Jones left."

"I am." *Not a poem. A clue.*

He nods and continues in silence.

"Look behind the cracks. For the truth you must set free." I move to the side wall, at the end of the mirror. I can feel through the gloves, so I run my fingers about midway up, across the wood wall. Halfway across, my fingers sink into a cushiony part, like foam or something. Sweat breaks out of my forehead. There's a crack. A crack in the foam! I push my fingers through it to something hard and bumpy, like a panel. I grab my iPhone and turn on the flashlight.

Oh God. Oh God. Oh God.

Numbers like a telephone pad.

"Tony! Read me the number on the first domino. The one in the center of the table. The one you'd start the game with." It's all starting to make sense.

"Double nines."

"Of course it is. You always throw out the double nines first if you have them." I press 99. Exhale when nothing blows up or ignites.

"Not always. Only a beginner thinks that," Tony says.

I turn to look back at him. Even though cortisol is shooting through me like a drug, he makes me smile. "When this is all done, game on."

"You're on." He's smiling back.

For one second, I forget what the hell I'm doing. "Next domino."

"Double threes. What's with the doubles?"

I hit 33. "Maybe part of the message?" Abuela told me you always try to get rid of your doubles first because they're harder to play. Still no movement, no action. Nothing. "Next number?" If I remember right, there are five dominoes on the table.

"The six and the four. You found something?"

"A keypad." I think for a minute and press 64.

"You're kidding," Tony says.

"We need to take a picture of it." Detective Smith is staying close by. The hair on the back of my neck rises as she walks up on me. But I'm focused and not moving.

"Five." Tony says, "But it's a four and a one. Okay, we can do it after she's finished with—"

Finished with what? That's the big question. I press 41. "Last number?"

"Double ones."

I take a deep breath, silently say a prayer to Chango that he's guiding my fingers, and I'm doing this right. I press 11.

Nothing.

My shoulders drop. Maybe I need to add the numbers. Maybe double nines should be 18?

Click.

It sounds like a lock unlocking. Another *click* and the wall moves back, contracting into the area behind the mirror.

All by itself.

I'm assaulted by a stench stronger than baby powder and stinky body parts. The scent of human waste attacks my nose, so I cover the bottom part of my face with my free hand. The room is dark. I hear movement. And mumbling. Zombie-like sounds.

I hit my flashlight app again and move it toward the room.

A scream. *¡Ay, Dios mío!* It's my own.

Three girls are chained to the wall.

Chained. To. The. Wall.

Two are slumped down and over. *Dead?* But the third is standing up, straining against the bonds that hold her. Her eyes are as wide as windows and her mouth is gaping. She appears to be screaming, too, but nothing is coming out. Her skin is ghastly white, dark hair matted like an animal's. It looks as if she's been stripped of almost everything that makes her human.

"I found you!" I'm yelling. But I'm not stepping into this shithole dungeon, should the door shut behind me, trapping me, too. "You're okay! You're okay!"

This is what I was supposed to do. I suck in air and with it, gratitude.

"Tony!"

But he's already right beside me.

"I've found more than broken girls. I've found witnesses."

CHAPTER FORTY-ONE

Firefighters freed the three young women in two hours. Paramedics tended to their most urgent medical needs and during all that, Tony and Detective Smith interviewed the girls.

Are there more girls trapped? Who brought them here? Did they see the murder?

Details rush out of that dungeon-like room, flying free like a flock of rabid bats.

I'm sitting in an ambulance outside the strip club talking with Lauren, the one awake when I opened the door to that soundproof, vile prison. A paramedic is starting an IV, so I jumped in to distract her and to take advantage of a few moments away from prying detective eyes and roaming news cameras. Ones that may not approve of my impromptu interview. But hey, I saved this girl's life, and I am not pressuring her to answer questions.

From Lauren, I learn City Council member Pedro Viaga trafficked girls for the sex trade and used this shithole to hide and train his newbies. They'd watch from the room, chained to the wall, drugged each day until they became complacent and cooperative. They'd practice at *The Pretty Pussy* until Viaga's team deemed them…perfect. If they didn't pass, they died here. Lauren counted two since she'd arrived weeks ago. The girls would pass out or pass away and be dragged from the room after meals and injections. She had no idea what happened to them after that.

So I was right when I accused Viaga of being a serial killer, even if he's not what you typically think of as one. I wish I could gloat, but there's simply nothing good about any of this.

If they survived, Viaga told them he'd move them, once cleaned up and groomed, to his high-end strip clubs in Downtown Tampa and on Dale Mabry. There, they could actually earn a wage and live outside of chains. But only once drug addicted and dependent on him for survival.

"Well, brave girl," I say to Lauren, "Viaga's high-priced, highly-placed attorneys can't save him now."

She continues speaking about the horrors she'd endured after drinking something spiked at a low-end club on Nebraska Avenue and waking up here.

I hold her hand for comfort and keep her looking at me while the paramedic works, but my mind is already drifting. The cops are so focused on the lives saved, they're missing a big point. Someone killed Pedro Viaga, the city councilman, the same way he killed. After his body had been taken down and the medical examiner got on scene, she found needle marks on Viaga's arm. But only a couple, indicating he wasn't an addict. More likely shot up to OD before he'd been strung up. Another eye-for-an-eye kill. Even if the other commonalities aren't there, I think the same serial killer committed this crime and dropped different clues meant for me, like the dominoes.

The poem on the ambulance pretty much assures

Hoodie Hannibal did it, right?

Can't rule out Sebastián Figueroa, especially if Pedro did something to piss off the West Tampa Kings. Maybe his thugs drugged a gang member's girl? Or encroached on their territory? The Kings were known to run a few low-end strip clubs.

I glance out the back windows of the ambulance. It's still storming. When I left the building, Hanks still hadn't shown up, despite Tony texting and calling him. I'm not sure if Tony wanted Hanks here because of potential tics to cold cases, or to question him about my theory.

The guy is recovering from a bullet plowing through him. Can pretty much rule out Detective Hanks. I think.

My phone *dings*.

I'm so deep in my head, I jump.

"You okay?" This mistreated young victim is worried about me?

"Yes." I want to hug her. "Yes."

My phone *dings* again. "A text is coming in."

You said I could always call if I need help.

"Izzy!" I haven't heard from her since the hospital when Abuela died. *Oh God, was that only yesterday?* It seems like a lifetime ago. "Where are you?" I say aloud as I text.

Izzy: *Come alone. I repeat, come alone.*

My body buckles as it becomes clear. "Someone's watching her."

"Who?" Lauren asks.

"My sister."

"Wha— ouch!" Lauren cries out as a needle is inserted into her vein. "It burns."

"I'm sorry." I squeeze her hand with my free hand. I text Izzy back using only my thumb: *Text me an address.*

She does.

My hand covers my mouth to keep a gasp from exiting, because I don't want to upset Lauren. The address Izzy texted me is an address I've been to before. It's the same place found on the last note left at our home. *You didn't meet me at El Reloj.*

I have a good idea what's going down.

I've got to get there.

I call for an Uber, which gives me time to send off another text. I forward the address with a few requests. *Will he do it?*

I'm not going to tell Tony. Not yet. He's busy, and he'll try to stop me. He'll send cops there. And that could be bad for Izzy.

"What happens next?" Lauren asks me, the color returning to her cheeks finally.

"Can you go home?" I ask.

"I ran away because…" She looks away.

I don't press. "Foster care."

Her shoulders shake, but she's biting back sound, only squeaking every few inhales.

I do the only thing I can think of because I have to go rescue another broken girl—my sister. Using a pen I found in the ambulance, I write my number on the inside of her palm. Hard to do because her hand is shaking. "I've got to go. But I'm here if you need me. Just call."

I don't look back as I jump out of the ambulance. I'm afraid if I see Lauren's face, I won't leave. But I'm taking my sister's text seriously.

Rain still beats the pavement. Lightning streaks across the night sky, reaching out like fingers of warning. *Stay inside. Don't go anywhere. Beware.*

When my Uber driver pulls up, I check to make sure it's not Hanks driving. *Paranoia will destroy you.* It's a normal looking forty-year-old American dude probably driving as his second job.

Ding. Another text from Izzy: *Hurry!*

I jump into the Uber, skip introductions since he already knows my name and where I want to go. "Hit the gas. I'm in a hurry. It's a matter of life and death."

CHAPTER FORTY-TWO

We pull up to La Chimenea, the one-hundred-ten-year-old brick cigar factory in Ybor City's National Historic District. The famous factory is known for its tall smokestack, so grand it can be seen by all driving in or out of Tampa on Florida's infamous Interstate 4. It's also famous for the giant clock inside called El Reloj.

I've covered stories here related to their well-known brand of cigars rolled with Cuban-grown tobacco.

I visited this factory for different reasons, too.

The one that matters the most today: it's owned by Andreas Santiago's family. My mamá's ex-lover grew up in a wealthy, renowned bloodline with suspected ties to the Cuban Mafia.

Although updated many times, the building aged. It looks spooky in the early morning darkness, with lightning flashing, casting a glow on shiny, cobbled streets. Heavy rain falls, a shroud between me and my destination.

"Sure you want to get out here?" the Uber driver asks.

I don't even answer. I jump out and run like hell, thankful for the flat shoes I'd slipped on as I left my house earlier. Abuela's slippers would have landed me flat on my ass in the wet street.

The thunderstorm, and the early morning hour, keeps people in their homes. My mad dash across the neighborhood street doesn't require any dodging of traffic or people. I do feel a little like a movie heroine in an Alfred Hitchcock thriller, as I splash through the puddles on the cobblestones. I hold the stupidly small umbrella I grabbed from Tony's car over my head, fighting the wind to keep it from flipping wrong side out. I'm using it mostly to keep the rain from beating at my eyes, so I can see my way to the factory.

I'm wet right down to my underwear, so when I first grab the handle of the large, metal factory door, my fingers slip off. The handle snaps back, and I catch the tip of my finger in it. "Coño!" I yell.

Just what I need. A bloody finger.

The door opens.

Someone has opened it from the inside?

I struggle to bring the umbrella down and push the door the rest of the way open with the strength I have left at this hour.

The air contracts around me.

Crack. Another zap of light close by, followed almost immediately by a loud, train-like rumble. I rush through the door.

Thud. It slams shut. I jerk around, shocked at how quickly I've been closed in. That was the wind, right?

The lights in the lobby are off, but I feel for the door handle and tug on it. It doesn't move. But my pulse does. I pull harder, fingers rushing over the metal until I find the lock and twist it. Hard. So hard, I lose my breath. It doesn't budge. Neither does the door. I kick it and instantly regret it. Should I call out to Izzy?

¡Carajo! Is this a trap?

Would my sister do this to me? No. No. She wouldn't. We're not close right now, but we are blood.

I fire off another text, typing quickly as my battery is dying.

Boom.

The door rattles with the thunderous sound but doesn't open.

"You're going to cut the top of the leaves and the bottom."

A voice.

"In a curve, like this."

Light at the top of a staircase. Should I use what battery I have left to shine a path to the bottom?

Ding.

My phone goes off again. I read the text. Stop to text back: *It's locked.*

Try the back employee entrance. Hurry.

I'm about to type, *I'm scared*, when my phone shuts off. *Arggh.* I stomp my foot, but it doesn't land on the floor. It slips off something thin and round and—

A high-pierced shriek followed by raw agony as claws rip down my left leg. "Ahhhhh!" I spring forward, despite the dark, and stop when my body connects with the wood railing of the staircase, which knocks the air out of me.

A hiss, and the sound of paws scurrying away.

A cat. A damn cat scratched me. Probably a black cat, too. *I'm not superstitious. I'm not superstitious.* I have to say it six times. I reach for my charm, but stop, disgusted with myself. I hope that cat wasn't diseased because blood is dripping down my calf.

"Cut between the veins."

What the hell?

"A little glue on the top."

I start up the stairs, toward the voice explaining how to make a cigar from scratch. My fingers climb the banister. Its smooth and cool, unlike my skin which is on fire. As are my nerves.

"Round, round. You're not doing it right!"

Is someone actually working at this hour? Rolling cigars? In the early morning? I count the steps as I climb—to focus on something other than my fear—because I recognize that voice. I know who's waiting upstairs, but I have no idea what he wants from me. Or my sister. Or who else is there.

I hit a step. It hisses like that angry cat.

I stop. Wait. A single drop of sweat slides down my forehead into my eye. I blink, afraid to move.

"Marisol Álvarez," the voice from upstairs says. "I know it's you."

What's the use of trying to be quiet? I'm a fly caught in sticky paper. I have to see if my sister is up there on the third floor, where the manual cigar rolling takes place. Usually during *normal* business hours. I continue to climb.

"Marisol, how many more steps will it take till you come to me? Shall I count with you?"

His voice is the same and yet different. The same cocky edge, but with this inhumane quality. Too calm, which makes him sound crazy, given the circumstances.

"One. Two." His voice follows my footsteps. "Three. Four…Five."

I don't know how he's doing it—I'm varying my speed trying to throw him off.

"Six. Seven. Eight-Nine. Oh my, you are excited to see me."

"Mari!" Izzy's voice!

"Shut up!"

The light from above bleeds down the stairway. I can finally see. I dart up the stairs, two at a time.

All goes dark.

My foot slips.

I grab the banister.

Bastard flipped off the lights.

"Mari! Watch out." Izzy is warning me. "He's got a gun!"

It goes off.

CHAPTER FORTY-THREE

The clock inside El Reloj chimes. I stand on the winding staircase and count the strikes. *Two. Three. Four.*

I don't feel pain. Just blood flowing down my calf. He didn't shoot me. Who did he shoot? Maybe it wasn't a gunshot. Just the damn clock.

Five.

Or maybe not.

Six.

Six chimes. It's six a.m. *Damn.*

"It's our time, Marisol." The man laughs, but it came out more like a crazed cackle. And sounds as if he was not only fine with it, but enjoying it.

In the midst of all this crazy, I resort to simplicity and common sense. "Turn on the lights so I can walk up the stairs and see what it is you want me to see."

The lights flicker. The staircase falls dark again. Full lighting blasts me, like after last call, when the bar manager blinds you with the reminder it's time to go home.

It takes a few seconds before I can see. I blink, hoping to wet my dry eyes, dry, despite the hurricane-volume of rain soaked into my skin. "Thank you."

I walk up the stairs, tired by the drama of all this, scared by what I might see when I enter the room, terrified by what I think is my little sister whimpering.

A door slams below me.

I halt. Wait for the lights to shut off again. They don't.

"Marisol?" The way he says my name makes me want to crawl back down the stairs and hide. "Was that you?"

I don't answer. Is it better to leave him guessing?

"You wouldn't leave your baby sister?"

Another pop. This time I know it's a gun firing.

"Stop!" I yell and sprint up the rest of the stairs like I'm at the Olympic trials.

In the room, finally, I come to a full stop. My gaze scans the room for Izzy.

She's tied to a chair in front of a cigar roller's wooden desk. Her hands are free, but her feet have been bound. Her always perfect hair is a tousled mess.

She's trembling, her body shaking so violently the legs of her chair chatter like teeth against the hardwood floor.

She's also crying, tears falling from her cheeks onto her lap.

"Izzy. Izzy. Izzy." I run to her, fall on my knees, and cover her trembling body with my own. "I'm so sorry." I squeeze her and wish she would hug me back. But her body is hard, like a statue. A cold, lifeless piece of art.

"Marisol, Marisol. What a martyr you are."

I look up.

The man sits in a chair like Izzy's, but up higher on a wood plank, just like the old Ybor City *lectors*

used to do. Of course, he'd see himself as the
storyteller—the one who sat above the common
cigar roller, weaving tales to entertain them while
they work. He has on black pants, a black hoodie,
pulled up over his head to cover his hair. A sling
over his right shoulder holds up his left arm, which
must be the arm the bullet went through. In his free
hand he has a newspaper. Oh, and he's wearing a
Batman mask. "Well look at you. If it isn't the Dark
Avenger." He's fucking nuts.

"I knew if I convinced your sister to join me,
you'd follow."

I snort. "Ingenious of you, Caped Crusader."

"What the fuck is going on here, man?"

My gaze darts toward the new voice, and my
heart turns to a lump of ice.

Andreas Santiago sits at another cigar roller's
desk a row back, to our left side. His feet are also
tied to chair legs. He's aged, and not nicely. His
hairline is receding to the point he should shave it
off like Pitbull. His belly protrudes, touching the
table. His jowls sag, and his nose and eyes have the
broken blood vessels of a man who drinks for a
living. I should be happy to see his fall. But all I see
when I look at him is the arrogant trust-fund baby
who stole my mother's heart. The narcissistic
playboy who seduced her with sex her hard-working,
tired husband couldn't deliver. The married husband
and father who destroyed my family and got away
with it.

The man I've wanted to see dead for about ten
years.

The lector's gaze heats me. He's staring at me,

waiting for me to react. "This is why you've summoned me here. To be forced into the same room with this—this—" I can't say murderer. Because now, I don't know. Maybe the West Tampa Kings did have something to do with my mother's murder. I never did see the license plate on the car to prove it was Santiago's. And even if he had been outside watching our house, it didn't mean he necessarily killed her. But he wouldn't have let anyone else kill her, either. So many questions still. And I know who probably has the answers.

The silence in the room is deafening.

Fine. I'll give him what he wants.

"Dígame, lector," I say. "¿Cómo termina la historia? Tell me, storyteller. How does this story end?"

CHAPTER FORTY-FOUR

"Please take a seat, and I will begin." Detective John Hanks, shooting survivor, now disguised as both a comic book hero and a historic figure in the Cuban American culture, sits on his wooden chair perched on a thick board, feet above us. Looking down at his three-person audience.

I sit at the cigar rolling desk closest to Izzy, staging myself between her and Santiago. *Just in case.*

"I will begin with a brief history of the importance of the lector to our ancestors," Hanks says.

He's gone insane.

"The lector read from sources selected by the cigar factory workers, usually from Cuban American newspapers. But some liked classic literature like *Don Quixote* or *The Count of Monte Cristo.*"

Or he had always been crazy.

"My story tonight will be different. Personal to those in attendance. If it is well received, you can rap your cutter on the desktop as a form of applause."

"What the fuck?" Santiago says.

"As our ancestors did," Hanks says.

¡Ay, Dios mío! I can't hold it in anymore. He's not even Cuban. "Get to the point, please. Why am *I* here?"

He ignores me and continues his *story*.

But I zone out. He's enticed me here by hanging the carrot of my sister in front of me. When I get here, he stabs me in my most sensitive spot by making our meeting at the historical palace owned by the untouchable family of the man I've spent ten years despising. He's pushing my buttons to see how far I'll go. Heat slaps my cheeks and irritation throbs at my temples. I interrupt his weird performance again. "What do you want?"

He puts down the newspaper he's holding in his free hand. "You're on to me."

I sit back. I didn't expect his honesty.

He leans forward in the chair, glaring right at me. Even through the mask, I see the fire in his eyes. Feel the heat of his anger. "I can't have you ruining what I've spent my entire adult life building."

I swallow. Maybe I should shut up. "And what is that?" But of course, I don't.

"The perfect way to seek justice for those victims the system failed."

And there it is. *Motive.* "What's with the mask?"

He chuckles and the sound bounces off the walls in the otherwise empty room. "Right now, you are the only one in the room who knows who I am."

My breath catches—there's still a chance to save Izzy. She's biting her bottom lip, staying quiet. But the fear is sizzling in her stare. It's palpable.

"Would you like me to take it off? Seal her fate?"

"No. Let my sister go." My heart is sliced like these precious leaves of tobacco. "She served her purpose. She got me here."

Izzy squeaks, "I'm sorry, Mari." She's been whimpering this whole time, but now her voice fills the space all the way up to the high ceiling. "I'm so sorry. I shouldn't have come here. But I thought I was meeting someone else. Someone—"

She doesn't finish, but I know who she thought she was meeting. The gangbanger. I thought he was in Cuba, based on what I saw in that brief call at his mother's. But I can't imagine anyone else, haven't seen anyone else, have that kind of pull over my sister. "It's okay, Izzy." My stomach is sick with her pain. Is it possible Raúl is in Tampa? Why would he lure her here, too?

"We're going to die, aren't we?" Sweat beads on her forehead. Her fingers nervously play with the rounded cutter that could easily take off a finger.

I reach out to her. "Put that down."

"Oh my God, we're going to die." She twirls the cutter. "You, me, Abuela, we'll all die the same day."

"Stop!" I issue an order, not bothering to tell her it's a new day already. "Put that down!"

She does, a look of fright directed at me this time. I take a few deep breaths. Calm settles over me. It's on me to soothe my sister and take control of this situation. If we're going to survive this night, this morning, if I'm going to save Izzy, it will take my brains, my will, and my faith.

I turn and look up. Right at him.

He's kicked back in the chair watching our little scene, smiling, I think, under that ridiculous mask.

He doesn't look like he's in pain. Maybe he's high on pain meds, which might explain why he's acting so differently. So would mental illness.

"I think I know why you are wearing a Batman mask." Estás loco. You *are* crazy. "Bruce Wayne's parents were murdered, as was your mother."

"And yours, too. We have much in common, Marisol."

I wish he'd stop using my full name. Makes the hair all over my body stand. "We do. It's how I connected the dots." The giant lightning bolt on his cap that had nothing to do with our local hockey team. His using the words ashe and understanding what the spiritual energy is. Throwing cowrie shells and looking for answers from the way they fall. These are all actions of someone who knows and practices Santería.

A family picture on a beach in Cuba. The tattoo of a double-headed ax. All signs of a man who is the child of the orisha Chango—my orisha—the orisha representing dancing and drumming, but also lightning and fire, and most importantly, justice and vengeance.

Hanks was at the first murder scene, even though his department handles cold cases, not current ones. He could have been at the second scene, too, much earlier than when we arrived. He has access to evidence, and he was in the ambulance with Hoodie. The only thing I don't know is what went down in that ambulance or how Hanks ended up surviving a battle over his own gun, but my gut tells me Hanks orchestrated Hoodie's escape. For his own benefit.

And if I play it right, if I survive, maybe I can get the details out of him. I have to try.

We may share a common desire: justice for our mother's murder. His life paralleling mine. Except, I've been working on the light side—Hanks in the dark, propelled by evil, dressed up—no, masked—in righteous, good intentions. "The crazy thing is, I understand your motivation. If not for you, Hanks, I never would have saved those three girls. The poem you left, you wanted me to find those girls, didn't you?"

"See how smart you are, Marisol? You knew it was me who wrote those words in blood. My own blood. I took a bullet for you. To get here and give us this chance. After I shot the paramedic dead, I gave Edward Jones an ultimatum to shoot me in the fleshy part of my arm or I'd kill you. I kept ahold of the gun, but he didn't hesitate. Then I shot the driver, and the ambulance went off the road in a rural area, giving me time to execute my plan."

"What plan?" I'm so riveted by his words and his cojones to pull that off, I can't even move.

"Ah, I've got you." He stands and walks toward the ladder next to his platform. "But you actually got me, first. You clued me in to the heinous crimes Pedro Viaga and his thugs were carrying out." The wood creaks as he steps. "They had a system perfected." He descends the stairs, never taking his gaze off me, his descent slow and deliberate because he can only use one hand to brace himself. "He'd drug the girls, have his goons kidnap them, take them to that hell on Earth, break their spirits and their will, and enslave them."

It's like we're now the only two people in the room.

"I would have never known about those girls being abused." He hits the bottom and walks toward me. "If you hadn't had the courage to speak out." He grunts and grabs for his shoulder. But pain clearly doesn't stop his advance.

"My City Council Killer story got my station sued and me fired."

As he gets closer, I see the outline of his gun tucked under his hoodie, worn on a strap, bracing it to the side of his belt.

Distract him by stroking that big ego. "But you pointed me toward redemption for both myself and for them."

He nods, in total agreement with his awesomeness. "Now you're beginning to feel it, the power of delivering justice to those who deserve it. The ability to seek vengeance against criminals who escape the law."

"Does it matter how justice is served if it's deserved?"

He cocks his head. "Are you asking me?"

"The Babalawo from Playa Hermosa asked me that."

"From Playa Hermosa?" He stops.

"Yes." We're silent for a moment. The only noise is my sister whimpering and Santiago shuffling his feet, surely in disgust, because he's so above any of this. I ask, "What does any of this have to do with Izzy or even Santiago?"

"I needed to get you alone, and there are two things most important to you—your family." He walks up to Izzy, lifting her chin. "Izzy is all you have left."

She jerks her chin out of his hold.

He grabs it again. "I'm sorry." This time with more force. "And revenge." He drops his hold on my sister and pivots toward Santiago's desk. "For the past ten years, you've wanted to see this man get what's due to him."

"Actually, I've wanted to see him dead." *Can't believe I let that truth out. I didn't even hesitate. Damn.*

"I knew you'd come." He walks toward my desk. "The other murder scene"—he waves a hand like that strip club revelation was a minor development—"it not only served my need to deliver justice, it also served your need to redeem yourself in your profession."

"And my mind."

"And it's a distraction that should keep Detective García and his team diverted."

I didn't think of that. *Brilliant.*

Hanks is right in front of me now. Towering over me, smelling of sweat, arousal, and tobacco. "Unless you told Detective García you were coming here?" Even with his arm in a sling, he's intimidating.

"I didn't." *I did tell someone else, though.*

"I didn't think you would. He would have stopped you. Or made you come with the SWAT Team. And if you had, we'd hear sirens by now."

He carefully squats so we're eye level. He wants to touch me—I sense the rising energy.

"If García and his team show up, I have a plan. I am, if nothing else, prepared. As you know, Marisol." His hand finds my knee. Maybe to balance himself but also, I think, to creep me out. His fingers are hot, even through the cotton material of my slacks. "So here it is."

"What?" I ask, tempted to brush his hand away. But I don't.

"The turning point." He squeezes my right knee till it's uncomfortable.

"What does that even mean?" I ask, taking deeper breaths now, trying to control my rising anxiety.

"What are we going to do now, Marisol?" He pushes off my knee to stand, rising to his full potential. "Now that you know. Now that I know, you know. How will this story end?"

I look up at him. "You're the storyteller."

His eyes blaze like two demonic windows to his damaged soul. "Here's how I'm writing it. One" —he holds up a long, thin finger—"I kill Santiago. He knows too much."

I glance at my enemy. He's fidgeting in his chair, but still in control, shooting *fuck you* bullets at Hanks with the confidence of a person raised with mafia support behind him.

"You can watch."

I smile at Santiago, but he refuses to look at me.

"Get the thrill of watching justice served. Live."

When he goes silent, I look back at Hanks.

"Reporting live from Ybor City, Marisol Álvarez."

He's mocking me. In this moment, I'm angry enough to kill him, too.

"This is fucking bullshit." Looks like Santiago wants to off Hanks, as well. "My family will know shit is fucked up," Santiago bellows. "They'll come looking for me as soon as the sun comes up, and my wife wakes up."

His reference to his wife brings a wave of old disgust rushing through me.

"My family will hunt you down and kill you like the fucking piece of shit you are. They will not rest until—"

"Shut up!" I can't even let Santiago finish his rant. His egotistical voice makes me grind my teeth.

"Next," Hanks continues, "I will kill your sister."

I stop breathing.

"She also knows too much."

I twist to face him.

"I can't take the chance you shared your suspicions about me."

I bolt out of the chair and face him down, even though I only reach his shoulder. It's an act of defiance. And he knows it. "She knows nothing. We aren't even close."

"She knows now." He shakes his head, mask and all. "And then"—he reaches down and slides a heated fingertip over my cheek—"I will kill you. And with you, goes all the suspicion."

If I punch him hard in his injured arm will he go down?

"Mr. Edward Jones, by the way, is already in the building. His dead body will burn, too, and with this fire goes all the proof of my involvement. As an added benefit, the next murders I commit will be blamed on Mr. Jones, who everyone will assume is still alive and killing."

"What if they find his bones, you fucking idiot." Santiago's words roll like boiling water. "Bones are some of the most resilient parts of the body and burn at higher temps than the rest of the body. Normal fires don't reach temps high enough to burn the evidence."

"Interesting that you would know that, Mr. Mafia."

Hanks says exactly what I'm thinking.

"This will be no normal fire. It will be spectacular!" Hanks throws out his good arm. "I'm burning this mother fucking palace down."

If I tackle him, can he still reach for his gun? "But if they do find them?"

"Then I, as a well-respected detective, will lead my colleagues to believe Mr. Jones killed the object of his obsession, her sister, and the man who happened to be at the factory—the owner. Then set off explosives and killed himself by shooting himself in the head. Dying in a blaze of glory. That's a narcissist killer's dream, don't you think, Marisol?"

With his one finger, he pushes my chin, making my head turn to one side.

I right myself and think about the murder wall I've built. I pray Tony gets back to it before Hanks has the chance to destroy it because there will be no one left to protect our home or anything in it.

He leans down. His breath tickles my ear. "Unless you have another ending in mind?"

My heart jumps to my throat. Blood pounds at my temples.

"Perhaps you like this way of seeking justice, too?" He steps back now.

I don't give him the satisfaction of looking away.

"How did it feel when you let those angels out of their living hell? How did it feel when you realized they're alive because *you* saved them?"

"We're not Gods," I whisper.

He nods. "But it's no coincidence we share an orisha. You could be my second set of eyes—investigate or do things I can't because of the badge."

His free hand is on my left shoulder.

"We could right wrongs."

My skin is going numb where he's pressing into my flesh.

"Chango and Saint Barbara. As one." He squeezes me until my nerves react with a jolt of pain.

"A king and a queen." I need to stall him. Get him to confess more.

"Yes!" He pulls me to him. "We share a belief in justice and revenge."

My face is in his chest, the rough texture of the sling pressing into my cheek. I can't stand the smell of his body.

"We could share a future."

I push away, unable to stand the closeness anymore. I see it now, even with his mask still on. The unease that assailed me when I'd see what I thought was fire in his eyes. It was the crazy. He's both the good boy who loved an adopted mom because she showed him love and compassion. But he is also a narcissistic killer who fancies himself a superhero, saving those broken and betrayed. There's such a blurred line between justice and revenge. It strikes me that in the beginning I wanted justice for the daughters of Deputy Rodríguez. But I wondered if it was Thomas Figueroa or his son who shot the deputy, and wouldn't their reason be the same? Justice for their murdered loved one. And Hanks seeking justice for his mother's death by killing the person who ran over her. When does one person's hunger for justice become the next person's trauma and spawn a new hunger for justice. When and where does it all end?

It also hits me with full power. It matters *how* justice is served, even if you can prove someone is guilty. Because, as Mamá taught me so many years ago, un error no se remedia con otro. One error doesn't remedy another error. "Taking an eye for an eye just makes the world blind."

Hanks unzips his hoodie and unsecures his gun. "Let's start with Santiago."

My skin starts to tingle, and I see stars, like right before you pass out. And I wonder, if I slam a chair into that arm will it be enough to make him drop his gun. I hold my breath. Can't take the risk.

"Don't shoot him," Izzy yells. "He didn't kill our mother."

I flip to face her, ten years' worth of wonder rising into the back of my throat. "How do you know?"

"Because I know who did."

CHAPTER FORTY-FIVE

"I didn't do it," Izzy says, her hands up.

The room is hazy; angst induced fog clouds my view.

"You *know* I didn't." Izzy's voice is tight. "I was sitting right next to you when Mamá got shot."

I close my eyes and I can see us doing homework in ignorant bliss. "But you know who pulled the trigger." Only one of us was ignorant that night. My voice sounds strange. I don't like it. I don't like where my thoughts are traveling, either.

"Raúl did it," Izzy whispers.

Fireworks ignite in my head. "You mean that loser gangbanger killed our mother?" My voice is rising. "Why?" But I know why.

"You know how much Mamá and Papi disliked Raúl," she says, leaning away from me as I fast approach. "She made me break up with him. You were there."

In fast motion, I run through that horrible night again. "When I see you again, I will be a different man," I mumble. "That's what he said, Izzy. That night in your bedroom, he said he'd be a different man the next time he saw Mamá. Not a better man. Just a different man." Now, I'm putting the missing pieces of the puzzle in place. "Raúl was a coward the last time I saw him, jumping out of your bedroom

window to avoid Papi's wrath, and to avoid the con-
sequences of his actions." I shake my head, seeing
my baby sister differently. "I actually applauded him
that night, thinking he was a smart man doing the
right thing. For you. Because he loved you. But by
'different man' he didn't mean better, did he? He
meant stronger. Better prepared. He meant the next
time he saw Mamá, he'd be a killer."

Izzy's gorgeous caramel skin blanches.

"When he saw her again, he was going to make
her pay."

"He was…was…he was angry." Izzy's words
stumble out of her mouth. "He thought if Mamá was
out of the way—"

"You let me think his own gang had killed him
for turning informant."

"Mari, I—"

"But the whole time he's been hiding in Cuba?"

"He couldn't take the chance that—"

"That what? He'd be punished for killing
someone? Do you even hear yourself?" The more
Izzy says, the more my control wobbles. "He shot
our mother, Izzy!" I'm towering over her. "Our
mother!" Thinking maybe I could strangle her.

She shrinks into her seat, quiet.

The whole room is quiet for a moment.

I hear a click.

Hanks turns toward a half open door at the back
of the big room.

I do, too. But only for a second. My focus is
quickly drawn back to my liar sister. "You let your
stupid boyfriend kill our mother."

"I didn't think he actually had a gun." Her voice

is now calm. Resigned.

"He was a member of the West Tampa Kings!" I'm seeing various layers of red, as if I'm on acid. "Of course he had a damn gun."

Izzy keeps talking, but her words blend into white noise. I remember the story I covered the week before Mamá's death—a fifteen-year-old girl and her then-boyfriend, a street kid living in foster care, injected the girl's mother with bleach. When that didn't kill the mom, they beat her to death. All because the mom wouldn't let the teens date. Was Raúl influenced by my story on those teens? "How could you not tell me?"

"Abuela was afraid—"

"Abuela." I'm not hearing right. "Abuela Bonita knew?" I feel my spirit leave my body.

"Mari—"

"You better tell me the truth, Isabella Álvarez." I lean over her. "I'm on the edge. I cannot be held accountable for my actions."

"Abuela thought if I confessed that my boyfriend suggested killing Mamá, I'd be arrested, too, and sent to jail as an accessory. Then she'd lose Mamá *and* me. She knew the truth would destroy you. She prayed to the saints, Mari. And the saints told her—"

Heat washes over me. "You don't even believe in the damn saints!"

"I do. I do. I do. Abuela made a sacrifice to Oshun and Chango." Izzy's words are for me, I know, but her eyes are now on Hanks.

Who, interestingly, is standing close, but is as still as one of the pillars in the room.

"She said the saints convinced Raúl's family to

send him to Cuba to live with relatives," Izzy continues. "He went by private boat and took his father's gun with him, so police would never find Mamá's murder weapon. Abuela told Raúl's mother if Raúl ever came back, or contacted me or any of our family again, she'd turn him into the police."

"And now our grandmother is dead. Isn't that convenient. He's back in Tampa, isn't he?" *That's why Mrs. Martínez lied to me.* "He left you those three notes, didn't he?"

"Three?"

"I found three. I also found a fucking rooster head on our front door. With a curse I thought was meant for me."

"He's been threatening me."

"Why?"

"He wants another chance."

"To do what, Izzy? You can't possibly still love that killer?"

"He's not—"

"He is! He killed our mother. Did he kill Abuela Bonita?"

"I don't know. When I found her, she was already unconscious."

"It was a warning. You know that!" My vision is fading, anger making everything red. "I visited his…" I almost say monster. "His mother."

"I know."

"I made her call Raúl. He was in Cuba."

"Mari, it's so easy to put any background behind you for fun."

"He faked it?" I only saw him for a few seconds.

"He was in the back bedroom hiding. His old bedroom—"

"His mother lied to me. Everyone has been lying to me."

"To protect him. Just like Abuela lied to protect me."

"How the hell did I fall for it? The cigar. The fucking burning cigar." I stomp, but even that isn't releasing the ferocious fury boiling inside me. "I knew it. But his mom began talking about Sebastián Figueroa."

"A diversion. To protect Raúl. And me."

"She wants you two to be together?"

"She wants her son to be happy."

"He had a newspaper article, Izzy, he—"

"When I wouldn't meet him, well, he threatened me. If I didn't go back to Cuba with him, he'd kill you and Abuela and blame it on the person committing these new murders in town. He's smart, Mari. He's devious and—"

"He's evil."

"Abuela liked him."

"Abuela always treated you differently." The spite rolls off my tongue, truth tasting like a sour ball.

"She always loved *you* more, Mari. You were always her perfect little angel, working so hard fighting for justice."

My heart is burning with disbelief. I can't believe the one person in the world I knew would never lie to me, *never lie to me*, lied to me over and over. "For ten years, you and Abuela let me believe Andreas Santiago killed Mamá! When you both knew it was Raúl."

"Do you think it was easy living with this all these years?" Izzy says. "Knowing our Mamá died because of me. Knowing Abuela lied to the police for me. Knowing she lied to you, too. Knowing she covered up a crime for me."

"Selfish. Selfish. Selfish. Selfish." I stomp my feet. But it still doesn't make me feel better.

"Stop! Don't say it six times." Izzy's rocking in her chair. "You drive me crazy with your superstitious shit." She grabs at the ties binding her ankles. Ripping at them.

Hanks doesn't stop her.

"Did you know about this?" I throw the question at him like one of Chango's lightning bolts. "Did you know about any of this shit?"

"I did not." He turns to me. "Interesting plot twist, though, don't you agree?"

I want to kill him. I hate myself for the thought, but I do.

In that calm psychopathic voice, he asks me, "*Now* would you like me to kill your sister?"

CHAPTER FORTY-SIX

"That last note, by the way, and the rooster head. That was me." Hanks eyes glow from behind the mask.

I shiver at the ill will shooting from that gaze. "You?" Hanks has been giving me the evil eye. *Hanks.* "How did you— I told you. I told you and García everything about those notes at my house. I gave you everything you needed to screw with me."

"Oh, I enjoy screwing with you."

"You cursed me. But you want to work with me? You want me to be your Saint Barbara? That doesn't make sense."

"There's a fine line, Marisol, between love and hate. And all it takes is one bad decision to cross that line. Don't make a bad decision, Mari rhymes with sorry."

"Kill me," Izzy says to Hanks.

Is she trying to pull Hanks's attention from me to her?

"Do it. I'm tired of living but feeling like I'm already dead inside. I'm trapped. I've been encased for a decade in a concrete tomb made of guilt."

I'm both horrified and amazed at her request. And its revelations. I had no idea my sister felt this way. I thought she hated me. Not herself.

"My future is shot anyway," she says.

"What do you mean?" I need to know.

"Raúl isn't going to let me go this time, Marisol." I hear the sadness in her tone.

"Ah, apparently we all have our secrets, Marisol." Hanks has his right hand on his mask. Like he's going to take it off.

I have to stop him. Maybe it's already too late for us.

Boom. Boom. Boom. "Open up!"

We all look at the doorway leading to the staircase. Someone is banging on the front door. *At six a.m.?* Orlando? I'd texted him about the back entrance. So, no, he wouldn't knock, would he?

"Open up."

Not O's voice.

Hanks is on me, jerking my head back with a fist full of my hair. "I thought you didn't tell García."

"I didn't." I close my eyes. Ignore the pain flooding the nerve endings. "I promise you, I didn't." But I did tell Orlando. Maybe he called 911, when he couldn't get in earlier? I cry as Hanks pulls my head back, straining the muscles in my neck. "What now?"

"A surprise ending," he says.

I lick my lips, pull against his hold. "You could let us go. That would be a surprise."

Surprisingly, he lets my hair free. I shuffle away from him, my breath leaving me in spurts. "At least let them go." I gesture to Izzy. "I no longer want to have blood on my hands." Blood is what's drilling through my veins, making my entire head throb.

Boom. Boom. Boom.

"Is that the lesson you've learned?" Hanks isn't done with me yet. "I was hoping you'd see it another way. I was hoping you'd make a different decision."

He's towering over me again, using his height and my obvious fear of him to intimidate me. Then he does the thing I dreaded most. He takes off the mask. Throws it at my feet. "I think maybe I've longed for a while to be unmasked."

I cry out, understanding this is a death sentence for us all. I flinch as he takes my face in his hands, both palms flat against my cheeks. "I've longed for someone to finally see me and recognize I am doing the work of the gods. I want someone to give me the credit I deserve. I thought that maybe that person would be you."

He applies pressure.

I stiffen against it.

"I began to believe Chango picked you, himself." He presses against my cheeks. His eyes go cold.

"You're hurting me."

"This is your last chance, Marisol Álvarez."

When I don't instantly respond, he lets me go.

I step back, my hands flying to my face, covering the imprint he's left there, "Chango doesn't advocate murder."

He drops his head. Stumbles back as if my words were bullets blasting him. His hand covers his heart. *Boom. Boom.* "Police. Last chance to open up."

When he looks up, it's the Devil I see possessing his eyes. "But Chango does love fire and brimstone."

"No, no, he doesn't. Not like that."

Hanks steps back, throwing his arms out, twirling around like the mad Joker himself. "I've rigged the doors. I let you in, dear Marisol, let you enter, but whoever else opens any door will set off explosives strong enough to burn this historic masterpiece down, along with everyone inside." He stops twirling and zeroes in on Izzy first. Next, me. "I'd shoot you all, to ensure I leave no witnesses."

"One, two, three!" The door cracks, as what must be the SWAT team tries to break it down.

"But I don't want any evidence left behind. Ropes"—he points to Izzy's feet—"will dissolve. Bullets only melt."

I'm already thinking I can use the tobacco cutter to free Izzy from her bonds. She's thinking that, too. She's fingering the sharp object, probably ready to use it as a weapon or an escape mechanism.

"And in case you do survive, Marisol…your future depends on your silence."

I sneak a look at Santiago—he's already sawing away at the ropes at his ankles.

"That's an old Cuban mafia rule, right Santiago?"

Santiago stops his sawing and flips Hanks off, to which the mad Joker laughs.

"You, of all men, know how this works. Remember this, I know where to find you. All of you."

Hanks slips through the door and out of our sight.

Just as the door downstairs is forced open, and the first explosion rocks me off my feet.

CHAPTER FORTY-SEVEN

I rush to Izzy. "Let's get you untied." My heart is skipping like a rock over rapids as I grab another cutter off the next desk and start sawing at the rope around her other ankle.

"Oh my God. Oh My God," Izzy is mumbling, her eyes unfocused. "I smell the smoke."

Acrid, dense, toxic fingers of it are already snaking their way up the stairwell. The *snip-snap-whoosh* of the flames pop in loud and soft continuous layers.

"We're gonna…we're gonna…we're gonna burn, burn, burn to death." Shallow breathing, flushed face, frantic movements.

My baby sister is experiencing a full-on panic attack. "Concentrate!" I order. I want to smack her back into reason, but I'm too busy sawing away on one of the ropes tying her to the chair. "Can you lift the chair up?"

"Bolted. Bolted to the floor."

Crazy guy thought of everything.

"Why don't you go, Marisol? Run!"

"Stop." I wish she'd pull it together.

"I…you hate me." She's sniffling, and it's affecting my concentration. "I know you do, I know you do."

Why have we never had this discussion before? Now we don't have time. "Izzy!" I yell louder than I intended. In doing so, I suck up a plateful of new smoke, causing my lungs to seize in revolt. The whole time I'm working the sharp edge of the cutter, back and forth. Back and forth. Hoping she doesn't jerk, and I cut her.

Another explosion rips through something below us. I jump back. "¡Carajo! Sounds like the back door."

"Tell them to stop." She found both her voice and courage.

"Tell who? My phone's dead."

"He crushed mine." She collapses back into a fit of tears.

Her body is rocking so hard now, I know I'm going to stab her. "Santiago!" I can't even stop long enough to look for him.

"Fuck you both."

Well, he's still with us.

The popping sound melts into one long hiss. My fingers are cramping. I take a break. Look up. And see a golden body of fire dancing in the doorway. It's like a molten ballet, the performing inferno twirling everything in its path into a beautiful, yellow, red, and gold tornado. Soon, the walls will be devoured, as will we. "Santiago, this is your factory. Do something."

"Mother fucker! Wooooo!"

Izzy and I look up.

"It's hot as witch's balls."

"Orlando!" He's entered from that back room, where we heard something earlier. "Was that you entering from downstairs?" He's hightailing it to my side.

"Employee entrance, like you said."

I'm so freaking glad to see him.

"I remembered the code the PR lady gave me."

"Here, help me free Izzy." She is rocking back and forth, unable to help herself. "You got my—"

Orlando drops to his knees.

I hand him Izzy's cutter.

"Yes ma'am, got your text. Got your instructions." He gets right to the effort. "Got the confession recorded on video. Already delivered it to the Cloud and our station Dropbox."

"Thank you." My whole hand is cramping now. The floor is starting to roast.

"Even if we don't survive, the evidence against Detective Hanks will."

Tears burn the back of my eyes. Fueled by emotion? Smoke? "We're going to get out of here alive."

Another detonation rocks the walls.

Heat slaps all sides of me, sweat dripping off every part of my body. "Go help Santiago," I say to O. "He knows how to get us out of here."

"I don't need your fucking help."

"Are you still here?" I ask, because the smoke is quickly clouding up the room.

No answer.

"Guess you do need our help." I barely spit out.

"Remember the story we came here to do that day?" Orlando asks between coughing.

"I do." The air is hot in my lungs. "The mafia tunnels underground in Ybor City—the ones criminals used to escape the FBI." I can barely get the words out and have no idea if Santiago is going to listen or answer.

"He's leaving," Orlando answers.

I catch Santiago near an exit. "Wait! Izzy isn't free, yet. Izzy! Snap out of it."

Orlando's on his feet. "Do I stop him or help you?"

"Don't leave us, Santiago," I plead to the man, who minutes ago, I admitted to wanting to murder.

Izzy springs up and grabs me, squeezing me until I can't breathe. Or maybe that's the smoke swirling around us now.

I push her away. I have to. Flames are on the roof above us. "Oh God." I run toward the departing Santiago, yelling with the air I have left. "Everything's recorded. Leave now and we die—" I leave the rest out there for him to figure out himself.

He stops. Does an about-face.

Fire rips away at a beam with the roar of a lion.

"Watch out!" Orlando yells.

Santiago gestures for us to move to the back of the room away from the dropping piling. "Drop to your knees. Crawl and follow me."

CHAPTER FORTY-EIGHT

Ybor City is often alive with vibrant colors and smells, roasting Cuban coffee, towering palm trees, Latin salsa beats blaring. Street lights and strands of multicolored bulbs line 7th Avenue, or La Septima, the equivalent to Bourbon Street in New Orleans. The whole area is known for its European look and its Cuban American influence. Like the towering cigar factories that employed the working class in this area.

Tonight, the historic district takes on a different look.

I'm walking down the cobbled street leading up to La Chimenea, the last working cigar factory in Ybor, and I'm stunned into silence by both the heat of the giant flames towering above the fire trucks with their ladders lifted, but also by the devastating realization that a part of our community's history is burning down. Although brick makes up La Chimenea's foundation, much of the top two stories were made of wood and filled with flammable products. Only a shell would survive tonight.

Orlando grabs my hand and squeezes. He understands. There are no words.

Thanks to Santiago, we got out of that fireball alive. We crawled through decaying, disgusting tunnels to a rundown building—once a speakeasy—and exited back out onto La Septima, only to walk directly back to where we came from.

I'm surprised Santiago is still with us. He hasn't spoken since we got near the factory. It's his family's life work charring before his eyes.

The arrogant asshole stops. He moves his hand to his heart in a gesture that makes compassion hit me like the burning embers falling in our hair, on our shoulders, and at our feet.

"Hey, there's Jessica and Chris." Orlando points to a street over, where the media are being staged.

Wannabe and the new photographer are on the story this morning. I guess neither are newbies any longer.

"I'm going to go talk to them," Orlando says. "Make sure they know about the video confession. Fill in the details." He grins. "It's our exclusive, you know."

I stop, exhale, wipe sweat off my brow. "Damn good job, my friend. You risked your life for this story."

"I risked my life for you." His Adam's apple moves.

I look away, moved by O's confession.

"Maybe you should go talk to them," he says. "You know the whole story."

I shake my head. "No, you go. I don't work there anymore." That fact hurts so much I can't even look at the media staging ground again.

"You okay?" Izzy is next to me. She pulled it together, thank goodness.

"No." I decide to tell her the truth, for once. "No, I'm not okay. And I'm not sure what I'm supposed to do next."

She looks down at the ground. "Neither am I."

"Maybe we start with working on our relation-ship." I turn to her, hopeful.

But she's looking down the street. I can't see at what.

Sirens blare, and I jump back to get away from another approaching first responder. Police cars, two ladder trucks, and numerous other fire vehicles litter the street. Water sprays the building in a useless flow.

La Chimenea is dying tonight.

And not one of us here has the power to save her.

I scan the scene, curious if Hanks is in custody. He has to be, right? He could have slipped out, but the police had already arrived. They would have captured him, right? A man slinking away from the scene of a cigar factory, exploding and on fire? That would catch their attention.

A man standing alone catches *my* attention.

Because I recognize that silhouette.

Detective García, Tony, is facing the factory, watching it burn.

Someone I don't know approaches him.

He waves them off, body stiff.

He's upset. I can tell. And it hits me—maybe he thinks I'm in there.

My feet move as if they're on fire. I walk up behind him. Tap him on the shoulder. "Tony."

He tenses up.

I step back. "I'm sorry. I didn't mean to—"

He flips around and pulls me to him, crushing me in that I-can't-believe-you're-alive way. "I can't believe—" He stiffens, as if suddenly aware this hug is unexpected and inappropriate. He pulls back. Lets me go. "I'm so mad at you." His words are a whisper in the middle of chaos, but his body language tells me something else. It tells me he's relieved.

"Why did you come here?" he asks. Flames flicker shadows across his face and sweat trickles down his hairline. "Hanks?" he asks.

I nod.

"Well, he got away." Tony turns back toward the fire. "Or maybe he didn't."

"You'll find him, and if you don't, Santiago's family will." I glance back at the multimillionaire. "Guess there is some truth to that whole Cuban mafia thing."

Tony shoots me a look I don't recognize. "You still want Santiago arrested?"

"Santiago? No." My shoulders ache with the heavy stories I must share with him. Some day. "He saved us tonight. I found out he didn't kill my mother."

"Who did?"

"Conversation for another night. But Hanks had nothing to do with it. Didn't even know. At least you have proof of Hanks's guilt in these other murders when you or they find him."

"Yes, we have your murder wall."

"Better than that, you have a confession."

The rising sun splashes new light on Tony's tired and confused features.

I call up Dropbox and play part of Orlando's video. When it's done, I say, "Compliments of Orlando, who snuck into the factory after I texted him and told him to meet me."

Instead of the joy and congrats I was expecting, I get, "You texted Orlando, but didn't tell me?"

"Tony."

He smiles. "It's okay. Orlando was smart enough to text me right after you texted him."

I tense. He starts laughing, which makes me relax instantly. "That's how the cops got here so quickly?"

He nails me with a stare. "If you ever do that again—"

I shrug. "Can't promise. I'm a bit of a rebel—but with a cause."

"Marisol Álvarez, what am I going to do with you?"

I hesitate, not sure how to answer because I'm not sure of the intention behind his words.

"Let me get you home," he says.

Is there a double meaning to his invitation? I can't decide if I'm going to let myself find out. I remember Izzy. I turn around. "Where is she?"

"Who?"

"Izzy. She was right with me."

"I didn't see her when you walked up."

"You sure?"

"I'm sure."

"¡Ay, Dios mío!" My shoulders drop.

"How about we look around for her?"

"You don't need to stay here? Interview people?"

"We have a few SWAT team members injured, but I'm homicide. This isn't my scene. I only came for, well, I came to check on you. Unless you know of any dead bodies inside?"

I'm about to say hopefully one Detective John

Hanks. But I stop and instead say, "Edward Jones. Hanks said he'd killed him, and his body is inside."

Tony whistles.

I can't tell if he's upset, he's got another murder victim, or relieved Jones isn't still out there to stalk me.

"Will tell the scene commander," Tony says. "We've had enough for one night."

"Thank you."

"For?"

"Coming to check on me."

He makes a sound, though I don't really understand what it means. But I do understand it's probably his way of handling embarrassment. And this weird thing between us. "All right, where is the last place you saw your sister?"

"Right over there." I point.

He places his hand on my back. Not in a romantic way. But in a protective way.

I like the feel of it.

"Let's go find her. So we can—"

I let the words he doesn't say hang out there in the humid, hot air, but only for a few seconds. "Right," I finish for him. "So we can both get home."

And despite the fire, the near-death experience, and Izzy going MIA once again, Detective Tony García makes me smile. And leaves me with hope for a brighter future.

CHAPTER FORTY-NINE

My brighter future will have to wait until after Abuela Bonita's funeral.

I didn't want to throw one. She didn't want one, either. Abuela Bonita gave me strict instructions to have her cremated and not to spend a dime on a fancy funeral she can't even enjoy.

I agree.

What's the point? She's not here to appreciate the white Mariposa orchids placed in the aisle of the sanctuary at Our Lady of Perpetual Help in Ybor City. She can't sit back and appreciate that most of West Tampa came out to say goodbye and show their respects.

She's ashes in an urn.

But I caved to the pressure of her friends and to our West Tampa leaders. I didn't have the energy to fight them. And many helped with arrangements.

I swallow. A single drop of sweat teeters on my right eyebrow, threatening to dive into my eye.

I just have to make it through this day. I just need to get through the visitation and the funeral without losing it or passing out. Then, I can go home and go back to bed. I've got a prescribed Xanax waiting. I want to bury myself deep into the blankets and fall asleep, into a blissful nothing.

But I'm not sure I can hold back the tsunami of

emotions threatening to roll me first. I'm not sure I can make it through this day.

Alone.

I stand next to a picture of Abuela Bonita. It was one of her favorite, taken about a decade ago. She'd been dressed to perfection in her favorite, white-orchid colored dress, with her cherished pair of white lace gloves, her rosary, and a second necklace with a Saint Barbara charm around her neck. She'd been getting ready for church when I caught her admiring her own reflection. I chose this picture out of respect, not only for my grandmother, but the one-hundred-twenty-seven-year-old church, one of the oldest in Tampa.

Our Lady is also where my mother and father married.

Now it will be where Abuela Bonita is celebrated before her ashes are spread and reintroduced to the earth. I didn't want to do this in a funeral home. They're so depressing. So I asked the priest for permission to hold a celebration of life.

A life now contained in a beautiful, ceramic holder.

My body tingles like I slept wrong on every part of my body. I wish every limb was asleep. Then this would only be a dream. And I could shake myself out of it.

I exhale, my mouth so dry even a bucket of Abuela's wash couldn't wet it.

Oh God, I miss her.

I force myself to glance around the sanctuary where Abuela's friends are gathering.

I know this is tradition. The greeting of family

and friends. The hugging, crying, even laughing over stories of Abuela's escapades in West Tampa. Of her kind heart and amazing arroz con pollo. I know it's supposed to make me feel better, knowing how much she was loved.

It doesn't make me feel better.

It makes me feel alone. Utterly, completely, heart-torn-open-like-a-festering-wound, alone.

I search the crowd for the only living immediate family member I have left. The one who should be by my side, her eyes as wet as mine, her heart as broken. Maybe even her hand in mine.

I don't see Izzy. She still hasn't reached out to me. My stomach tumbles.

I see Abuela Bonita's pharmacist, the one who holds domino competitions on his front porch. He is crying. My grandmother always brought over rice pudding to his friends during those competitions. And she brought him home-cooked meals for weeks after his wife died of cancer.

I see the Babalawo and Santera walking down the aisle to take a seat in the pew and nod as they walk by me. The Babalawo nods back. Something new reflects in his eyes, but I can't put a name to it. It's not empathy. It's not compassion. It's, I don't know, maybe concern? Or maybe even fear? *What does he know that he isn't telling me?*

"I'm sorry for your loss."

I jump and turn toward the voice. It's Tony. His eyes are full of sympathy, but he extends his hand, like we're strangers or something.

"Thank you." My voice shakes. His palm is warm against my ice-cold flesh.

"Mari, I—"

"Marisol!"

I tear my gaze from Tony's. His mother is coming up the aisle behind him, reaching for me, arms extended, tears tracking down her face. "Your abuela was such a lovely woman. She loved you so much." She pulls me into a hug, much too intimate for the time we've known each other.

I start to pull away, my gaze searching for Tony.

She grips my upper arms.

I still.

She pulls me closer and whispers, "I have something for you. It's important. I must give it to you before you speak today."

She's pushing something onto my wrist. It's cool and—I look down at the intersection of our hands. She's given me an azabache bracelet. "But"—I pull back and show her the one I'm already wearing.

"You already have one?" She cocks her head. "Antonio told me you gave yours away."

"I did. Tony gave this to me but said it was from you."

She shakes her head, fingering the beads as if they're precious diamonds. "I've never seen that bracelet before."

We both look at Tony.

He looks away.

Beatriz looks back at me with what looks like new understanding. She smiles but says nothing. Then she hugs me again, pulling me close like I'm her own daughter. "Whatever you need. Whenever you need it. I am here for you."

And that makes me cry. I'm not even sure why

this woman opened the spigot with her hug. But the tears flow and my shoulders shake, and Beatriz continues to hold me.

Like my mamá would have had she lived to be here.

At some point, the tears clear, and I catch Tony watching us. And I wonder why he didn't tell me the truth—that he'd bought this bracelet for me because he knew I thought I needed it. I did need it. It was a thoughtful, kind act.

His back is to us now. But he doesn't move down the church aisle to take a seat.

I wonder if he did it because he's developing feelings for me. Because it is a strange gift from a man who won't open himself up to the possibility that spiritual things happen in our world outside of the church.

I think Tony has a lot of work to do on himself.

As do I.

And this uncomfortable, awkward moment between us only makes me like him more.

Forensics Freddy is taking a seat. I offer an unsteady smile.

Orlando is here, standing awkwardly behind Beatriz, probably because he's unused to having to wait to get my attention.

"I'm sorry, Mari." He opens his arms to hug me.

I leave Beatriz's embrace for his, wiping my eyes and then throwing my arms up and around his neck.

"I know how much you loved your abuela."

"Thank you, O." Warm tears threaten to push through. Again. I need to blow my nose.

"I love you, M," he whispers in my ear.

"I love you, too," I say. And I do, even though I'm still hurting from our fallout.

Despite all the bodies heating up the room, I'm chilled by the thought I'm an orphan, because frankly, my little sister has been a stranger to me since our mother's death a decade ago, and she's clearly not interested in working on our relationship.

She chose not to be here.

Unless she's unable to attend.

My heart twinges at that thought.

In my peripheral vision, I catch a couple entering the sanctuary. My back stiffens. Mr. and Mrs. Martínez, Raúl's parents. I leave Orlando's embrace, fully intending to storm up to them and demand they tell me where Raúl is. If he's with my sister.

Orlando is still talking to me. As is Beatriz. But their words are like bees buzzing by me.

Mrs. Martínez is as pale as the white lace on the table where Abuela's urn is. She looks cold, like Abuela's icy hands I held at the hospital. It hits me. If Raúl has fled to Cuba again, if he killed my abuela and he told his parents what he'd done, if he's taken Izzy, if any of those things occurred, they must carry a weight of guilt so heavy it could crumple them. It took cojones grandes to show up here. Mr. Martínez catches my eyes, and I see a flash of regret. I can't bring myself to smile at him, signaling it's okay for them to stay. I know that's what Abuela would have wanted but my heart still burns with anger, and I cannot yet forgive or forget. So I just turn away. Better to not cause a scene today. If it gives them relief to attend Abuela's service, I will turn a blind eye. I will swallow my anger and suspicion.

My stomach gurgles. I haven't been able to eat anything. My stomach feels like it's actually eating itself.

"You okay?" Tony has his protective hand on my back again.

"Yes. Yes." I look up at him, needing that hand on my back while also needing him to give me some space. "Please, take a seat. Thank you for coming."

Those words are generic, too cold, and not worthy of the developing relationship Tony and I have, but I don't have the energy for other emotions right now. I can barely stand here on two feet. And I see a group from my former job approaching. *Great.*

O told me Jessica is the proud owner of my former crime beat. Chris Jensen is her photographer. A clump forms in my throat when Mr. Payton walks in. I don't know why his being here is so important to me. He fired me. Who am I kidding? His opinion of me has always been important. I still long to earn his respect back and the thought, in this moment, brings heat to my face. He's dressed to the nines, leading a small group of people I was also close with at work. I haven't talked to Mr. Payton since I walked out of his office in a just-fired bubble of WTF and what do I do next. He nods at me. I nod back. He didn't know my abuela, so it's clear he's here for me. And I'm not quite sure what to make of that. Does he have guilt he needs to assuage, too? Like the Martínezes? Or is his opinion of me higher than I thought? I wish I didn't care what he thinks.

Chris Jensen waves.

My hand is too heavy to lift and wave back.

I'm alone in the middle of a crowded room. And

I want to be anywhere but here.

"It's time." The priest gestures for me to head toward the front of the sanctuary, take the stage and address my West Tampa family, my work family. Wait, my *former* work family, and my friends.

These people are here to pay their respects to my abuela, but many are also here to comfort me.

I should feel their love.

But what I feel is the evil eye upon me.

It's heavy like syrup, smothering my heart until I can barely breathe.

CHAPTER FIFTY

What does one say about the central figure in your life for a decade? A day after finding out she'd been lying to you for that entire time. And you can't confront her and find out why.

When your heart is shattered, and your soul is battered, and you stand before a room full of people, all of whom know you, but none of whom know your truth.

I step to the mic on the pulpit. The air in my lungs flies out of me in shallow spurts, words taking flight with little to no air beneath them. Will they flutter and fall? Or fly free, lifting the darkness over me?

"Marisol Álvarez was easy to love. To all of you who knew her, she was the heart of our West Tampa neighborhood. She had the attributes to which many of us aspire. She was beautiful on the outside, which is why I always called her my Abuela Bonita. She smelled of lavender, and that smell always gave me peace."

Until it didn't.

"She was both strong—"

"Go do your wash, Marisol."

"And tender."

Her bony hands cradling my face, her fingers chilly, but her lips warm, pressing against my forehead, whispering, "I love you, Marisol." *Then why did you leave me?*

"She was both smart and understanding."

She was also a liar.

My gaze catches Orlando's. He looks down and away as if he hears my internal thoughts.

"She was a mother and grandmother first, putting our family above all else."

Putting Izzy first. Lying to me to protect their secret. And yet, I still love her.

"She made her West Tampa neighborhood her priority, and that's why so many of you showed up for her today. Abuela Bonita never met a neighbor she did not welcome into her home, no matter what the time of day. She never met a hungry person she would not feed with both her delicious arroz con pollo or her award-winning black beans. She never met a sick neighbor she would not try to heal."

With a wash or prayer to the saints.

"In the end, it will be her compassion and kindness she will be remembered for. She'll be remembered for her rice pudding on domino days and her chicken fricassee for the latest quinceañera. She'll be remembered for her door always being open and unlocked."

But I'll never know why she locked away the truth from me.

"My Abuela Bonita believed in an afterlife. She believed in God, and she believed in angels."

She also believed in the saints.

We are all complicated creatures, aren't we? Fighting with our two sides, the good and evil, angels and devils, different sides of us all woven together.

"And I know she is with us today, watching over all of us, determined to live within all of us a wonderful, warm memory. So please, remember Marisol Álvarez when you eat your next bowl of rice pudding, when your fifteen-year-old has her first dance, when you sit down to play your next game of dominoes. Her spirit will be with all of us—in the air we breathe, the food we taste, in the love we let into our hearts. Thank you for coming."

I exhale, thankful I let the right words fly while the real words stayed inside my head.

Isn't that what life is? A constant struggle with ourselves?

A rope woven with both positive and negative experiences? Rope we can use to both hang ourselves or pull ourselves out of the quicksand of despair and to a shore of safety where happiness awaits?

When I leave this sanctuary today, which waits for me?

CHAPTER FIFTY-ONE

I exit through the back door of Our Lady of Perpetual Help while most of the guests exit the front. I entered today's service sad that I'm alone. But right now, I need to be alone.

I carry Abuela's urn and something almost as valuable in the pocket of my suit jacket.

The air is heavy with approaching rain and soon, I will either be drenched with sweat or raindrops. A low rumble of thunder rolls my way. I love a good thunderstorm. It reminds me we are not in control. Something greater is.

Something powerful.

I'm wandering through the parking lot, trying to find my thoughts. That's when I see it, the remnants of La Chimenea, the last working cigar factory in Ybor City burned to the ground.

Like my life.

I can't swallow the knot stuffed down my throat.

"Well, now is as good of a time as any time," I whisper to no one.

I pull a letter from my pocket, one I found last night while going through Abuela's altar room, looking for something. A message. A direction. A hope.

Under the picture of my mamá I found an envelope, sealed, with Abuela's handwriting on it:

My dearest Marisol. TO BE OPENED IN THE
CASE OF MY DEATH Abuela Bonita.

I open it.

Dearest Marisol,

*If you are reading this it means I have passed into
the next world.*

*I have had some time to think about dying, and so
I decided to write this note to you.*

*There is really no reason to tell you how much I
love you, because I know you know that. I just want
to put it in writing. I love you so very much. If you
weren't my granddaughter I would seek you out and
want to get to know you and be your friend. That's
the kind of person you have become. Watching you
develop and grow has given me such pleasure and
happiness. I am so proud of you. My life has been
complete having you as my granddaughter. Believe
me when I say my life has been full and I've had such
opportunities and done so many things that leaving is
not all that hard. What I really regret is that I won't be
around to see you in the future and getting to know
and love my son-in-law and great-grandchildren*

*Having you as my best friend is one of the nicest
gifts I've ever received. Thank you for that and for all
the wonderful things you've done for me.*

*Marisol, you and Isabella share blood. Family is
really important. Please keep in touch and forgive all
past transgressions.*

Forgiveness is what heals.

*You should have my necklace of Saint Barbara. I
do want you to have that protection.*

Marisol, I won't say goodbye as I will always be a

part of you. And I believe we will meet again. Until
that day know that despite my actions, despite me
holding the truth from you, I always loved you and
your best interest always came first.

I leave you with one last thought.
Broken girls blossom into warriors.
Be a warrior, Marisol.
Be a warrior.

I can't be sure if the wetness on my face is from
tears or the sprinkle preceding the downpour of
August rain. I don't bother wiping either away. For
the first time I feel comfortable in my grief and pain.

I rub the charm of Saint Barbara I'm wearing
around my neck. My new touchstone. I will cherish it
forever.

"What should I do now?" I speak to Abuela and
know that our relationship is not dead. I will
continue to talk to her in a way I never really felt
comfortable talking to my mother, and she will
answer.

"Should I go back to Cuba and spread your ashes
in the garden behind your childhood home? The one
you always used to describe to me in rich detail. You
could grow into the beautiful flowers you so
appreciated. And I could meet your family members,
the ones you talked about. I've seen pictures, but
I've never met my Cuban relatives. Maybe it's time
to connect to my heritage. To the only family I have
left."

A rooster crows as it waddles past me, a solo
parishioner outside the church.

I smile. That is a sign, for sure.

I've never been to Cuba. Maybe like a Phoenix, I can rise from the ashes of my life and rebuild what has been charred.

There.

I will be a warrior.

A door creaks open.

The hair on the back of my neck stands.

I feel someone watching me. Could Hanks be here?

A clap of lightning startles me. One thousand one. One thousand two. One thousand three.

Boom.

The thunder is closer. Time to make a move. Maybe it's Izzy.

I turn to see who's found me in my garden of silence and reflection.

Tony is standing by the back door. He doesn't move when our gazes lock. It's like he understands I need this moment by myself. He's just checking on me.

Again.

Is this going to become a thing?

My heart stretches.

Not if I leave for Cuba.

Truth is, I'm scared to be alone. Even though I'm clutching Abuela's remains, I'm still technically alone.

I could walk up to Tony, or meet him halfway and let him drive me home. I know he will offer. I could let him take me to dinner and talk to me to keep my mind off the fact I have an empty house full of a lifetime of memories waiting for me to go through. Maybe he'd even offer a hug, or a more pleasant kind of distraction. That would be the easiest thing for me to do. Lean on him. Let him lead.

Or I can be strong. I can stand on my own two feet on this, the second worse day of my life.

I smile at him. I really do like him. I want him to know I'm okay.

But "I want to be a warrior." I know he can't hear me. Those words aren't really for him or anyone else anyway. "I want to feel strong again. Whole." I turn away from Tony and take the first step forward.

My cell rings.

I jump, because another flash of lightning streaks across the sky at the exact same time.

The rain grows heavier, fat drops plopping on my head and my nice suit jacket. I glance at my phone.

My heart flutters with new wings. It's a number I never expected to see come up on my home screen again, especially right now.

I hesitate. What could he possibly want from me right now?

Be a warrior! I hear Abuela's voice in my head. *Be a warrior, Marisol.*

And so I do the brave thing.

I answer the call.

CHAPTER FIFTY-TWO

ONE WEEK LATER

Walking into the lively afternoon TV news meeting, the disgraced crime reporter back from being fired and then rehired, I feel my center spinning in one pride-fueled funnel cloud. A couple of weeks ago, I tiptoed into the room late, with a list of four or five feature stories to pitch, eager to stay out of trouble with El Jefe and continue—in secret—an investigation I'd hoped would change my life.

But this is not a few weeks ago.

I still haven't heard from Izzy. My heart catches like it's been scraped over rough concrete.

But I did point the finger at a serial killer—two actually—and get a confession out of one of them. Which should put Hanks away, when García arrests him. Unless Santiago locates him first. Then who knows?

And I did hear from Mr. Payton, who called after the funeral to offer me the condolences he didn't have the chance to offer in person at the church. Not his fault. I'd avoided him at the funeral, not having the emotional bandwith to deal with our baggage then. He also offered me my job back. I told him no thank you, I had to go to Cuba to spread my abuela's ashes. He told me I'd be entitled to family leave, earned and well deserved.

So today, I present my best journalistic poker face as I move through the room, praying my upturned lips and vibrant eyes don't give away my current state of mind and body. I'm trying not to gloat on this first day back to work. Or worse, brag. Pitch your story. Don't say *I told you so*. Don't mention how no one but Detective Tony García believed in you. And he was right.

Sencillo. No hay problema.

My various coworkers stop the daily debate over story priority and stare. Once again, I'm the fish food for their curiosity. I smile at the afternoon anchor with the perfectly blown-out hair. She raises her eyebrows, smiles, and glances to the other side of the room. As do I.

The only open seat in the room packed with managers, producers, writers, reporters, and photographers is at the end of the elongated conference table, directly across from El Jefe.

Of course.

I'm five minutes early, unheard of for me, and wearing my signature high heels that are clicking on the uncarpeted floor like my Abuela Bonita's disapproving tongue. All I can think of is how proud she'd be of me today.

Both stories—the vigilante, serial killer police detective, and the sex trafficking city council member—made national news. The big boss in New York insisted I be rehired and do live shots for the morning news program. ASAP. Because Hanks is on the run, his story leads almost every day on cable news. And no one knows his story as well as I do.

García is leading the task force looking for Hanks. Detective Smith, who took over Hanks's job, is heading the team looking into old murders with either a broken doll or references to the evil eye listed as evidence. The charges against Hanks could grow.

I am technically still on probation, but I'm not worried. I nailed these investigations and the stories that followed. And I feel vindicated. I need this job to continue crime reporting and helping victim's families. Like Hanks, I feel compelled to help all the broken girls. The difference is, I plan to do it the legal way.

I rub my right wrist. The gold chain García gave me is there, the little black gemstone dangling from the chain. I no longer feel the urge to roll the azabache charm between my fingers six times. But I like that it's there. I also have my Saint Barbara charm almost directly over my heart. Tomorrow may still bring another crisis, due to that thirty-day curse. But I feel protected now in a different way.

I pull out the chair across from El Jefe and accidentally scrape the floor. It's loud… ¡Qué escándalo! More stares cut my way. Even without the air conditioning blowing, today I'm already feeling pretty damn cool.

El Jefe drills me with that intense stare that says everything he's not allowed to vocalize, for fear HR will reprimand him. "Welcome back, Mari." And it's Mari now. No longer Ms. Álvarez.

Today, I think he actually means it.

"Thank you, Mr. Payton. It's good to be back.

I've got a great story to pitch."

"You've got the floor." He smiles.

"Remember the two girls who lost their mother, Natasha Rodríguez?"

He nods.

"Detective García says the Sheriff's Department is awarding them full scholarships to college. The check presentation is today, at the foster home they are currently staying at. I want to do a series on these two young women, and the girl Lauren who we saved from the sex trafficker."

"You saved," Mr. Payton clarifies, bragging for me.

¡Gracias! "I want to follow them for the next year and make sure these girls are healed and headed in the right direction."

"I like it. Let's start with the check presentation today. Taking Orlando?"

"Of course." I turn to look at Jessica, crime reporter wannabe. "I have another story to pitch."

The buzz that usually hangs in the air during our content meetings slows to barely a whisper.

"Hanks's brother has agreed to an exclusive interview with our TV station. Today. Since I can't be in two places at once, I thought Jessica and Chris Jensen could to it." I believe in lifting other women up. There's enough crime in this city for both of us to cover.

She smiles at me. You know, I think she actually looks up to me. I'm going to help her all I can.

"Good idea. You couldn't do it anyway. Conflict of interest," Mr. Payton says what I was thinking. "You're on it, Jessica."

Her cheeks are flushed with that excitement of youth heading out for what is surely a lead story. Go get 'em, Jessica.

I could gossip with my coworkers about being fired, eventually being right, and making my boss apologize before agreeing for me to not only come back but do interviews with our national network's morning show. I could make a big deal of it, but I don't. And won't. El Jefe and I, we've both made mistakes. What I like about him is he admitted to his. What he likes about me is I've admitted to mine. We've got a clean slate between us.

Especially after the city council member's attorney dropped the lawsuit, helping to restore my damaged reputation. And the station's.

And Mr. Payton already approved my time off to spread Abuela's ashes. I'm appreciative of that.

Then there is García. *Tony. Tony. Tony. Tony. Tony. Tony.* I think about him a lot. See him as the real superhero. Chide myself for silly schoolgirl thoughts. I haven't seen him since the morning at the church.

Ding. A text comes in. I sit up, not believing what I'm seeing. I text back. My heart is skipping, waiting for the reply.

"Álvarez?" Mr. Payton's executive assistant is sticking her head in the door. "You have a visitor up front."

My heart swells with hope.

"It's a police detective," she says. "He says it's important. He needs to speak with you right now."

Now fear whips through me. Izzy?

I glance at the boss, whose eyebrows are raised.

What in the hell could be happening now? "Maybe it's about Detective Hanks?" *I can only hope.* "They could have found him." My pulse jumps through dueling ropes of hope and fear.

El Jefe nods toward the door. "You're excused."

CHAPTER FIFTY-THREE

I head toward the lobby of the TV station, my heart doing repetitive backflips. This is the first time I've heard from Izzy since the night of the fire when she disappeared near La Chimenea. I don't recognize the number she's texting from.

I've already filed a missing person's report, convinced local TV stations to run a picture of her and of a 1980's Ford Mustang, red with a black stripe. But Santiago is the only one who's given us any clues. He saw her get into the Ford Mustang the night his cigar factory burned. A guy he didn't know drove her away. Proof it was Raúl. It had to be. Much to my surprise, Santiago offered to help in the search. Says he knows people, and I'm sure he does. Wonder if his network reaches more than ninety miles south? Cause I'd bet Raúl is already back in Cuba with my sister.

I figure Izzy ran away because she feared getting arrested for her part in Mamá's death, and for never telling the police. Part of me is okay with that—her making a new life elsewhere—if it means she stays out of jail. And trouble. I've made peace with the past, and I don't want her punished. Living with guilt has to be punishment enough.

But after the text I just got, I have to make sure it *is* her, and that she's okay.

I have to be honest with myself. I won't be happy if she's with him.

The enemy.

The gangbanger.

The guy who's loved Ford Mustangs since his youth.

I'm afraid he'll hurt her. Violence is just his way.

I hope he hasn't killed her already.

And then, there's Abuela's last request. Stay in touch with Izzy. Forgive past transgressions. Forgiveness heals.

Pressing my head against the door, I take six deep breaths. Whatever awaits me on the other side of the lobby door, I'll handle it with my newfound grace and gratitude. *I will survive*. That's my new mantra.

The lobby is empty, except for one homicide detective, whom I haven't seen in a while. I say, "You here about Izzy?"

His lips roll in, and he shakes his head. He doesn't break eye contact.

I appreciate that.

"Hanks?"

He shakes his head. "I brought you something." Tony walks to me, a folder in his outstretched hand.

"My mother's case file." It's the only file he'd have I want to see.

"I think you've earned the right to look through it." He hesitates before handing it to me. "Some of the pictures are graphic."

"I was there, remember."

"What are you looking for?" He hands me the file. "We know who did it."

"Closure." I take it. "I'm looking for closure." I tuck it under my arm. I need to go over this alone. "Do we know where Raúl might be?"

"*We* do."

My pulse skips.

"I've traced him to family in Cuba. A little beach town in the western outskirts of Havana. Playa Hermosa. Heard of it?"

I nod, my whole body tingling. "That's the town that famous ceramist is from. The one who puts his art on the streets and transformed the whole beach area into a unique work of public art. I hear people from all over the world come to see it. Looks like a Cuban Disneyland, minus the rides." But here's what will change Tony's professional and my personal investigation. I'm sure of it. "It's also the hometown of my new Babalawo. And where Hanks and his family took a picture I saw in his office."

I fill García in on that. And about my text that just came in. "Izzy lost her phone the night of the fire. Said Hanks destroyed it. But right before you showed up I got this text, but from a different number: *Sorry about everything. I want you to know I'm safe.* I texted back, but so far no answer. I was going to call you about this but—"

"But I'm here," Tony says.

We're like two sides of the same piece of paper.

"Recognize the new number?" Tony asks.

"No. I wouldn't know Raúl's cell number, though."

"Text again."

I do. *Izzy, I need you to answer me. If you don't, I'm tracking this phone.*

"Nice subtle touch." Tony grins.

I'm about to toss back a smart-ass reply when my phone *dings*.

Don't come looking for me. I'm safe in a place you know. Don't come looking for me. Izzy

My fingers grow cold. My body stiffens. "That's our secret sister code."

"Your what?" Tony asks. "What does it mean?"

"I think it means she's probably in Playa Hermosa. But I think it also means she's in trouble. She's asking me to come look for her. Do we have an extradition treaty with Cuba?"

"We have a memo of understanding that still stands today. Our two countries are supposed to work together, but the reality is, if Raúl is already back in Cuba, it's unlikely Cuban officials will extradite a Cuban national to stand trial in the United States, even if he's kidnapped Izzy."

This is what I feared. "Raúl was born in Playa Hermosa. Hanks and my Babalawo have ties there." The connections raise the hair on the back of my neck. "If Raúl is back there, he's probably living a great life, getting away with murder." I don't have to say that's unfair. I'm sure Tony hears the anger in the tone of my voice.

"Do you think Izzy is with him willingly?" he says.

"If she's hanging out on the beach with her ex, that would piss me off. I want her to be safe. But not with him."

"But it's a possibility?"

"It is. It's also possible she's there because she didn't have a choice." I hated the way Raúl used to control her. "And that's why she used our secret sister code Raúl doesn't know about. Nobody does."

Except you. Now.

"Well then, that's where we're heading." He pulls me into a hug I really needed. "We'll find her and that asshole who killed your mother. We'll figure it out." He pulls back and looks into my eyes with confidence. "I promise."

My center fills with hope. I already have plans to go back to Cuba to spread Abuela's ashes.

"Is your passport up to date, Ms. Álvarez? Because you and I are going to Cuba."

I am still a warrior. But that doesn't mean I have to stand alone.

I close my eyes and my heart opens again.

Abuela, I understand now. This is what you meant. I can feel myself blossoming.

ACKNOWLEDGEMENTS

Many thanks to Team Bond. I could not have done this without you.

First, to my husband Jorge for his patience and support. I love you for that. To his wonderful mother, Fina, you are the inspiration for my Abuela Bonita. I love you.

To my writer's coven, Sorboni Banerjee, Dominique Richardson, and Kelly Coon, thanks for reading the very first chapters—over and over again. Your cheerleading makes even the toughest edits fun! To freelance editor and awesome beta reader Katherine Caldwell, you helped shape this book, and I'm forever grateful. Lissette Campos Perez, your friendship is so valued, your cultural check invaluable, too. And Audrey, I hope your dream of becoming an editor comes true. To Chris Cato, my coanchor at Fox 13 news in Tampa, Florida, thank you for going through my book and noting where I made your eyes roll with romancelandia language that makes men, well, roll their eyes. LOL, you're a great writer and a fabulous partner. And to Veronica Forand, thanks for the late minute dive into *All the Broken Girls* to help me meet deadlines and word count. I have a great team!

USF Religion professor Tori Lockler, thanks for fact-checking me on Santería. Investigator Dale

Stockton and Carrie Horstman of the Polk County Sheriff's Office, you made sure my scenes with law enforcement remained on point. *¡Gracias!*

Morgan Barse, Wing Woman extraordinaire, thanks for your assistance and your social media and brand excellence.

Barbara Rosenberg, you are a joy to work with. Exactly what I've wanted in an agent. Robin Haseltine, we are making magic again. Love working with you and think you are a great person.

Liz Pelletier and Jessica Turner, you are the genius behind Entangled Publishing, and I am thrilled to not only work with you all on this project, but excited to take a spin inside your brilliant brains.

Thanks to all of you who have helped me by reading early versions, commenting on details like log lines, and generally, just giving a—you know what. I appreciate you all!

*A DEA special agent and his K-9 team up
with an ER doctor to find the distributor of
the deadly new drug, but the danger is far
closer than they know.*

TOUGH
▓▓▓JUSTICE

TEE O'FALLON

It should have been a routine investigation. Instead,
DEA K-9 agent Adam "Deck" Decker watches in horror
as one Denver hospital seems to be Ground Zero for
overdoses of a new drug. Now Deck can only hope a
certain icy, green-eyed ER doctor will help him and his
canine partner track down the deadly source.

Dr. Tori Sampson has her reasons for not trusting
federal agents, especially ones working for the DEA. But
the rash of overdoses—including a heartbreaking case
involving a teen—is alarmingly high. And the new
opioid is not only extremely dangerous, it defies all the
usual medical treatments. So Tori has a choice: work
with the big, brawny, and annoyingly hot DEA agent…
or watch more innocent people die.

Tori's the only person who can help Deck break the
case, and they'll need to trust each other, no matter how
high the tension and attraction sizzling between them
runs. But with every question answered, they realize
there's something more behind these typical teen
overdoses. There's a pattern here, and a pattern can only
suggest one thing. There's a killer on the loose.

New York Times *bestselling author Lisa Renee Jones delivers a gripping new thriller that will keep you on the edge of your seat until the very end.*

P⊙ET

A detective with a dark secret...
Samantha Jazz used to be one of the top profilers in the Austin PD, living for the chase of hunting down a killer and bringing him to justice. That is, until one bad case nearly destroyed her.

A killer with a hidden agenda...
There's a new kind of serial killer on the loose—and people are turning up dead. The only clues to their murders lie in the riddles the killer leaves behind. A mystery with more questions than answers, and a suspicion that he's taunting Samantha.

A dead body wrapped in a riddle...
Samantha will have to use all her wits to solve each new puzzle before the killer can strike again. But the closer she gets to the killer, the more she draws him to her as well. And in this thrilling game of cat and mouse—only one of them will survive.

AMARA
an imprint of Entangled Publishing LLC.